HALO

PRIMORDIUM

BOOK TWO OF THE FORERUNNER SAGA

GREG BEAR

TOR

First published 2012 by Tor, Tom Doherty Associates, New York

This edition first published 2012 by Tor
an imprint of Pan Macmillan, a division of Macmillan Publishers Limited
Pan Macmillan, 20 New Wharf Road, London N1 9RR
Basingstoke and Oxford
Associated companies throughout the world
www.panmacmillan.com

ISBN 978-0-330-54563-1

9 8 7 6 5 4 3 2 1

A CIP catalogue record for this book is available from
the British Library.

Printed and bound by CPI Group (UK) Ltd, Croydon CR0 4YY

Visit **www.panmacmillan.com** to read more about all our books
and to buy them. You will also find features, author interviews and
news of any author events, and you can sign up for e-newsletters
so that you're always first to hear about our new releases.

Greg Bear and the team at 343 would like to
dedicate this volume to

Claude Errera

in gratitude for ten years of faithful support
for the Halo universe.

ACKNOWLEDGMENTS

343 Industries would like to thank Greg Bear, Alicia Brattin, Scott Dell'Osso, Nick Dimitrov, David Figatner, James Frenkel, Stacy Hague-Hill, Josh Holmes, Josh Kerwin, Bryan Koski, Matt McCloskey, Paul Patinios, Whitney Ross, Bonnie Ross-Ziegler, Christopher Schlerf, Matt Skelton, Phil Spencer, and Carla Woo.

None of this would have been possible without the amazing efforts of the 343 staffers, including: Nicolas "Sparth" Bouvier, Christine Finch, Kevin Grace, Tyler Jeffers, Tiffany O'Brien, Frank O'Connor, Jeremy Patenaude, Corrinne Robinson, Kenneth Scott, and Kiki Wolfkill.

Greg Bear would again like to thank the 343 team and Erik Bear for their continuing help and creativity, and take this opportunity as well to extend his thanks to Halo fans and readers for their support and input—which have been nothing short of extraordinary!

HALO®
PRIMORDIUM

HALO/SHIELD ALLIANCE 631

Record of communications with Autonomous Mechanical Intelligence (Forerunner Monitor).

SCIENCE TEAM ANALYSIS: Appears to be severely damaged duplicate (?) of device previously reported lost/destroyed (File Ref. Dekagram-721-64-91.)

Machine language records attached as holographic files. Incomplete and failed translation attempts deleted for brevity.

TRANSLATION STYLE: LOCALIZED. Some words and phrases remain obscure.

First successful AI translation: RESPONSE STREAM

#1351 [DATE REDACTED] 1621 hours (Repeated every 64 seconds.)

What am I, really?

A long time ago, I was a living, breathing human being. I went mad. I served my enemies. They became my only friends.

Since then, I've traveled back and forth across this galaxy, and out to the spaces between galaxies—a greater reach than any human before me.

You have asked me to tell you about that time. Since you are the true Reclaimers, I must obey. Are you recording? Good. Because my memory is failing rapidly. I doubt I'll be able to finish the story.

Once, on my birth-world, a world I knew as Erde-Tyrene, and which now is called Earth, my name was Chakas. . . .

Multiple data streams detected. COVENANT LANGUAGE STREAM identified.

SCIENCE TEAM ANALYSIS: Prior contact with Covenant likely.

Break for recalibration of AI translator.

SCIENCE TEAM LEADER to MONITOR: "We realize the difficulty of accessing all parts of your vast store of knowledge, and we'd like to help you in any way we can, including making necessary repairs . . . if we can be made to understand how you actually work.

"What we're having difficulty with is your contention that you were once a human being—over a thousand centuries ago. But rather than waste time with a full discussion of these matters, we've decided to proceed directly to your narrative. Our team has a dual focus for its questions.

"First question: When did you last have contact with the Forerunner known as the Didact, and under what circumstances did you part ways?

"Second question: What goals did Forerunners hope to achieve in their ancient relations with humans? . . ."

RESPONSE STREAM #1352 [DATE REDACTED] 2350 hours
(first portion lost, nonrepeating):

ONE

. . . **LOOKED ACROSS THE** deck of the star boat at the Didact—a massive, gray-black shadow with the face of a warrior god. He was impassive, as usual. Far below, at the center of a great gulf of night filled with many ships, lay a planet under siege—the quarantined prison world of the San'Shyuum.

"What will happen to us?" I asked.

"They will punish," Riser said gloomily. "We're not supposed to be here!"

I turned to my small companion, reached to touch the long, dry fingers of his outstretched hand, and shot an angry glance at Bornstellar, the young Manipular that Riser and I had guided to Djamonkin Crater. He would not meet my eyes.

Then, faster than thought or reflex, something cold and bright and awful carved up the distance between us, splitting us apart in blue-white silence. War sphinxes with passionless faces moved in and scooped us up in transparent bubbles. I saw the Didact and Bornstellar packed away in their own bubbles like trophies. . . .

The Didact seemed composed, prepared—Bornstellar, as frightened as I was.

The bubble sucked in around me. I was caught in sudden stillness, my ears stuffed, my eyes darkened.

This is how a dead man feels.

———

For a time, surrounded by senseless dark or flashes of nothing I could understand, I believed I was about to be ferried across the western water to the far grasslands where I would await judgment under the hungry gaze of sabertooths, hyenas, buzzards, and the great-winged eagles. I tried to prepare myself by listing my weaknesses, that I might appear humble before the judgment of Abada the Rhinoceros; that Abada might fend off the predators, and especially the hyenas; and that his old friend the Great Elephant might remember me and nudge my bones from the dirt, back to life, before the time that ends all.

(For so I have seen in the sacred caves.)

But the stillness and silence continued. I felt a small itch in the pit of my arm, and in my ear, and then on my back where only a friend can reach. . . . The dead do not itch.

Slowly, with a flickering rhythm, like the waving of a fan, the stiff blue silence lifted, scattering visions between shadows of blankness and misery. I saw Riser wrapped in another bubble not far from me, and Bornstellar beside him. The Didact was not with us.

My ears seemed to pop—a painful, muffled echo in my head. Now I heard distant words . . . and listened closely. We had been taken prisoner by a powerful Forerunner called the Master Builder. The Didact and the Master Builder had long opposed each other. I learned as well that Riser and I were prizes to be stolen from the Didact. We would not be destroyed right away; we had value, for the Librarian had imprinted us at birth with ancient memories that might prove useful.

For a time, I wondered if we were about to be introduced to the hideous Captive—the one my ancient ancestors had locked away for so many thousands of years, the one released by the Master Builder's ignorant testing of his new weapon-toy, a gigantic ring called *Halo*. . . .

Then I felt another presence in my head. I had felt this before, first while walking over the ruins at Charum Hakkor, and then later, witnessing the plight of humanity's old allies, the once beautiful and sensuous San'Shyuum, in their quarantined system. Old memories seemed to be traveling across great distances to reassemble, like members of a tribe long lost to each other . . . struggling to retrieve one personality, not my own.

In my boredom, thinking this was merely a strange sort of dream, I reached out as if to touch the jittering pieces. . . .

And was back on Charum Hakkor, walking the parapet above the pit, where the Captive had been imprisoned for more than ten thousand years. My dream-body—oft-wounded, plagued with aches and motivated by a festering hatred—approached the railing and looked down upon the thick-domed timelock.

The lock had been split wide like the casing of a great bomb.

Something that smelled like thunder loomed behind me. It cast a shimmering green shadow—a shadow with far too many arms! I tried to turn and could not. . . .

Nor could I hear myself scream.

———

Soon enough I lapsed back into a void filled with prickly irritations: itching but unable to scratch, thirsty but without water, muscles both frozen and restless. . . . Viscera trying to writhe. Hungry and nauseated at the same time. This long, weightless suspension was suddenly interrupted by violent shaking. I was falling.

Through the filters of my Forerunner armor, my skin sensed heat, and I glimpsed blossoms of fire, searing blasts of energy trying but failing to reach in and cook me—then, more buffeting, accompanied by the gut-wrenching shudder of distant explosions.

Came a final slamming impact. My jaw snapped up and my teeth almost bit through my tongue.

Still, at first there was no pain. Fog filled me. Now I *knew* I was dead and felt some relief. Perhaps I had already been punished sufficiently and would be spared the attentions of hyenas and buzzards and eagles. I anticipated joining my ancestors, my grandmother and grandfather, and if my mother had died in my absence, her as well. They would cross rich green prairies to greet me, floating over the ground, smiling and filled with love, and beside them would pad the jaguar that snarls at the sabertooth, and slither the great crocodile that darts from the mud to put to flight the ravenous buzzards—in that place where all hatred is finally extinguished. There, my good family spirits would welcome me, and my troubles would be over.

(For so I had seen in the sacred caves.)

I was not at all happy when I realized yet again that this darkness was not death, but another kind of sleep. My eyes were closed. I opened them. Light flooded in on me, not very bright, but after the long darkness, it seemed blinding. It was not a spiritual light.

Blurry shapes moved around me. My tongue decided to hurt horribly. I felt hands tugging and fumbling at my arms and legs, and smelled something foul—my own scat. Very bad. Spirits don't stink.

I tried to raise my hand, but someone held it down and

there was another struggle. More hands forcibly bent my arms and legs at painful angles. Slowly I puzzled this out. I was still wearing the broken Forerunner armor the Didact had given me on his ship. Stooped and bent shapes were pulling me from that stinking shell.

When they had finished, I was laid out flat on a hard surface. Water poured cool and sweet over my face. The crusted salt of my upper lip stung my tongue. I fully opened my puffy eyes and blinked up at a roof made of woven reeds thatched with leaves and branches. Sprawled on the cold, gritty platform, I was no better than a newborn: naked, twitching, bleary-eyed, mute from shock. Cool, careful fingers wiped my face clean, then rubbed grassy juice under my nose. The smell was sharp and wakeful. I drank more water—muddy, earthy, inexpressibly sweet.

Against flickering orange light I could now make out a single figure—black as night, slender as a young tree—rubbing its fingers beside its own broad nose, over its wide, rounded cheeks, then combing them through the hair on its scalp. It rubbed this soothing skin-oil on my chapped, cracked lips.

I wondered if I was again being visited, as I was at birth, by the supreme Lifeshaper whom the Didact claimed was his wife—the Librarian. But the figure that hovered over me was smaller, darker—not a beautiful memory but solid flesh. I smelled a woman. A young woman. That scent brought an extraordinary change to my outlook. Then I heard others murmuring, followed by sad, desperate laughter, followed by words I barely understood . . . words from ancient languages I had never heard spoken on Erde-Tyrene.

How then could I understand them at all? What kind of beings were these? They looked human in outline—several kinds of human, perhaps. Slowly, I reengaged the old memories within me, like digging out the roots of a fossil tree . . . and found the necessary knowledge.

Long ago, thousands of years before I was born, humans had used such words. The assembled shadows around me were commenting on my chances of recovery. Some were doubtful. Others expressed leering admiration for the female. A few grinding voices discussed whether the strongest man in the village would take her. The tree-slender girl said nothing, merely giving me more water.

Finally, I tried to speak, but my tongue wouldn't work properly. Even without being half-bitten through, it was not yet trained to form the old words.

"Welcome back," the girl said. Her voice was husky but musical. Gradually my vision cleared. Her face was round and so black it was almost purple. "Your mouth is full of blood. Don't talk. Just rest."

I closed my eyes again. If I could only make myself speak, the Librarian's imprint from ancient human warriors might prove useful after all.

"He came in armor, like a crab," said a low, grumbling male voice. So many of these voices sounded frightened, furtive—cruel and desperate. "He fell after the brightness and burning in the sky, but he's not one of the Forerunners."

"The Forerunners died. He did not," the girl said.

"Then they'll come hunting him. Maybe he killed them," another voice said. "He's no use to us. He could be a danger. Put him out in the grass for the ants."

"How could *he* kill the Forerunners?" the girl asked. "He was in a jar. The jar fell and cracked open when it hit the ground. He lay in the grass for an entire night while we cowered in our huts, but the ants did not bite him."

"If he stays, there will be less food for the rest of us. And if Forerunners lost him, then they will come looking for him and punish us."

I listened to these suppositions with mild interest. I knew less about such matters than the shadows did.

"Why?" the dark girl asked. "They kept him in the jar. We saved him. We took him out of the heat. We will feed him and he will live. Besides, they punish us no matter what we do."

"They haven't come for many days to take *any* of us away," said another voice, more calm or more resigned. "After the fires in the sky, the city and the forest and the plain are quiet. We no longer hear their sky boats. Maybe they're all gone."

The voices from the milling circle dulled and faded. None of what they said made much sense. I had no idea where I might be. I was too tired to care.

I don't know how long I slept. When I opened my eyes again, I looked to one side, then the other. I was lying inside a wide meeting house with log walls. I was naked but for two pieces of worn, dirty cloth. The meeting house was empty, but at my groan, the dark girl came through the reed-covered doorway and kneeled down beside me. She was younger than me. Little more than a girl—not quite a woman. Her eyes were large and reddish brown, and her hair was a wild tangle the color of water-soaked rye grass.

"Where am I?" I asked clumsily, using the old words as best I could.

"Maybe you can tell us. What's your name?"

"Chakas," I said.

"I don't know that name," the girl said. "Is it a secret name?"

"No." I focused on her, ignoring the silhouettes of others as they filed back in through the door and stood around me. Other than the tree-slender female, most of them kept well back, in a wide circle. One of the old men stepped forward and tried to pluck at the girl's shoulder. She shrugged his hand away, and he cackled and danced off.

"Where do you come from?" she asked me.

"Erde-Tyrene," I said.

"I don't know that place." She spoke to the others. No one else had heard of it.

"He's no good to us," an older man said, one of the shrill, argumentative voices from earlier. He was heavy of shoulder and low of forehead and smacked his thick lips in disapproval. All different types of human being were here, as I had guessed—but none as small as Riser. I missed Riser and wondered where he had ended up.

"This one fell from the sky in a jar," the older man repeated, as if the story was already legend. "The jar landed in the dry short grass and cracked and broke, and not even the ants thought he was worth eating."

Another man picked up the tale. "Someone high above lost him. The flying shadows dropped him. He'll just bring them back sooner, and this time they'll take us all to the Palace of Pain."

I did not like the sound of that. "Are we on a planet?" I asked the girl. The words I chose meant "big home," "broad land," "all-under-sky."

The girl shook her head. "I don't think so."

"Is it a great star boat, then?"

"Be quiet and rest. Your mouth is bleeding." She gave me more water and wiped my lips.

"You'll have to choose soon," the old, cackling one said. "Your Gamelpar can't protect you now!"

Then the others went away.

I rolled over.

Later, she shook me awake. "You've slept long enough," she said. "Your tongue isn't bleeding now. Can you tell me what it's like where you come from? Up in the sky? Try to speak slowly."

I moved lips, tongue, jaw. All were sore, but I could talk easily enough. I propped myself up on my elbow. "Are you all human?"

She hummed through her nose and leaned forward to wipe my eyes. "We're the Tudejsa, if that's what you're asking." Later I would put this word in context and understand that it meant the People from Here, or just the People.

"And this isn't Erde-Tyrene."

"I doubt it. Where we are is a place between other places. Where we came from, we will never see again. Where we are going, we do not want to be. So we live here and wait. Sometimes Forerunners take us away."

"Forerunners . . . ?"

"The gray ones. The blue ones. The black ones. Or their machines."

"I know some of them," I said.

She looked dubious. "They don't like us. We're happy they haven't come for many days. Even before the sky became bright and filled with fire—"

"Where do *they* come from—these People?" I waved my arm at the silhouettes still coming and going through the door, some smacking their lips in judgment and making disapproving sounds.

"Some of us come from the old city. That's where I was born. Others have gathered from across the plain, from river and jungle, from the long grass. Some walked here five sleeps ago, after they saw you fall from the sky in your jar. One fellow tries to make people pay to see you."

I heard a scuffle outside, a yelp, and then three burly gawkers shuffled in, keeping well back from us.

"The cackling bastard who fancies you?" I asked her.

She shook her head. "Another fool. He wants more food. They just knock him down and kick him aside."

She didn't seem to like many of the People.

"Valley, jungle, river . . . city, prairie. Sounds like home," I said.

"It *isn't*." She swept her gaze around the gawkers with pinched disappointment. "We are not friends, and no one is willing to be family. When we are taken away, it brings too much pain."

I raised myself on my arm. "Am I strong enough to go outside?"

She pressed me back down. Then she pushed the gawkers out, looked back, and stepped through the hanging grass door. When she returned, she carried a roughly carved wooden bowl. With her fingers she spooned some of the contents into my mouth: bland mush, ground-up grass seed. It didn't taste very good—what I could taste of it—but what I swallowed stayed in my stomach.

Soon I felt stronger.

Then she said, "Time to go outside, before someone decides to kill you." She helped me to my feet and pushed aside the door-hanging. A slanting burst of bluish white glare dazzled me. When I saw the color of that light, a feeling of dread, of not wanting to be where I was, came on me fierce. It was not a good light.

But she persisted and pulled me out under the purple-blue sky. Shielding my eyes, I finally located the horizon—rising up like a distant wall. Turning slowly, swiveling my neck despite the pain, I tracked that far wall until it began to curve upward, ever so gently. I swung around. The horizon curved upward to both sides. Not good, not right. Horizons do not curve up.

I followed the gradually rising sweep higher and higher. The land kept climbing like the slope of a mountain—climbing but narrowing, until I could see both sides of a great, wide band filled with grassland, rocky fields . . . mountains. Some distance away, a foreshortened and irregular dark blue smear crossed almost the entire width of the band, flanked and interrupted by the nearest of those mountains—possibly a large body of water. And everywhere out there on the band—clouds in puffs and swirls and spreading white shreds, like streamers of fleece in a cleansing river.

Weather.

Higher and higher . . .

I leaned my head back as far as I could without falling over—until the rising band crossed into shadow and slimmed to a skinny, perfect ribbon that cut the sky in half and just hung there—a dark blue, overarching sky bridge. At an angle about two-thirds of the way up one side of the bridge, perched just above the edge, was the source of the intense, purple-blue light: a small, brilliant sun.

Turning around again, cupping my hand over the blue sun, I studied the opposite horizon. The wall on that side was too far away to see. But I guessed that both sides of the great ribbon were flanked by walls. Definitely not a planet.

My hopes fell to zero. My situation had not improved in any way. I was not home. I was very far from any home. I had been deposited on one of the great, ring-shaped weapons that had so entranced and divided my Forerunner captors.

I was marooned on a Halo.

TWO

HOW I WISH I could recover the true shape of that young human I was! Naïve, crude, unlettered, not very clever. I fear that over the last hundred thousand years, much of that has rubbed away. My voice and base of knowledge has changed—I have no body to guide me—and so I might seem, in this story, as I tell it now, more sophisticated, weighted down by far too much knowledge.

I was not sophisticated—not in the least. My impression of myself in those days is of anger, confusion, unchecked curiosity—but no purpose, no focused ambition.

Riser had given me focus and courage, and now, he was gone.

When I was born, the supreme Lifeshaper came to Erde-Tyrene to touch me with her will. Erde-Tyrene was *her* world, her protectorate and preserve, and humans were special to her. I remember she was beautiful beyond measure, unlike my mother, who was lovely, but fairly ordinary as women go.

My family farmed for a while outside of the main human city of Marontik. After my father died in a knife fight with a water baron's thugs, and our crops failed, we moved into the city, where my sisters and I took up menial tasks for modest pay. For a time, my sisters also served as Prayer Maidens in the temple of the Lifeshaper. They lived away from Mother and me, in a makeshift temple near the Moon Gate, in the western section of the Old City. . . .

But I see your eyes glazing over. A Reclaimer who lacks patience! Watching you yawn makes me wish I still had jaws and lungs and could yawn with you. You know nothing of Marontik, so I will not bore you further with those details.

Why are you so interested in the Didact? Is he proving to be a difficulty to humans once again? Astonishing. I will not tell you about the Didact, not yet. I will tell this in my own way. This is the way my mind works, *now*. If I still have a mind.

I am moving on.

After the Librarian (I was only an infant when I saw her) the next Forerunner I encountered was a young Manipular named Bornstellar Makes Eternal Lasting. I set out to trick him. It was the worst mistake of my young life.

Back before I met Riser, I was a rude, rough boy, always getting into trouble and stealing. I liked fighting and didn't mind receiving small wounds and bruises. Others feared me. Then I started having dreams that a Forerunner would come to visit me. I made my dream-self attack and bite him and then rob him of the things he carried—treasure that I could sell in the market. I dreamed I would use this treasure to bring my sisters back from the temple to live with us.

In the real world, I robbed other humans instead.

But then one of the cha*manune* came to our house and inquired after me. Despite their size, cha*manush* were respected and we rarely attacked them. I had never robbed one because I heard stories that they banded together to punish those who hurt them. They slipped in, whispering in the night, like marauding monkeys, and took vengeance. They were small but smart and fierce and mostly came and went as they pleased. This one was friendly enough. He said his name was Riser and he had seen someone like me in a dream: a rough, young ha*manush* who needed his guidance.

In my mother's crude hovel, he took me aside and said he would give me good work if I didn't cause trouble.

Riser became my boss, despite his size. He knew many

interesting places in and around Marontik where a young fellow such as myself—barely twenty years old—could be usefully employed. He took a cut of my wages, and his clan fed my family, and we in turn protected his clan from the more stupid thugs who believed that size mattered. Those were exciting times in Marontik. By which I mean, stupid cruelties were common.

Yes, cha*manush* are human, though tinier than my people, the ha*manush*. Indeed, as your display now tells you, some since have called them Florians or even Hobbits, and others may have known them as *menehune*. They loved islands and water and hunting and excelled at building mazes and walls.

I see you have pictures of their bones. Those bones look as if they might indeed fit inside a cha*manush*. How old are they?

INTERRUPTION
MONITOR HAS PENETRATED AI FIREWALL
AI RECALIBRATION

Do not be alarmed. I have accessed your data stores and taken command of your display. I mean no harm . . . *now*. And it has been ever so long since I tasted fresh information. Curious. I see these pictures are from a place called Flores Island, which is on Erde-Tyrene, now called Earth.

In reward for their service, I can now see that the Lifeshaper in later millennia placed Riser's people on a number of Earth's islands. On Flores, she provided them with small elephants and hippos and other tiny beasts to hunt. . . . They do love fresh meat.

If what your history archives tell me is correct, I believe the last of Riser's people died out when humans arrived by canoe at their final home, a great island chain formed by volcanoes that burned through the crust. . . .

I see the largest of those islands is known as Hawaii.

I am getting distracted. Still, I notice you are no longer yawning. Am I revealing secrets of interest to your scientists?

But you are most interested in the Didact.

I am moving on.

————

Soon after Riser took charge of my life, following a decline in our work opportunities, he began to direct his attentions toward preparing for "a visitor."

Riser told me he had also seen a young Forerunner in a dream. We did not discuss the matter much. We did not have to. Both of us lay under thrall. Riser had met male Forerunners before; I had not. He described them to me, but I already saw clearly enough what our visitor would look like. He would be a young one, a Manipular, not fully mature, perhaps arrogant and foolish. He would come seeking treasure.

Riser told me that what I was seeing in my dreams was part of a *geas*—a set of commands and memories left in my mind and body by the Lifeshaper who touches us all at birth.

As a general rule, Forerunners were shaped much like

humans, though larger. In their youth they were tall and slender, gray of skin, and covered nape, crown, shoulders, and along the backs of their hands with a fine, pale fur, pinkish purple or white in color. Odd-looking, to be sure, but not exactly ugly.

The older males, Riser assured me, were different—larger, bulkier, less human-looking, but still, not exactly ugly. "They are a little like the *vaeites* and *alben* that come in our eldest dreams," he explained. "But they are still mighty. They could kill us all if they wanted to, and many would. . . ."

I took his meaning right away, as if somewhere within my deep memory, I knew it already.

The Manipular did indeed arrive on Erde-Tyrene, seeking treasure. He was indeed foolish. And we did indeed provide him with what he sought—guidance to a source of mysterious power. But where we took him was not a secret Precursor ruin.

Following our *geas*, we led Bornstellar into the inland wastes a hundred kilometers from Marontik to a crater filled with a freshwater lake. At its center this crater held a ring-shaped island, like a giant target waiting for an arrow to fly down from the gods. This place was legendary among the cha*manune*. They had explored it many times and had built trails and mazes and walls across its surface. At the center of the ring-shaped island stood a tall mountain. Very few cha*manush* had ever visited that mountain.

As the days passed, I came to realize that despite my urges, I could not hurt this Manipular—this young Forerunner. Despite his irritating manner and obvious feeling of superiority, there was something about him that I liked. Like me, he sought treasure and adventure, and he was willing to do wrong things.

Meeting him, I began my long fall to where I am now—*what* I am now.

The Didact was in fact the secret of Djamonkin Crater. The ring-shaped island was where the Librarian had hidden her husband's warrior Cryptum, a place of deep meditation and sanctuary—hidden from other Forerunners who were seeking him, for reasons I could not then understand.

But now the time of his resurrection had come.

A Forerunner had to be present for the Cryptum to be unsealed. We helped Bornstellar raise the Didact by singing old songs. The Librarian had provided us with all the skills and instincts we needed, as part of our *geas*.

And the Didact emerged from his long sleep. He plumped out like a dried flower dipped in oil.

He rose up among us, weak at first and angry.

The Librarian had left him a great star boat hidden inside the central mountain. He kidnapped us and took us aboard that star boat, along with Bornstellar. We traveled to Charum Hakkor, which awoke another set of memories within me . . . then to Faun Hakkor, where we saw proof that a monstrous experiment had been carried out by the Master Builder.

And then the star boat flew to the San'Shyuum quarantine system. It was there that Riser and I were separated from Bornstellar and the Didact, taken prisoner by the Master

Builder, locked into bubbles, unable to move, barely able to breathe, surrounded by a spinning impression of space and planet and the dark, cramped interiors of various ships.

Once, I caught a glimpse of Riser, contorted in his ill-fitting Forerunner armor, eyes closed as if napping, his generous, furred lips lifted at the corners, as if he dreamed of home and family. . . . His calm visage became for me a necessary reminder of the tradition and dignity of being human.

This is important in my memory. Such memories and feelings define who I once was. I would have them back in the flesh. I would do anything to have them back in the flesh.

Then what I have already told you happened, happened. Now I will tell you the rest.

THREE

THE HUTS STOOD on a flat stretch of dirt and dry grass. A few hundred meters away was a tree line, not any sort of trees I recognized, but definitely trees. Beyond those trees, stretching far toward the horizon-wall and some distance up the thick part of the band, was a beautiful old city. It reminded me of Marontik, but it might have been even older. The young female told me that none of the People lived there now, nor had they lived there for some time. Forerunners had come to take away most of the People, and soon the rest decided the city was no longer a safe place.

I asked her if the Palace of Pain was in this city. She said it was not, but the city held many bad memories.

I leaned on the girl's shoulder, turned unsteadily—and saw that the trees continued in patches for kilometer after kilometer along the other side of the band, for as far as the eye could see . . . grassland and forest curving up into a blue obscurity—haze, clouds.

The young woman's hand felt warm and dry and not very soft. That told me she was a worker, as my mother had been. We stood under the blue-purple sky, and she watched me as I turned again and again, studying the great sky bridge, caught between fear and marvel, trying to understand.

Old memories stirring.

You've seen a Halo, haven't you? Perhaps you've visited one. It was taking me some time to convince myself it was all real, and then, to orient myself. "How long have you been here?" I asked her.

"Ever since I can remember. But Gamelpar talks about the time before we came here."

"Who's Gamelpar?"

She bit her lip, as if she had spoken too soon. "An old man. The others don't like him, because he won't give them permission to mate with me. They threw him out and now he lives away from the huts, out in the trees."

"What if they try—you know—without his permission?" I asked, irritated by the prospect, but genuinely curious. Sometimes females won't talk about being taken against their will.

"I hurt them. They stop," she said, flashing long, horny fingernails.

I believed her. "Has he told you where the People lived before they came here?"

"He says the sun was yellow. Then, when he was a baby, the People were taken inside. They lived inside walls and under ceilings. He says those People were brought here before I was born."

"Were they carried inside a star boat?"

"I don't know about that. The Forerunners never explain. They rarely speak to us."

Turning around, I studied again the other side of the curve. Far up that side of the curve, the grassland and forest ran up against a border of blocky lines, beyond which stretched austere grayness, which faded into that universal bluish obscurity but emerged again far, far up and away, along that perfect bridge looping up, up, and around, growing thinner and now very dark, just a finger-width wide—I held up my finger at arm's length, while the female watched with half-curious annoyance. Again, I nearly fell over, dizzy and feeling a little sick.

"We're near the edge," I said.

"The edge of what?"

"A Halo. It's like a giant hoop. Ever play hoop sticks?" I showed how with my hands.

She hadn't.

"Well, the hoop spins and keeps everyone pressed to the inside." She did not seem impressed. I myself was not sure if that indeed was what stuck the dirt, and us, safely on the surface. "We're on the inside, near that wall." I pointed.

"The wall keeps all the air and dirt from slopping into space."

None of this was important to her. She wanted to live somewhere else but had never known anything but here. "You think you're smart," she said, only a touch judgmental.

I shook my head. "If I was smart, I wouldn't be here. I'd be back on Erde-Tyrene, keeping my sisters out of trouble, working with Riser. . . ."

"Your brother?"

"Not exactly," I said. "Short fellow. Human, but not like me or you."

"You aren't one of *us*, either," she informed me with a sniff. "The People have beautiful black skins and flat, broad noses. You do not."

Irritated, I was about to tell her that some Forerunners had black skins but decided that hardly mattered and shrugged it off.

FOUR

O N OUR SECOND outing, we stopped by a pile of rocks and the girl found a ready supply both of water from a spring and scorpions, which she revealed by lifting a rock. I remembered scorpions on Erde-Tyrene, but these were bigger, as wide as my hand, and black—substantial, and angry at being disturbed. She taught me how to prepare and eat them. First you caught them by their segmented stinging tails. She was good at that, but it took me a while to catch on. Then you pulled off the tail and ate the rest, or if you were bold, popped the claws and body into your mouth, *then* plucked the tail and tossed it aside, still twitching. Those scorpions tasted bitter and sweet at the same time—and then greasy-grassy. They didn't really taste like anything else I knew. The texture—well, you get used to anything when you're hungry. We ate a fair number of them and sat back and looked up at the blue-purple sky.

"You can see it's a big ring," I said, leaning against a boulder. "A ring just floating in space."

"Obviously," she said. "I'm not a fool. That," she said primly, following my finger, "is toward the center of the ring, and the other side. The stars are there, and there." She pointed to either side of the arching bridge. "Sky is cupped in the ring like water in a trough."

We thought this over for a while, still resting.

"You know my name. Are you allowed to tell me yours?"

"My borrowing name, the name *you* can use, is Vinnevra. It was my mother's name when she was a girl."

"Vinnevra. Good. When will you tell me your true name?"

She looked away and scowled. Best not to ask.

I was thinking about the ring and the shadows and what happened when the sun went behind the bridge and a big glow shot out to either side. I could see that. I could even begin to understand it. In my old memory—still coming together, slowly and cautiously—it was known as a corona, and it was made of ionized gases and rarefied winds blowing and glowing away from the nearby star that was the blue sun.

"Are there other rivers, springs, sources of water out there?"

"How should I know?" she said. "This place isn't real. It's made to support animals, though, and us. Why else would they put juicy scorpions out here? That means there might be more water."

More impressive by the moment! "Let's walk," I suggested.

"And leave all these scorpions uneaten?"

She scrambled for some more crawling breakfast. I left my share for her and walked around the rock pile, studying the flat distance that led directly to the near wall.

"If I had Forerunner armor," I said, "I would know all these words, in any language. A blue lady would explain anything I ask her to explain."

"Talking to yourself means the gods will tease your ears when you sleep," Vinnevra said, coming up quietly behind me. She wiped scorpion juice from her lips and taunted me with one last twitching tail.

"Aii! Careful!" I said, dodging.

She threw the tail aside. "They're like bee stingers," she said. "And yes. That means there are bees here, and maybe honey." Then she set out across the sand, dirt, and grass, which looked real enough, but of course wasn't, because the Forerunners had made this ring as a kind of corral, to hold animals such as ourselves. And it cupped the sky—a still river of air on the inside. How humbling, I thought, but I don't think my face looked humble and abject. It probably looked angry.

"Stop grumbling," she said. "Be pleasant. I'll take back my name and stitch your lips shut with dragonfly thread."

I wondered if she was beginning to like me. On Erde-Tyrene, she would already be married and have many children—or serve the Lifeshaper in her temple, like my sisters.

"Do you know why the sky is blue?" I asked, walking beside her.

"No," she said.

I tried to explain. She pretended not to be interested. She did not have to pretend hard. We talked like this, back and forth, and I don't remember most of what we said, so I suppose it wasn't important, but it was pleasant enough.

I could not avoid noticing that the angle of the sun had changed a little. The Halo was spinning with a slight wobble. Twisting. Whatever you call it when the hoop . . .

Precesses. Like a top.

The old memories stirred violently. My brain seemed to leap with the excitement of someone else, watching and thinking inside me. I saw diagrams, felt numbers flood through my thoughts, felt the hoop, the Halo, spinning on more than one axis. . . . What old human that came from, I had no idea, but I saw clearly that based on *engineering* and *physics*, a Halo would not be able to *precess* very quickly. Perhaps the Halo was slowing down, like a hoop rolling along. . . . When it starts to slow, it wobbles. I didn't like that idea at all. Again, everything seemed to move under me, a sickening sensation but not real, not yet. Still, I felt ill. I dropped to my haunches, then sat.

I hadn't earned any of this knowledge. Once more, I was haunted by the dead. Somebody else had died so that this knowledge would be left inside of me. I hated it—so superior, so full of understanding. I hated feeling weak and stupid and sick.

"I need to go back inside," I said. "Please."

Vinnevra took me back into the hut, away from the crazy sky. Except for us, the hut was empty. I was no longer much of a curiosity.

I sat on the edge of the platform of dried mud-brick. The young female sat beside me and leaned forward. "It's been five days since you arrived. I've been watching over you ever since, to see if you'd live or die. . . . Giving you water. Trying to get you to eat." She stretched out her arms and waggled her hands, then yawned. "I'm exhausted."

"Thank you," I said.

She seemed to be trying to decide something. Her manners and a certain shyness would not allow her to just stare. "You lived inside . . . on Erde-Tyrene?"

"No. There's a sky, ground, sun . . . dirt and grass and trees, too. But not like this."

"I know. We don't like it here, and not just because they take us away."

Forerunner treachery . . .

I shook my head to clear away that strange, powerful voice. But the existence of that voice, and its insight, was starting to make a kind of sense. We had been told—and I still felt the truth of it—that the Lifeshaper had made us into her own little living libraries, her own collections of human warrior memory.

I recalled that Bornstellar was being haunted by a ghost of the living Didact, even before we parted ways. All of us—even he—were subject to deep layers of Lifeshaper *geas*.

Even though it looked as if I had fallen out of somebody's pockets, I might still be under the control of the Master Builder. It made sense that if Riser and I had value, he would move us to one of his giant weapons, then return later to scour our brains and finish his work.

But there was no Riser. And no Bornstellar, of course.

I had an awful thought, and as I looked at the woman, my face must have changed, because she reached out to softly pat my cheek.

"Was the little fellow with me when I came here?" I asked. "The cha*manush*? Did you bury him?"

"No," she said. "Only you. And Forerunners."

"Forerunners?"

She nodded. "The night of fire, you all leaped through the sky like falling torches. You landed here, in a jar. You lived. They did not. We pulled you out of the broken jar and carried you inside. You were wearing *that*." She pointed to the armor, still curled up on one side of the hut.

"Some sort of capsule," I said, but the word didn't mean much to her. Perhaps I had just been tossed aside. Perhaps I did not have any value after all. The people here were being treated like cattle, not valuable resources. Nothing was certain. What could any of us do? More than at any time before, my confusion flared into anger. I hated the Forerunners even more intensely than when I had seen the destruction of Charum Hakkor. . . .

And remembered the final battle.

I got up and paced around in the hut's cooler shade, then kicked the armor with my toe. No response. I stuck one foot inside the chest cavity, but it refused to climb up around me. No little blue spirit appeared in my head.

Vinnevra gave me a doubtful look.

"I'm all right," I said.

"You want to go outside again?"

"Yes," I said.

This time, under the crazy sky, my feet felt stable enough, but my eyes would not stop rising to that great, awful bridge. I still wasn't clear what information any of these humans could provide. They seemed mostly cowed, disorganized, beaten down—abused and then forgotten. That had made them desperate and mean. This Halo was not the place where I wished to end my life.

"We should leave," I said. "We should leave this village, the grassland, this *place*." I swung my arm out beyond the tree line. "Maybe out there we can find a way to escape."

"What about your friend, the little one?"

"If he's here—I'll find him, then escape." Truly, I longed to start looking for Riser. He would know what to do. I was focusing my last hopes on the little cha*manush* who had saved me once before.

"If we go too far, they'll come looking and find us,"

Vinnevra said. "That's what they've done before. Besides, there's not much food out there."

"How do you know that?"

She shrugged.

I studied the far trees. "Where there are bugs, there might be birds," I said. "Do you ever see birds?"

"They fly over."

"That means there might be other animals. The Life-shaper—"

"The Lady," Vinnevra said, looking at me sideways.

"Right. The Lady probably keeps all sorts of animals here."

"Including us. We're animals to them."

I didn't know what to say to that. "We could hunt and live out there. Make the Forerunners look hard for us, if they want us. At least we wouldn't be sitting here, waiting to be snatched in our sleep."

Vinnevra now studied me much the same way I studied the distant trees. I was an odd thing, not one of the People, not completely alien. "Look," I said, "if you need to ask permission, if you need to ask your father or mother . . ."

"My father and mother were taken to the Palace of Pain when I was a girl," she said.

"Well, who *can* you ask? Your Gamelpar?"

"He's just Gamelpar." She squatted and drew a circle in the dirt with her finger. Then she took a short stick out of the folds of her pants and tossed it between two hands. Grabbing the stick and holding it up, she drew another circle, this one intersecting the first. Then she threw the stick up. It landed in the middle, where the two circles crossed. "Good," she said. "The stick agrees. I will take you to Gamelpar. We both saw the jar fall from the sky and land near the village. He told me to go see what it was. I did, and there you were. He likes me to bring news."

This outburst of information startled me. Vinnevra had been holding back, waiting until she had made some or other judgment about me. Gamelpar—the name of the old man no longer wanted in the village. The name sounded something like "old father." How old was he?

Another ghost?

The shadow racing along the great hoop was fast approaching. In a few hours it would be dark. I stood for a moment, not sure what was happening, not at all sure I wanted to learn who or what Gamelpar was.

"Before we do that, can you take me to where the jar fell?" I asked. "Just in case there might be something I can find useful."

"Just you? You think it's about you?"

"And Riser," I said, resenting her sad tone.

She approached and touched my face, feeling my skin and underlying facial muscles with her rough fingers. I was startled, but let her do whatever she thought she had to do. Finally, she drew back with a shudder, let out her breath, and closed her eyes.

"We'll go there first," she said. "And then I will take you to see Gamelpar."

The site of my "jar" was about an hour's walk. She led me out
of the reed-hut camp and across a shallow stream, through a
spinney of low, heat-shriveled trees, where the air smelled
bittersweetly of old fires and drying leaves. Up a low hill, and
down again, we finally came to a flat meadow that had once
been covered with grass—familiar, I thought, very like home.
But the grass had been burnt up in a fire and was now gray
and black stubble. The char and dust burst up around our
feet and blackened our legs.

Finally, I saw a grouping of large, grayish white, rounded
objects I took to be boulders—and then I realized they were
not boulders, but fallen star boats, larger than war sphinxes
but much smaller than the Didact's ship.

Vinnevra showed no fear as we approached these vessels.
There were three of them, each split wide open, surrounded
by deeper char and scattered debris. She stopped at the periphery of the rough oval they formed. It took me a moment
to understand what I was seeing. The hulls were not complete, and yet they had not just broken apart or burned up—
parts had simply gone away. These boats, I remembered,
were not just made of solid stuff. They were spun out of
temporary stuff as well, what the Forerunners called hard
light.

The Forerunners that had flown inside the first boat—
six or seven of them, if I counted the pieces correctly—lay
sprawled in the wreckage, most still wrapped in their armor.

On four, the armor was cluttered with strange attachments, like fist-sized metal fleas. The fleas had gathered along the joints and seams.

Fearful myself now—visualizing the fleas leaping loose and landing on me—I backed off, hunkered down, and studied them carefully from a distance. The fleas didn't move. They were broken.

The bodies still smelled bad. They had swollen out of their armor, what parts had not been cooked away by the impact.

The emotions I felt were confused, exultant, and sad at once—and then alarmed. I walked around the first hulk and wondered if Bornstellar was among these dead.

After a few minutes, Vinnevra called to ask when I was going to be done here. "In a while," I said.

Now I moved a few dozen paces to the second star boat. It was of a different design, more organic, like a seed pod, with short spikes covering its surface. The Forerunners left inside—three of them—wore no armor and had been reduced to blackened skeletons. They seemed different—different styles of boats, different types of Forerunners. Had they fought each other?

If this Halo was a gigantic fortress—as it certainly had the potential to be—then perhaps it had its own defenses, and I was looking at a sad remnant of a much larger battle—what the People here called the "fire in the sky." I could not know that for sure, of course. I could not know anything for sure.

Dead Forerunners, it seemed, decayed much as dead humans do, yet I knew that the armor, if active, would have done all in its power to protect them while alive, and even to preserve them after death. Therefore, the armor had failed before the crash. It seemed reasonable to assume that the strange flea-machines had something to do with this. My old memories had no experience of Halos and knew nothing of current Forerunner politics. But I could feel an interior tickle of speculation, and wondered if there was any way I could coax it out—bring it forward.

"Tell me what these are," I said, and shivered despite my attempt at bravado. Waking ghosts was never a good idea.

Armor cracking units.

The old memories—the dominant old spirit within me—suddenly revealed its own mixed emotions about the carnage.

"Human-made—human weapons?" I whispered.

Not human. Forerunner. Fratricide. Civil war.

I had been present on the periphery of a few Forerunner disputes and power plays. Ten thousand years ago, the Forerunners had been united in their conquest of my ancestors. Now, it seemed clear that they were even more deeply divided.

"The fleas got into the star boats and cracked the crew's armor before the boats crashed," I speculated. "Is that what happened?"

You are young. I am old. I am dead, the old memory said, like a low hum inside my thoughts.

"Yes, you are," I agreed. "But I need you now to tell me—"

I am Lord of Admirals!

The sudden strength of the inner voice staggered me. I had never felt such a powerful presence in my head before, even when being possessed during the scarification ceremony celebrating my manhood—not even when being suffused in smoking leaves and led through the caves.

"I feel you," I said, my voice shaky.

I fought the Didact and surrendered Charum Hakkor, but not its secrets.

I knew nothing of this.

We survived the Shaping Sickness. Forerunners hoped to learn the secret of how we survived the Shaping Sickness, but we would not give it to them, even under torture!

And with that, the old memory did an awful thing—it spasmed in rage. The effect almost knocked me over, and I knelt down in the dirt, by the second vessel, clutching my head. For sanity's sake, I pushed back the old spirit—and heard Vinnevra calling from outside the ellipse of fallen star boats.

"Why are you talking to yourself? Are you mad?"

"No," I called back, and muttered, "not yet."

"The Flood," I said to the old spirit. "That's what they call it."

Our bodies died; our memories linger. Is this what the Librarian did?

"You knew her?"

She it was who executed us. Or preserved us.

I found this more than disturbing. The image I had within my head, formed in childhood, was of infinite kindness, infinite compassion. . . .

Clearly, the Lifeshaper was more complicated than anything I could easily encompass. Or the old memory, the Lord of Admirals, was wrong.

We are here, true? Within you, within . . . others . . . true?

"I think so," I said. Riser had also experienced the old memories. "We are all visited by the Lifeshaper at birth."

I very much wanted to get away from these ruins and remains—this graveyard. Abada the Rhinoceros would never remember these Forerunners in their time of judgment, that much I knew; no Great Elephant would rustle through their bones and save them from the ravages of the hyenas, if any such beasts were here.

I had no idea what Forerunner spirits were now set loose or whether they would blame me if they did show up and find me here. Both gods and spirits are unpredictable and quick to judge the living—for whom they feel both lust and envy.

But I could not leave yet. I had to find my "jar." And soon enough I did, all the way across the ellipse: six meters wide, split open like a seed pod, purple-brown, burned and pitted on the outside, smooth and polished black on the inside.

Empty—now.

Who had had charge of me at the last—the Master

Builder's forces, or those in charge of the Halo? Had the Halo defenders snatched us away? Had they juggled Riser and me between them . . . ?

I stooped beside the jar, the pod, and felt around inside, grimacing at my lack of memory. Nothing remained that I could use. Nothing here but quiet and mystery and sadness—and awakenings that neither the Lord of Admirals nor I wished to encompass all in a rush.

I returned to Vinnevra and stood with her for a moment, my back to the wreckage, having trouble breathing.

"What did you find?" she asked.

"Just as you said—dead Forerunners," I said.

"We did not kill them. They were already dead."

"I see that."

"Will they punish us anyway, when they return?"

"What's the difference?" I asked.

She looked at me with a squint. "Gamelpar knows more than I do. He's very old."

I glanced down at the filthy rags that covered me, then raised my arms in query—was I presentable?

"He doesn't care about that," she said. "Mostly, he goes naked, night and day. But sometimes he talks like you—crazy talk. Nobody wants him in the village now. They'd kill him if they could. But they don't dare hurt him because he knows the great way, *daowa-maadthu*."

Again the Lord of Admirals stirred. *Daowa-maadthu* . . .

Fate is off-center, the wheel of life is cracked, the wagon will hit a rock, jolt hard, and fall apart for all of us—eventually.

"You know that truth?" she asked, studying my expression.

"I know of the broken wheel." How odd that we were now actually riding inside one. I had first heard of the great way from Riser. He had called it *daowa-maad*. If the Lord of Admirals knew of this, then it was a very old teaching indeed. I felt a spark of hope. Maybe this Gamelpar had heard about the great way from Riser. Riser might be out there now, waiting for me, afraid to enter a village of large, strange humans.

"Sometimes it's all Gamelpar talks about." Vinnevra shrugged. "He wishes I understood more. Maybe he'll stop pestering me if I take you to him. Are you coming?"

Dark was perhaps an hour away. "Yes."

She walked ahead quickly on long, skinny legs. I had to hurry to catch up. We skirted the confines of the village—really just a circle of huts around the central meeting house.

"They say Gamelpar brings them bad luck," she said. "I suppose he could if he wanted to, but around here, bad luck comes all by itself."

In a few minutes, we crossed the bare, tramped-down dirt and entered a forest of low trees and brush. At last, night slipped down over us, and we followed the distant light of a campfire.

———

The old man was squatting and tending the fire. He was as black as the girl. His long legs and long arms were like gnarled sticks, his fingers like square-cut twigs, and his square head was topped by a pure white fringe. His mouth still held a few yellow teeth, but if he let it, his chin could almost meet his nose.

Around the fire he had laid out the skin of a small animal he had skinned and cleaned, which he had roasted in the coals and was now eating. The second he had cleaned but not skinned. They looked like rabbits, and confirmed my suspicion there were other familiar animals here on the hoop. The Librarian's collection might be large and diverse.

Vinnevra stepped forward out of the reflected glow from the sky bridge and into the firelight. "Old Papa," she said. "I bring a fig from the first garden."

The old man looked up from the bone he was gnawing, somewhat ineffectually. "Come close, fig," he said, his voice a soft, rattling squawk. He was looking at me. I was the fig.

Still chewing, he waved greasy fingers that glinted in the firelight. Meals for him were no doubt long affairs. "Tell the fig to strip away those rags."

Vinnevra cocked her head at me. I pulled off my rags, then stepped in toward the fire, feeling a little awkward under the old man's calm scrutiny. Finally, he turned away, smacked his gums, lifted the bone to his lips, and took another bite. "Human," he said. "But not from the city dwellers, nor the ones near the wall. Show me your back."

I slowly turned and showed him my naked back, looking over my shoulder.

"Hm," he murmured. "Nothing. Show him your own back, daughter's daughter."

Without shame or hesitation, Vinnevra turned and lifted her ragged top. The old man waved his greasy fingers again, for me to look close. I did not touch her, but saw imprinted, in the skin of the small of her back, a faint silvery mark, like a hand clasping three circles.

She lowered her top. "This is the one who fell from the sky and lived," she said. "He claims to come from a place called Erde-Tyrene."

The old man stopped chewing and lifted his head again, as if hearing distant music. "Say that again, clearly."

"Erde-Tyrene," she obliged.

"Have *him* say it."

I spoke the name of my birth-planet. Now the old man rotated on his ankles and rearranged his squat, arm resting on drawn-up knee, the half-eaten rabbit leg dangling from one outstretched hand. "I know of it," he said. "Marontik, that's the biggest city."

"Yes!"

"Outside lie the lands of grass and sand and snow. There is a place where the land splits like a woman, deep and shadowed, and mountains of ice roll between mountains of rock and grind and drop big stones from their jaws."

"Have you been there?" I asked.

He shook his head. "Not since I was a babe. I don't remember it. But my best wife was older. She came from there before me," he said. "She called it Erda. She described it. Not like this place."

"No," I agreed.

Now the old man switched over to the language I had been raised with. He spoke it fluently enough, but with an odd accent, and using some words that were not familiar. He motioned me to come closer and sit beside him, while he said, in my birth-tongue, "That wife was a teller of the finest stories. She filled my life with great flares of passion and dream."

"What's he saying?" Vinnevra asked me.

"He's telling me about his favorite wife," I said.

Vinnevra lay down on her elbow on his other side. "My mother's mother. She died in the city before I was born."

"We have been here for many long nights—many *years*," Gamelpar said. "My best wife would be eager to hear about Marontik. How is it now?"

I described the old city and its balloon rafts and farm-to-market squares, and the power stations left nearby by the Forerunners. I did not go into my experiences with the Manipular or the Didact. Now was not the time.

"She said nothing of balloon rafts," he said. "But that was long ago. Vinnevra tells me you lost a friend somewhere out there. Was he one of the small people with sweet voices?"

"He is," I said.

"Well, some of them are here, too, but not in the city or nearby. Way over toward the far wall. We saw them long ago, and then they walked a long walk. They were honest, in their way, but had little respect for size or age."

Riser had been quite old when he took me under his guidance. Cha*manush* lived long lives.

Finally, Vinnevra said, "Gamelpar, we are hungry. We have come from the village where there is no good food. You remember."

"I sent you there to look when the sky burned and the stars fell," the old man said, nodding. "They still don't like me there."

I could not keep track of the windings of all these stories. Which were true? Perhaps for these People, on this broken wheel, it didn't matter.

"They have no rabbits," Vinnevra wheedled.

"They eat all the game and leave none to breed, and then they go hungry. They burn all the wood and then go cold, they flee the city but live nearby and fear to leave . . . and then they vanish. But it is not their evil. Forerunners carry some off to the Palace of Pain, and now the villagers are stiff with fear and don't want to do anything. Pfaaah!" He threw the bare bone out into the bushes.

"Share your meat and I'll tell you what I know," I said.

Gamelpar stared into the fire and softly cackled. "No," he said.

Vinnevra glanced at me reproachfully. She knew how to deal with Gamelpar, it seemed, and I did not. "We went back, and the dead Forerunners are still there. Nobody has come for them."

The old man looked up, reconsidered for a moment, then made up his mind. "Here, clean this branch," he said to Vinnevra, "and I will spit and cook the second rabbit. It will be for both of you. I have eaten my fill." When Vinnevra had stripped away the bark with teeth and nails, he thrust the stick through the rabbit, then tossed it directly into the fire, skin and all, and used the end of the stick to shift and turn it.

And so we settled next to him, waiting for the second rabbit to cook, beneath the fitful stars, with the bright silvery band of the sky bridge high above.

Gamelpar turned the rabbit again on the coals. The smell of burned fur was not appetizing. Was he trying to punish me for my presumption?

"Rabbit cooked in its skin is most succulent," Vinnevra explained.

"Smells bad, eats fine," Gamelpar agreed. "Tell me what you saw. The fire in the sky, and the brightness, and you falling—what did it look like, from up there?"

I told him a little of what had happened. "The Forerunners were angry at each other, last time I was with them. And the dead ones—"

"You were with *them*?" Gamelpar lay down on his side, then on his back, and contemplated the bridge.

"I did not know them. It could be they were carrying me someplace."

He nodded. "Shooting stars—dying ships. Lots of ships. But the brightness—the sky turning so white the eyes and head hurt—I don't know what that is. Do you?"

Gamelpar was proving remarkably astute. Still, he wasn't exactly telling me the truth, about not understanding—not knowing. He knew something, or at least he had made a decent guess, and now he was testing me.

Ask him who else he is.

"Why are you scowling?" Vinnevra asked me.

I shook my head. I was not about to serve as a go-between for two old, dead warriors—not yet. I fancied I was still my own person. For now.

"There," he said, indicating a blotchy patch about a third of the way up one side of the band, "is where a big ship crashed into the hoop, before the brightness and the shooting stars, just before you fell from the sky." He reached for another, thicker stick, handed it to Vinnevra, and blew out through his lips. She showed the stick to me. There were many notches already. "Mark another double handful," the old man instructed. "A day or so doesn't matter."

Vinnevra took the stick and removed a sharp rock from her pocket. She began to carve.

"Many mysteries," the old man said. "Why are we here? Are we like animals in a pit that fight to amuse the Forerunners?"

"We have something they want," I said.

The old man shifted the rabbit again and bright orange sparks flew up into the cool air. "Can't let the skin go black all over," he murmured. "Can't let the legs burn through. Why do they move us around, why do they take us to the Palace of Pain . . . why treat us so?"

I itched to ask about this Palace of Pain, but the time did not seem right—the look on his face as he said those words . . .

"Humans defeated Forerunners, long ago," I said. "Forerunners still resent it."

Now the old man's expression really sharpened. His jaw firmed and dropped a little, making his face look younger. "You remember such times?" he asked. He fixed me with an intense, if rheumy-eyed, stare, then leaned toward me and whispered, "Are there old spirits inside your head?"

"I think so," I answered. "Yes."

Vinnevra considered both of us with alarm and moved away from the fire.

"Does he have a name?"

"No name . . . just a title. A rank."

"Ah. A highborn, then."

"You're *encouraging* him!" Vinnevra accused from the shadows, but who was encouraging whom, she did not make clear.

"Pfaah," the old man said, and lifted the rabbit. "Break off a leg. I wish we had some salt." He poked the now-bare spit over his shoulder, toward the part of the bridge spinning into shadow. The blotch where a ship had crashed was a dark gray smear, tapering in one direction, and then flaring outward with the marks of burning debris.

"Before the strange brightness, the sun was different—true?" I asked.

Vinnevra had moved closer again, and she answered this time. "Golden-red," she said. "Warmer. Larger."

"Did you see the sky bridge—the hoop in the sky—disappear into the brightness, before all the rest?"

The old man favored me with a gap-toothed grin. "So it did."

"Then it *is* a different sun," I said.

"Not different," Vinnevra insisted, her brows arching. "It changed color. That's *all*." Any other explanation was too vast for her. Perhaps too vast for me as well. Moving something the size of this Halo the way the Didact had moved us from Erde-Tyrene to Charum Hakkor, then out to the San'Shyuum world . . .

But I did not back down. "Different suns," I insisted.

The old man pondered, his nearly toothless jaw moving up and down. I began to regret this discussion—we were distracting him from portioning out the rabbit.

He raised himself up in his seated posture and squared his hands on his knees. "I was brought here when I was an infant," he said. "I do not remember much about Erda, but my best wife told me it had a flat horizon, but when you are high up, the end of the world curves down to each side, not up. Makes you wonder what's on the other side of the wheel, down there . . . doesn't it?"

He caught me staring at the rabbit. I wiped drool from the corner of my lips. He tapped his finger lightly on the ground, then lowered his head, as if in mourning. "I remember the long journey in the gray walls and no way to see the sky, with air that smelled of closeness and sweet and bitter herbs, like perfume. Herbs that kept us quiet during the voyage. And then . . . the first ones were brought *here*, to the hoop." He tapped the ground again. More firmly. "I was just a babe. We had lived for many days within gray walls, but now the great ship shook us like ants from a cup. None were hurt; we drifted like fluff to the dirt and rocks.

"Then, so I was told, we stood together, holding each other, and looked up, and saw the sky bridge, the way the land rose up, and there was much wailing. Finally, we separated into families and small tribes, and wandered this way and that—"—he swung his arms—"outward. We came to forests and plains and we made our homes there, as we were used to living. For this while, in my youth, we were tended like cattle, but because there was little pain and we were fed, we came to believe this was where we should be.

"The Forerunners gave us bricks. We used the bricks and made walls and houses and great buildings. We lived in peace and raised children, and the children were touched by the Lady, and when they could speak, they told us of this beautiful Forerunner, so tall, who spoke to them in their first days and filled them with light. I already knew her. She had come to me on Erda."

"When you were born?" I asked.

Gamelpar nodded. "But it was not the same, how the Lady touched those from Erda and how she touched the children born here. As I grew up, I sometimes remembered things that I never lived." His voice grew thin. He lifted his gnarled hand, pointed in a broad sweep, up toward the center of the Halo's spin, then down, as if poking his finger through to the other side. "So many memories," he whispered. "Old, old memories—in dreams, in visions. Weak and frightened . . . old, lost ghosts.

"But years later, the old memories became stronger—after we finished the city, long after I was husband and father. After the sky changed five times. Those were great darknesses, long, long nights. Different suns, different stars, came and went.

"Each time, glowing bars climbed across the sky and a big, pale blue disk appeared inside the hoop, like the hub of a wheel. Each time came the white brightness, then a great darkness. . . ." He swept his hand across the welkin. "Spokes shot out from the hub, and glowing fires burned on the ends of the spokes, to warm us in that darkness. And twice we saw something other than brightness and darkness—something terrible that came out of the hub and the center of the wheel—something that gave us fits and hurt the soul."

He rubbed his forehead and looked away from the fire. "But we did not die. We moved again. Under the orange sun, where Vinnevra was born."

Vinnevra stared intently at her grandfather.

"It was under that sun that the Forerunners came in their boats and carried us off to the Palace of Pain. They stole away my daughter and her mate, and many, many others. They came so often we were afraid, and we abandoned the city, crawled back out onto the plain. And there, as we huddled in fear, the beast came among us and pointed its awful arms, and raised its jeweled eyes."

I started at this. "Beast?"

"Bigger than men, bigger than Forerunners. Many arms, many small legs, curled up like a shriveled spider. It sat on a big dish, flying this high over the ground." He raised his arm as high as he could. "Beside it flew a large machine with a single green eye." He laced his gnarled, knobby fingers together, shaping a kind of complicated ball. "These two spoke in our heads as well as in our ears—telling us of our fates. The Primordial and Green-eye were deciding who would live and who would die.

"But some who had been taken to the Palace of Pain returned. At first we were happy that they were back, but then we saw how some had changed. Some grew other skins, other eyes, other arms. They broke apart and joined together, then made others sick. They wailed in pain and tried to touch us. These poor monsters died, or we killed them later.

"And Green-eye said to the Beast, 'Not all resist . . . not all survive.' But most do. Why? Why do many survive, but some do not?" Gamelpar shuddered. "Twisted death. Death that spreads like spilled blood. Those who survived . . . who did not die . . . the Forerunners took some back to the Palace of Pain, and some they left behind. We do not know how they chose. And then . . ."

He could not finish. He looked at the ground and held up his hands, stretching his fingers to the sky. Then he began a low keening, like the wail of a weary, hopeless child.

Vinnevra finished for him. "Gamelpar went to the Palace of Pain, but he did not become ill. He never tells that tale."

The old man stopped keening, straightened as tall as he could, and wiped his hands on his thighs.

"We camped on the outskirts of the city. The little village, you have seen. Me. And my daughter's daughter. Alone of all my kin. That is the truth of it." He stood and brushed sand from his long black legs, then pointed vaguely at the backside of the rushing shadow. "Then they pushed me out here, to be done with me."

"I told them he had died out in the bush, but his spirit still keens, and he will haunt those who hurt me. Nobody touched me after that," Vinnevra said. "He knows how to hunt and take care of himself. Still, he is old. . . ."

I did not know whether to speak, their sadness was so profound. But Gamelpar was not finished.

He looked fondly upon her. "Just before you fell, the sky changed again. As the machines fought and killed each other, great ships passed over, splitting open and spinning away in flames, and smashing—up there." He pointed toward the black streak, or where it would have been, were it not now hidden by errant clouds. "And then came the last hurtful whiteness."

"Tell me again about the Beast," I said.

His jaw grew strong again, and he held out both arms. "He flew on the large disk, and his eyes were like gray jewels, and Green-eye flew beside him, and they talked, and the

People were taken away. After that time, no longer did we have children, and no longer was there enough food. The water turned bad. Forerunners fought each other and died . . . all because of the Beast . . . the Beast. . . ."

He repeated this over and over, as if it had been burned by a hot iron into his memory. Finally he could stand it no more, and he seemed to fall into a brief fit, prancing around, shaking out his arms, babbling in a singsong, until he had cleansed himself. "Pfaah!"

He spat, then jabbed his splayed hand at the darkness beyond the dying fire. "Let us leave this place. Nothing here but fools and twisted ghosts."

Gamelpar eased back down on his haunches, then began to break up the rabbit. He handed the pieces to us. Vinnevra regarded me with caution and curiosity. I had almost lost my appetite. But not quite. The girl and I settled down to eating, and I thought: the Beast Gamelpar had seen, and the Captive from Charum Hakkor, were they one and the same?

I say yes.

My old spirit had seen the Beast; that's how I could see it, as well.

The old man watched us as we gobbled down the rabbit. "Tell us what you learned in your travels," he said softly.

"Long, long time past," I said, "we fought the Forerunners and nearly won."

"Yes," he said.

"But then they defeated us and pushed us down. They

turned us into animals. The Librarian raised us up again, and gave some of us old memories from dead warriors."

"Why do they torture us?" Vinnevra asked. She did not like this talk of carrying ghosts.

"Forerunners worry we will become strong and fight them again. They will keep us down any way they can—some of them."

"You know about the Beast, I am sure of it," the old man said.

"I visited where it was once imprisoned. An ancient being older than humans or Forerunners. Forerunners freed it from its trap and it came—or was brought—here."

The old spirit within approved.

We ate for a while in silence while Gamelpar absorbed this. "Who rides you?" he asked.

Without thinking, I said, "Lord of Admirals."

We stared hard at each other. "We *knew* him," the old man said. "My old spirit fought under his command. . . ." His voice trailed off. Then he reached up and again swept his char-smudged fingers across the glittering sky. "The voices ride us," he said. "They hope to live again, but do not know what we face. We *are* weak, like animals. There will be no return to that old war."

He looked away, but not before I saw a glint of tears on his cheeks. "Finish this poor rabbit before it gets cold." He pointed toward the near wall. "My daughter's daughter tells me we should go over there, where the land stays in shadow longer."

Vinnevra had already finished. She stood up, as if ready to leave right away. "You want him to come with us?" she asked the old man. I could never tell what she thought about me. Her eyes seemed dangerous, the way they peered and examined from under her brows.

"Yes," the old man said.

For her, that was enough. "Gamelpar, can you walk?"

"Cut a big stick from the brush. With that, I can walk as well as you."

"He fell a few days ago," Vinnevra explained. "He hurt his hip."

"My hip is fine. Eat. Sleep. Then we leave."

He looked back up at the stars and the sky bridge. His face grew sharp again, more interested, and again he looked younger.

As I tossed away the final clean-stripped rabbit bone, we felt something rumble beneath the dirt, far below us, like some huge, restless animal. The sound made the pebbles dance, but I followed the old man's upraised hand and trembling finger to the sky.

High on the bright arc of the sky bridge, where the black mark and rays had once been, an emptiness had suddenly appeared—a gap in the continual sweep of the band through which I made out two bright stars, quickly hidden by the hoop's spin.

"I have never seen *that* before," Gamelpar said.

"That's where the big boat crashed!" Vinnevra said.

The grumbling continued, and we moved in close and

hugged each other, as if together we might weigh enough to hold down the dirt. Finally, the vibrations dropped to a faint trembling—and soon I wondered if I was feeling anything at all.

The gap in the sky bridge remained.

We did not say much for the rest of that night. Vinnevra curled up close to the dying fire, at the feet of Gamelpar.

Even with the missing square, the sky bridge was as bright as a long ribbon of moon, and that made seeing the stars difficult.

FIVE

FIVE

PRETTY SOON, AFTER a small and troubled sleep, sunlight crept down the band like a descending river and caught us. Clouds crossing the band took fire, rose up in mountainous billows, and spread orange glow even into the tilt-shadow and wall-shade.

Halo dawn.

Then it was light all around, and after several loud thunderclaps and brief shower of warm rain, the old man got up and took his new long stick from Vinnevra, and we started our walk away from the village and the deserted city. Gamelpar did indeed walk faster and better with a stick, but Vinnevra and I slowed to allow him his dignity.

We walked together just behind him.

"Time to tell this one where we are going, daughter of daughters," the old man said.

"I'm going to find my friend," I said.

"The little one," Vinnevra explained.

"Do you know where he is?"

I had to admit, I had no idea.

"Vinnevra knows where to go."

"I have seen it," Vinnevra said, with a sidelong and almost guilty glance.

"Seen what?" I asked.

We crested a low hill. "A place where I should go when I am in trouble," she said. She turned to look back over the meadow and plain that held the scattered village, the hut where she had tended to me, and beyond that, stretching wide to either side, the brown mud and stone walls and towers of the city where she had grown up . . . and lost her parents to Forerunners.

She pointed inland, away from the wall, then led us down the opposite side of the hill.

Gamelpar followed and did not look back.

I had no idea which way Riser might be, so I followed as well—for now. "What kind of place is it?" I asked.

"I will know it when I see it," she said.

"The Lady's touch?"

She nodded.

"A *geas*. All right. That's a start," I said. The Lifeshaper was kind. "If we get away from here, maybe you can remember more."

"We *are* getting away," Gamelpar said over his shoulder.

"I don't see any Forerunner machines," Vinnevra said hopefully. "Maybe they're all broken."

We walked for several kilometers through the forest of low trees, then beyond more hills covered with ditches and wide pits long ago dug out for their stone and clay. Then we paused.

Vinnevra closed her eyes and turned her head back and forth, as if searching the darkness behind her lids.

"Are we going in the right direction?" I asked.

She wrapped her arms around herself and soberly returned my look. "I think so." Then her face fell and tears streaked her cheeks. "Everything's changing! I don't see it now."

That stopped us for a time.

An idea struck me. "Look around with your eyes closed and point at something."

"What?" Vinnevra asked.

"Maybe you're just getting your bearings, or something's distracting you. Look around at anything—at the wall and the old city and where we are, then turn . . . just hold out your hand and *point*."

The old man leaned on his stick.

"That's stupid," Vinnevra said. The old man did not disagree.

"The Lifeshaper—the Lady—touches us all for a reason," I said. "Maybe she touched you with a sense of direction, not just the memory of a place."

"Is it *our* reason, or hers?" Gamelpar asked.

"I don't know. She gave Riser and me a *geas* which we had to fulfill. She gave us old memories that come awake when we visit certain places. But I wasn't born here, so she didn't tell *me* what I need to know, or where to go when I'm in trouble. You . . . were born here. Try it."

Vinnevra shook her head and looked miserable. I paced away, again wishing Riser were here; he was so much better with people—even big people—and so much older and more experienced. "If we don't know where to go, we'll wander until we starve," I said. I was petulant, hungry again, angry at being stuck.

The girl dropped her arms and took a deep breath, then squinted at the sky. Gamelpar had raised his stick and seemed to be drawing a circle in the air.

Then I saw he was pointing at something. A great grayness with a long, straight side was rising over the near wall, far above the wispy clouds. It cast a broad black silhouette across the clouds and the far land. We watched, shivering even before the black line moved over us and we were surrounded by almost complete darkness, darker than Halo night, for the gray shape had obscured nearly the entire sky bridge, seeming to cut it in two.

Despite my fear, I tried to reason it out. There was a purpose here—there had to be. Something might have been detached from the outside of the wheel—a *huge* something, square or rectangular—and now it was being hauled along over the wall, angled inward, squared off—

And then what? I tried to visualize gigantic blue hands passing this object from one to the other, or some other Forerunner tools . . . and failed.

Whatever it might be, it was already larger than any star boat I had seen. The far side extended all the way to the opposite horizon. Having cast its shadow from one side of the band to the other, the great mass stopped moving. It was as wide as the Halo itself—perhaps wider.

Then the great square mass moved again. The shadow moved in parallel with the edges of the band, sliding at some great distance—but a tiny distance for the Halo itself—and allowed light to return.

I dropped to the ground and looked up at the sky bridge, swept my eyes along the curve—and found a second gap about a third of the way up. It might have appeared while we were walking and talking—paying no attention. It was twice as large as the first gap—many thousands of kilometers in length. *Two* parts from the hoop had been removed, one from the underside and one entire section from between the walls—and both, it seemed, were now being transported around the curve, perhaps a thousand kilometers above the inner surface.

Repairing what has been damaged.

I muttered at this inner voice, but kept watching. The Lord of Admirals was probably correct. The battle around the Halo had done significant damage and now repairs were being made. Pieces were being moved just as a mason cuts stone tiles to fit a floor and transports them to where they are needed.

Gamelpar and Vinnevra were transfixed by the gigantic tile and the darkness it cast. Vinnevra wiped tears from her cheeks. "I am so scared," she said. "Don't they *want us* anymore?" The resentment in her tone was puzzling.

"Don't talk foolish," Gamelpar said, but gently. He, too, was frightened, *but the fear of an old man is not like the fear of a young female, or one would be afraid all the time.*

The Lord of Admirals again.

"You should know all about being old," I said under my breath. Then, out loud, "Their damned Halo is broken and they're patching it up. That's more important than we are—for now."

Gamelpar leaned on his stick. His right leg twitched. The old man watched his granddaughter closely.

"How could something *they made* break?" she asked.

The shadow slid farther along the curve.

"They're not gods," I said. "They make mistakes. They're mortal. Things they build can be destroyed."

I have destroyed many Forerunners and their ships, their cities—the things they made.

Suddenly, the old spirit—so far happy to volunteer his opinions—seemed to hitch up and fade. For a few minutes, nothing—then, his abrupt return caused a tingling in my head.

What is this—hell? But the body is young!

The Lord of Admirals was slowly coming to grips with his true situation.

I focused on the girl. Gamelpar was right. What she had to say was far more important right now than any of my old memories. I pretended a kind of calm, but decided to push her a step further. Riser would have done the same to me in a tough situation.

"So tell us—did you *ever* really know?" I asked.

She gave me a feral look, pushed between the old man and me, turned away from both of us, and closed her eyes again. For a moment she swayed back and forth and I thought she would fall over, but instead, she spun around several times—then jerked out her arm and pointed a finger.

"There!" she cried hoarsely. "I feel it again! We need to go *there*." She jabbed her finger at a diagonal to the far gray wall.

"Not away from the wall?" Gamelpar asked.

"No," she said, face radiant. "We need to move *that* way."

"That takes us back to the city," Gamelpar said.

This confused her. "We don't want to go back there," she admitted, her voice low.

"Why not?" I asked. In truth, I was curious to see the city.

"Bad memories," Gamelpar said. "Are you sure that's the way?"

"We could walk *around* the city. . . . ," she ventured. Then she shook her head. "No. I need to go there . . . into the city, through the city—first." She took Gamelpar's hand. "But we'll go around the village. They don't want you there."

"Are you sure the city's deserted?" I asked.

She nodded. "Nobody goes there anymore," she said.

"Not even Forerunners?" I asked, but neither of them seemed to think that was deserving of an answer.

SIX

W E TOOK THE long way around the village toward the old city.

As we walked, I decided on my own terms for directions on the wheel. Inland or inward meant away from an edge wall—until, I supposed, one reached the midpoint of the band, and then one would be heading outward, or outland, toward the opposite wall. East was the direction from which light swept around to wake us each "morning." West was the direction of the fleeing light.

We rested as night came down. I lay on my side, several paces from the old man and the girl, and tried to anticipate what might happen next. Wherever the Didact and Bornstellar had taken me, memories and ideas and even indelible instructions had popped up in my thoughts, in my actions. Vinnevra was now experiencing the same troubling gift.

Maybe the Librarian wants only the girl—not you or the old man.

The old spirit again.

"Go to sleep," I muttered.

Death has been sleep enough.

Gamelpar had pointed out that my skin was not marked. I presumed that would reveal to Forerunners that I was a recent arrival. My thoughts grew hazier and wilder. Having seen my lack of a mark—or my strangeness—could have triggered Vinnevra's urge to travel. I could almost imagine the instructions the Lifeshaper had laid down in our flesh: See this, do that. Meet this visitor, take him there. Face this challenge, behave this way. . . .

Like puppets, at times we seemed to be motivated only by the Lifeshaper's omnipresent touch.

But going into the city—despite my curiosity, the necessity of that was less than obvious to Gamelpar and me.

The next day, we stood before a broken wooden gate on the western side of the old city. The thick mud and rock rampart stretched unbroken for hundreds of meters in either direction. There were no other gates.

The gate gave entrance to a tunnel about twenty meters long.

82

"Thick walls—to keep Forerunners out?" I asked Gamelpar.

He shook his head, leaning on his stick before the gate, staring into the gloom. "Other cities, roving bands . . . raiders. Humans were on their own for centuries before I came here."

"War and pillage," I said.

He blinked at me, nodded, then turned to face Vinnevra, who was steeling herself to go through the tunnel.

"You are still sure?" he asked her.

She stubbornly lifted her shoulders and sprinted ahead, eager to get through the darkness.

Gamelpar regarded me again with weary eyes. "The Lady has her ways."

As we followed the girl, I told them my words for directions, describing where we were going on the wheel. We emerged from the tunnel into the light, stepped over another broken gate, and stood in a narrow lane that followed the wall and separated most of the buildings from the wall itself.

The old man listened intently. When I finished, he said, "*East, west, north, south* . . . new words. We say turnwise, lightwise, crosswise. I suppose they're all the same. Vinnevra hasn't traveled far enough to care much for the old words. The new ones will work just as well."

Above us, a parapet leaned out, crossing the top of the gate and meeting a stone tower on either side. Guards had seen fit to look within as well as without.

"War," I said. "The Lady always allows us the freedom to fight each other. . . ."

Gamelpar lifted his lips in a gap-toothed smirk. "Where there is freedom, there will be war," he said. "We covet. We hate. We fight. We die."

"Was it that way before we met the Forerunners?" I asked. My old spirit did not express an opinion.

"Probably," Gamelpar said. "It's likely the same for Forerunners. But who will ask them?"

Vinnevra circled back and glared at us. "Keep close," she said. "We shouldn't stay here any longer than we have to." She looked around, lips drawn tight, then moved off again, running like a young deer on her long, skinny legs.

———

I have no doubt you have seen marvels of architecture on the worlds you know—Earth today, perhaps. And I had seen great marvels—or their ruins—on Charum Hakkor, revealing the genius of humans before the Forerunner wars brought us low. But this old city reminded me of Marontik—though surrounded by thicker walls.

The mud-colored buildings were never more than three stories high, the third stories on both sides leaning in and almost touching over narrow dirt or cobble streets. The second and third floors were supported by wooden beams which poked through the walls—old wood no doubt cut from the nearby forests until only stunted trees remained.

But if anything, as we walked and walked, I suspected

that this city had once been larger and more populous than Marontik, though its true scale was difficult to judge. I would have liked to see it from above—a layout of all its streets and neighborhoods.

From the Didact's ship, before being sealed into our bubbles, Riser and I had looked down upon entire worlds— cities no more than tiny smudges. A revelation at the time.

The old spirit observed this, to him, primitive yearning for a map—but again, did not comment. I wasn't sure which was more irritating—his comments or his silence.

As we penetrated deeper into the winding lanes, Vinnevra seemed to lose confidence in her *geas,* her sense of direction. Several times she turned around and doubled us back. But we tended—I noticed, and no doubt Gamelpar noticed as well—ever toward the diagonal she had first pointed out, cutting, I judged, across one-third of the old city.

The low oval doors of the buildings were dark and silent but for a mournfully hooting wind. Hangings or rough fiber curtains still hung like drooping eyelids in a few higher windows. The streets were filled with windblown clutter from the last inhabitants: rotting sandals, scraps of filthy cloth, broken wood—no iron or other metal. The city had been stripped of anything valuable, leaving only the walls.

That meant, of course, we would not find caches of food or anything remotely like treasure. I thought sadly of Bornstellar and our shared quest for treasure. Which of us had been the most naïve?

You have affection for a Forerunner.

"Not really," I said. "We traveled together."

It is no crime. I once felt affection for a Warrior-Servant as I hunted his ships and destroyed his fighters. No lover ever felt my attentions so fiercely.

The old spirit suddenly burned. For a while, his questing intensity made me feel as if I held a caged animal—but it passed. One can grow used to anything, I suppose.

I have grown used to the way you find me now, after all. I barely remember the flesh. . . . No. That's a lie. I remember it too clearly.

At least the Lord of Admirals, back then, was still lodged in flesh. My flesh, to be sure.

———

The shadows grew long, the lanes dark enough to let us see stars overhead—stars, and something larger: a round planet the width of my outstretched thumb—as wide as the moon as seen from Erde-Tyrene, red and gray and foreboding.

This was the first time I saw the object that would cause so much disaster—but I am getting ahead of myself.

SEVEN

THE DEEPER WE traveled into the old city, the softer and sadder sang the breezes. Gamelpar kept up with us well enough, but Vinnevra and I were more eager than ever to leave these ruins behind. Ghosts within are one thing—ghosts without, another.

Down one long, straight lane, wider than any of the others, we debouched onto a wide circle, marked off by flat platforms and stone walls barely higher than my waist. From the walls poked the remains of broken-down sheds with gaping fronts.

"Market?" I asked Gamelpar.

He nodded. "Been here many times," he said. "Happy times." He looked fondly at Vinnevra, who rubbed her nose and looked suspiciously around the broad circle. "My daughter had stalls . . . here, and . . . there." He pointed out the spaces. "We sold fruit and skins and ceremonial flutes—whatever we could gather or grow or make. We had no idea how happy we were."

We kept walking. A sudden gust brought with it flurries of dust that spun up and over the flat platforms, rustling shreds of woven mats. I shielded my eyes as the flurries passed—and then, on the opposite side of the circle, saw that we had come upon something different and unexpected. Half-blinded by grit, I bumped against the girl, who under ordinary circumstances would have delivered me a wallop—but now she just stood her ground.

I wiped the dust from my eyes and looked over a platform of Forerunner metal, about fifty meters wide and shoulder-high. It supported a great, egg-shaped structure as high as the platform was wide. This central egg, the color of beaten copper laced through with swirls of dusky sunset sky, was incised all around by smooth vertical grooves spaced an arm span apart.

"A boat?" Vinnevra asked.

Gamelpar shook his head, as puzzled as we were. "Never saw it before. But it's been here a long time," he said. "Look—the shops were built around it."

Vinnevra squatted, picked up a pebble, and threw it at the egg. The pebble bounced off without making a sound.

"The Lady has eyes everywhere," Gamelpar said. "We never know when she is watching."

"Hidden . . . camouflaged," I said. "Why?"

"If she sees our plight, why doesn't she protect us?" the old man asked. He worked his jaw. "We should find water. There used to be good wells." He hobbled off on his stick. Vinnevra and I chose to study the tall, sunset golden egg for a while longer.

The old spirit was shaping a vague explanation.

From here she can reach out and touch all the newborns. I resented his swifter analysis, but could not deny it.

"Unseen, central—like a lighted tower, a beacon," I told Vinnevra. "Maybe this is where the Lady sends out her voice to touch your People."

"Maybe," she said, with only the barest scowl. "Does it still send out messages?"

"The children stopped being born," I said. "Right? No more children—maybe no more messages." Then I had a discouraging thought. "Is this where you're supposed to go when you don't feel safe?"

"No," she responded quickly. "That's over there." She pointed in the same direction as before, arm steady.

Gamelpar called out that he had found a little water left in a well. We walked around the Forerunner beacon—or whatever it was—and joined him at the lip of a circular wall made of bricks and stones. He had pulled up a wooden bucket on a decaying length of rope, and offered us a drink of muddy brown water—probably old rain.

"All there is," he said.

We drank despite the smell. On Erde-Tyrene, I thought, the water would probably be filled with wrigglers—but here in the city, nothing wriggled that I could see.

Even the mosquitoes had abandoned this place.

We walked on. Vinnevra led us down another winding lane. All the lanes looked alike to me. Many of the buildings had fallen in, revealing sad little rooms filled with drifting leaves. Once these places had held real people, real families.

There had been communities all across the Halo, I suspected, filled with people touched by the Lifeshaper—the Lady. They had been allowed to be completely human, to find their own strengths, succumb to their natural weaknesses—to fight their wars. Humans allowed to be human, left like a garden to grow wild, just to see what new flowers might sprout up.

But were we always observed by the Lifeshaper herself—or her cadres?

And had she watched over us—them—through the successive times of brightness, darkness, new skies, new suns? Had she watched when, years ago, the wheel had been taken to Charum Hakkor, to unleash the bitter brilliance that burned the soul?

Had she herself offered refuge to the Captive—the Primordial?

My old spirit expressed skepticism at that. *If the Primordial were allowed to rule and control this place, it would conduct its own experiments*, the Lord of Admirals suggested.

"What sort of experiments?" I asked.

What the old man has seen . . . the Shaping Sickness. It is the Captive's great passion.

But the old spirit could not convey things too far beyond what my mind had already experienced. I would not comprehend until I myself had seen more.

We found another straight road. At its end, we saw a larger gate opening to the plain beyond. Vinnevra chose that direction, to my relief. We helped Gamelpar along.

Just a few hundred meters from the gate and the boundaries of the city, as the wheel's shade again slipped over us and a fine rain drizzled down, we took refuge in a tumbledown home that still had part of a roof.

That night, Gamelpar tossed and turned, no doubt because of the aches and pains of age—but he also cried aloud, calling names, so many names, until he jerked upright. Vinnevra tried to soothe him. Then she motioned for me to join them, and we all lay beside each other.

To these two, the ruins of this old city spoke of lost glory and family and happiness.

To me, and to the old spirit within, the city spoke of Forerunners deigning to allow us a crude, limited sort of freedom—but only for a time.

Had it really been any different back on Erde-Tyrene?

EIGHT

A T FIRST LIGHT, we passed through the gate and saw the near-edge wall much more clearly. Vinnevra spun around again, eyes closed, and flung out her arm to establish our direction.

Where she pointed, I could see a brown smudge along the wall's gray horizon—dust rising high in the air.

Gamelpar leaned heavily on his stick, his right leg still trembling. "You're sure?" he asked.

"I'm sure."

The great double-square tiles of Halo had continued to move along the inside of the wheel. Now the sun shone on their upper surfaces and revealed geometrically patterned

Forerunner metal, as with the bare segments we could see spaced at intervals along the sky bridge.

Whatever landscape—if any—that had been layered on the tiles had been sacrificed, atmosphere spilled out into space along with land, animals, and, yes, perhaps even *people*— all to repair damage suffered during the war between the Forerunners.

It is her way, to allow us to suffer.

"No," I said under my breath. "I feel *her* in me, it is not *her* way." My experiences on the Halo had not yet rubbed out all my hopes for the Lifeshaper.

Then streaks crossed the sky, —silvery, darting, like heaven-made swallows chasing swift insects. I grabbed Vinnevra's arm. She trembled at the sight.

"Sky boats," Gamelpar said. "From the Palace of Pain. They're coming for the rest of the People in the village."

At this, we moved on as fast as we could and still have the old man keep up with us. Soon, the city was hidden by rolling hills. We stopped when Gamelpar tired and lagged. Concealing ourselves among another patch of low trees, we tried to keep still and quiet.

We had traveled perhaps a dozen kilometers outland. Fog crept over us, but the moisture did not quench our thirst. None of us slept.

But the boats did not come for us. We never saw the streaks in the sky descend, and I do not know what happened to the People in the village.

The fog lifted with the passage out of shadow. No rain followed and the land was soon as dry again as old bones. In silence, Gamelpar suffered pain in his joints from the night's damp and cold.

I wondered what the old spirit he carried thought about this aging, primitive vessel. He or she—or it, who could know?—might have wished for a younger, stouter container. But in the old man's stolid, wrinkled face I read a different kind of courage, one new to me.

Vinnevra and I offered to help carry him, but he waved us off and used his stick to push to his feet. He then swung the stick around, limbering up for the morning journey, and headed off before we began, leaning on the stick and swinging his sore leg out in an arc with each step. Again we followed a few paces behind, allowing him some dignity. Truthfully, I was in no hurry to discover what might be raising so much dust near the edge wall.

The next day and night we found very little in the way of food—just a few dry, greasy berries that made my stomach grumble. For water we had only the morning dew from the rocks and leaves and grass. The land we crossed was like a squeezed sponge. No springs, no rivers . . .

On the third morning of our journey, we licked up as much dew from the rocks and grass as we could. The hills had become more prominent and rugged, some rising several hundred meters and studded with rocks. The dust towered high beyond. We pushed between the hills, skirting cracked boulders and spiky, cone-shaped trees. Their bristles left small, itching welts. Wisps of fog mixed with dust swirled over our heads. A few small birds flew back and forth, but the sky seemed as empty of sustenance for them as the land was for us.

The air twisted and whistled through the hills and the trees.

The next morning, the fog carried as much dust as moisture. An hour after first light, as we trudged along, half-blind, the dirty curtains of mist blew aside in ragged ribbons—and Vinnevra, intent on following her *geas*, nearly walked over a crumbling rim of rock and dirt.

I grabbed her arm forcibly—she hissed and tried to pull away—but then she saw, and gasped, and ran back. Gamelpar leaned on his stick and took deep breaths, letting each breath out in a low, curling sort of song whose words I did not understand.

This did not seem to be a valley, a canyon, or a river run. It was simply the deepest, ugliest ditch I had ever seen.

The old man ended his song and swept out his arm, fingers clutching, as if trying to grab at any answer to the mystery.

"The land here pulls back like drying mud," he said. "This is new. I don't like it." He walked back to squat in the shade of a high boulder.

Vinnevra and I carefully approached the ditch's crumbling rim. The last few meters, we got down on our hands and knees and crawled. An alarming cascade of dirt and pebbles fell away beneath my outstretched hands. I tried to guess how deep and how far across the ditch was. I could no longer see the edge wall, nor could I see the ditch's bottom.

The dirty fog crept along like a filthy, useless river.

"You want us to go down *there*?" I asked Vinnevra. "That's where your *geas* leads you?"

She regarded me glumly.

"Well, with all that dust, something's definitely on the move," I said.

"What?"

"Animals, maybe. Like wildebeest."

"What are . . ." She tried to say the word but gave it up. "What are they?"

I described them and said that on Erde-Tyrene I had seen such herds raising great clouds of dust and trying to forge broad rivers, where many drowned or fell prey to crocodiles. As a boy I had sat on the riverbank and watched the jaguars and sabertooths wait patiently on the far shore for the animals who survived, grabbing a few more, while the drowned ones swept away to become food for other crocodiles and fish. And yet, by sheer numbers, the wildebeests overwhelmed even these predators, and most reached their destinations.

By now, daylight had warmed the fog and I could dimly make out the bottom of the ditch. Gamelpar was right: the land had indeed pulled away from the great blue-gray wall, leaving a slope of broken rubble, and beyond that, about a kilometer of revealed foundation. It was easy to see how deep the land was here, on the inside of the Halo: eight or nine hundred meters. Not much thicker, relatively, than a layer of paint on the wall of a house.

I thought of one of my mother's bond-friends, with whom she would meet and chew leather and stitch cloth. The bond-friend kept a gray parrot that spoke as well as I did (I was just a child). To amuse the parrot, the bond-friend had arranged, within the bird's large wicker cage, a small forest of old tree branches stuck into a shallow dirt floor. The Librarian or some other Forerunner had painted the inside of this hoop with dirt and trees and animals to make us feel at home. All illusion, like the parrot's forest.

I drove this idea from my thoughts and focused on what I had seen and what I could know. There *were* things on the move down there, probably tens of thousands of them—but they were humans, not animals, walking over the bare foundation and around the slopes of rubble, following the great ditch westward.

For minutes, Vinnevra and I watched the crowds, stunned silent by their numbers and steady, united motion. Were all of them heading where Vinnevra had pointed? Had the beacon in the old city—if that was what it was—sent out a signal, a message so old that it had become outdated and pointless? Or had they become lost, slid into the ditch, and now followed it wherever it took them?

Soon I spotted other objects in motion—objects I definitely did *not* want to see. Only by their shadows, rippling like banners across the haze, did I first spot them: ten war sphinxes. From this distance, their paleness almost blended into the dust. They hovered, moving slowly back and forth above the masses, whether urging them along or just keeping watch I could not tell.

I pointed them out to Vinnevra. She groaned deep in her throat.

Gamelpar had crawled to a spot just behind us, still well back from the chasm. "Be quiet!" He cocked his head. "Listen!"

I heard little but the steady rush of wind from behind, cooler air seeking lowness. Finally, the wind subsided enough for me to pick up a distant, deeper note. Vinnevra heard it, too, and her face brightened.

"That's the sound of where I'm supposed to go if there's trouble!" she said.

"They're moving toward that sound?" I asked.

The old man crawled forward some more, turned slowly, head still cocked, and faced me. "What do our old ghosts say about *that*?" he asked.

"The memories are quiet," I said.

"Biding their time," Gamelpar said. "It will be a real struggle, you know, if the old spirits want to take charge."

I had not thought of this possibility. "Has that happened to you?"

"Not yet. Fight them if you will." He took the weight off his sore leg, then lifted his stick and pointed in the direction of the noise. "There's no bridge and nothing in the way of a path down—so, not much choice, eh?"

Vinnevra agreed. We walked on, keeping well back from the edge of the ditch, until the night shadow swept down upon us and the stars came out. I thought about the chance that Riser was down there in that crowd.

"Are they all going to a good place, or a bad place?" I asked Vinnevra. She turned away.

"It's all I have," she said.

As we rested against an embankment, I could feel the old spirit's deep curiosity at work again, and together, we studied those stars. The Lord of Admirals, finding new life within me, was so dismayed by the changes since his (I assumed) violent demise that more often than not he kept to the background, a kind of brooding shadow. I did not know whether I preferred his silence or his frustrated attempts to rise up and discover what he could do. He could not control me; he was little more powerful than a babe in a sling, not yet a willful force. My reaction to his growing strength was mixed. I worried about what might happen, yet took pride in flashes of remembered battles between humans and Forerunners, especially the victories. I shared his pain and shock at the power the Forerunners now wielded, the fates they had meted out to humans since the end of the old wars, our weakness—our divisions—our diversity.

Once, we were one great race, united in power and concerted in our goals. . . .

But I saw quickly enough that this was not precisely true, and soon realized that what the Lord of Admirals *believed* and what he *knew* were at times quite separate matters. Even alive, it seemed, the original mind that had lived these ancient histories had shared the contradictions I was all too familiar with in myself and in my fellows, back on Erde-Tyrene and here on the great wheel.

Vinnevra cut and prepared a new walking stick for Gamelpar. "Recognize any of those stars?" he asked me. His face was like a dark wrinkled fruit in the sky bridge's cool, reflected glow.

"Not yet," I said.

"Stop talking about *that*," Vinnevra demanded. She chopped away the last few twigs and presented him with the stick, greener and less crooked than the previous one. "We need to find food and water."

The dew that gathered here was muddy and bitter. We could drink from pockets of rainwater in the depressions in the boulders that lay along the edge of the chasm, but even those were drying up or thick with scum. It had been days since rain had fallen.

At first light, the noise from the chasm rose like a faraway torrent—the People were on the move again after a night's rest. We listened, then got up and walked on through the gray light, each of us casting two shadows, one growing from the light cast by the brightest arc of the band, the other dimming and shortening as shadow swept the other side.

"Does everyone have a *geas*?" Vinnevra asked. "Everyone down there, too?"

Gamelpar shook his head. "The Lady seeds her gardens, but she may also pluck weeds."

"What if *we* are the weeds?" Vinnevra asked.

The old man chuckled. He sounded young. If I did not look at him, I could almost imagine he *was* young, but the impression was fleeting. The Librarian—the Lifeshaper—the Lady, as these two called her—did not seem to care if those who bore her imprint grew old or suffered and died. That obvious fact seemed important, but I was too tired and thirsty to think it through.

Cool air crept down the embankment and spilled into the chasm.

"Tell us more about Erda," Gamelpar said to me, his voice growing hoarse.

"Is that where all the People come from, long ago?" Vinnevra asked. "Not even *you* remember that far back, Gamelpar."

"Too thirsty to talk," I croaked.

Without warning, my ears popped and the dust in the chasm bellied upward, lapped over the edge, and billowed toward us. Along with the dust came the strange, high sound of thousands of people screaming.

Gamelpar groaned and clutched his ears. Vinnevra leaned forward, hands on her knees, as if she were about to be sick. The sky above darkened, stars twinkled—breath came harder. Discouraged, gasping, my head throbbing and chest burning, I lay beside Vinnevra and the old man. Vinnevra had closed her eyes tight and was trembling all over like a fawn. Gamelpar lay on his back, the new green stick held across his chest. Grit floated everywhere, wet and clinging—clogging our noses and getting in our eyes. We could barely see.

All around the land again began to shake. Boulders rocked ponderously in their sandy beds, and a few started to lean, then tumble over. Some rolled to the edge of the chasm and vanished in swirls of muddy vapor. I could swear I felt the entire land beneath us *rippling* like the hide of a water buffalo tired of stinging flies.

The old man painfully dragged himself beside Vinnevra and laid his arm over her. I joined them. I saw streamers of dust ascending like thunderheads many thousands of meters, obscuring the sky bridge as well as the stars. Then a great wide shadow of dust covered us. Lightning played nearby, diffuse flashes followed nine or ten finger-clicks later by thunder—thunder that would once have terrified me, but now seemed nothing. I wondered if the entire Halo were about to shiver itself to pieces. Was it possible for such a great Forerunner object to be destroyed?

Of course! We laid waste their fleets, attacked their outpost worlds. . . . And the Forerunners themselves found a way to bring down the indestructible architecture of the Precursors, on Charum Hakkor. . . . Charum Hakkor, once called the Eternal.

The Lord of Admirals had no fear—he was already dead!

Then came the deluge. It fell of a sudden, curtaining sheets of water that pounded the ground until we started to sink. With an effort, I pushed against the suck of the mud, then dragged Vinnevra to firmer sand and the overhang of a very large boulder that did not seem interested in either shaking or rolling. My motive was simple: Vinnevra knew where we should go, the old man did not.

But that did not stop me from crawling back to get him. Walking was impossible in the thudding rain, each drop the size of a grape and cold as ice. Gamelpar, half buried in mud, struggled feebly to free himself. I rose on my knees, sank immediately to my thighs, and, reaching down, took hold of the center of his stick. His fists grabbed the stick tight and I half dragged, half carried him through the muck to where Vinnevra waited.

We lay under the rock overhang as the land continued to shake. Sleep was impossible. We stared out into the plashing, thundering dark, wretched, chilled to the bone—but no longer thirsty. We took turns drinking from water that quickly filled a fold in one of my rag-garments—cold and sweet, even if it wanted to drown us, even if it wanted to be our death.

At one point during the darkness, the boulder gave out a mighty crack, louder than the thunder, and sharp chips sprayed down over us. I reached up and found a fissure wide enough to accept the tip of a finger. Feeling in the fissure, I imagined it closing suddenly—and jerked back my hand, then wrapped myself in my arms and settled down. We were convinced that it would crash down on us at any second, yet we did not move.

———

The overhang did not fall, the boulder did not split apart. We saw little or nothing through that long, dark day, beyond the occasional silvery flash. Numbness overtook us. We did not sleep, neither did we think. Misery filled the void behind our eyes. We were waiting for change, any change. Nothing else would rouse us from this mortification of fear and tingling boredom.

———

Day passed into night, followed by another day.

Finally, both rain and the rippling ground ceased abruptly, as if at the wave of a masterful hand. We stared out across the mud at wan, milky sunlight, condensing over the chasm into a double—no, a *triple* rainbow, each brilliant, gaily-colored streamer intersecting, fading slowly from one end, brightening at the other—and disappearing.

Vinnevra ventured out first. She pulled and plunged through the mud for a few paces, then stood upright, lifting her arms to the light, moving her lips but making no sound— silent prayer.

"Who does she pray to?" I asked Gamelpar, who lay on his side, the green walking stick still clutched in one hand.

"No one," he said. "We have no gods we trust."

"But we're alive," I reasoned. "Surely that's worth thanks to somebody."

"Pray to the *wheel*, then," Gamelpar said. He crawled out from under the overhang, pushed up on his stick, and stood for the first time in many hours. His legs trembled but he kept upright, lifting first one foot loose from the mud, then another.

I was the last but I moved quicker and boldly walked along firmer, stony ground to the chasm. The migration below had stopped. I thought for a moment, peering down through the clear air, that those thousands were dead—drowned or struck down by avalanches.

But then I saw some of them move. One by one, individuals, then groups, and finally crowds picked themselves up, stumbled about in confusion, then coordinated, touched each other—and continued in the same direction as before. Just like wildebeest.

But much closer to us than before.

The floor of the chasm—the foundation material—had heaved itself up as if on the shoulders of a giant, rising almost halfway in the ditch. The great scar was closing. Soon, the chasm would be gone, filled in with Forerunner metal.

Here was a force, a presence—a monstrous god if you will—that could undergo great change, suffer hideous injuries, yet still heal itself. There was nothing mightier in our lives. Praying to the Halo might not be a bad idea after all.

I held out my hands like a shaman, as if to personally tap into the power of what had just happened. Vinnevra looked at me as if I were crazy.

I smiled, but she turned away without a word. There had been no end of fools in her life.

———

We moved on roughly parallel to the chasm. Vinnevra, puzzling out the failure of her *geas*, seemed to be trying to find a way around this obstruction. For a few hours, she led us inland, walking this way and that, stopping to pick up and drop pebbles, as if hoping to somehow sense the land. She would shake her head . . . and walk on.

The Lifeshaper had her in thrall, no doubt about it.

By noon—the sun a palm-width over the sky bridge directly above us—we had only wandered back in a loop, closer to the chasm, closer again to the edge wall. This time, looking across the chasm, we saw no dust or fog. Visibility was good right up to the wall itself. But that only revealed the futility of her quest.

At the end of the chasm, blocking the flow of the People, a great Forerunner building stuck up from the foundation through a ruckled chaos of rock and crust: a huge, square pillar curving in to lean against the wall, then thrusting high above both the wall and the air itself.

The pillar was about a kilometer square around the base. Clouds obscured its top.

I took Vinnevra aside. "Is this our destination?" I asked.

She had a dazed expression, eyes almost blank with the power of her inner drive, and it took some moments for her to stop pacing. Gamelpar squatted nearby, racked by coughing. When that stopped, he lifted his eyes toward the wall and slowly shook his head. He was almost worn out.

Vinnevra suddenly straightened, stuck out her jaw, and walked on at a brisk trot. I caught up with her and tried to flank her. She gave me a sidewise glare.

"The old man needs time to rest," I told her. Her mouth worked without making a sound. Finally, I took her shoulder and grasped her chin in one hand and swung her about, forcing her to face me. Her eyes went wild and she reached up with clawing hands to scratch my face. I batted her hands aside and held them down. At this, she leaned forward as if to take a bite out of my nose.

I dodged her teeth and pushed her back. "Stop that!" I said. "We're going to wait here for a while. Enough of the *geas*. You need to find yourself again!"

She swung back and glared, but there were tears in her eyes. Strangely, that look made my own breath hitch in sympathy.

Then she spun around and stalked off.

Gamelpar watched wearily from where he had stopped. "Leave her go," he called. "She won't wander far."

I returned to squat beside him and we observed in silence as the girl moved away to the rim to study the leaning pillar that blocked the chasm.

"Is that the Palace of Pain?" I asked the old man.

"I never saw the Palace of Pain except from the inside," he said.

"What was it like, inside?"

He hooded his eyes with his hands, as if not to remember. "Anyway, it's not what she's looking for," he concluded. "The People in the ditch must not know where they're going, either."

"How can you be sure?" I asked.

His face had grayed. "That she has not led us to where we need to be . . . that's a disappointment." He rubbed his trembling leg. He was thinking he might not finish the journey.

Restless, I walked back to the girl, now standing stiffly a few meters back from the chasm, tossing her head like some lost farm animal.

I walked right up to the rim and glanced down at the masses, milling around the base of the monument like so many turbulent pools, raising another great cloud of dust.

Then my blood seemed to stop and freeze.

There was something different moving now among the hordes, a kilometer or two away, half-obscured by the dust, hovering over the silent crowds. At first I could not tell whether it was a variety of war sphinx. But the dust raised by tramping feet briefly cleared and I saw a huge, curled-up spider with many legs, nine or ten meters wide, resting on a round disk and floating with insolent majesty above the migration. Sparkling glints shone from the facets of two oval, slanted, widely spaced eyes on the front of its broad, flat head.

The Captive.

The Primordial.

Vinnevra came up beside me. "Is that . . . ?"

For a moment, I could not say a word—made dumb by the old spirit's memories: raw fear and the intensely cutting realization that this thing was now free, perhaps in control of the migrations—or at least patiently observing.

She grabbed my arm. "I've been taking us toward *that one*, the Beast, haven't I? That's where they're all going!"

A wide gate opened in the base of the leaning monument. Slowly at first, then with steady determination, the crowds began to flow into the gate. Two war sphinxes emerged from the sides to guide and guard them.

The disk carrying the Captive also approached the gate, dipped a little, making the crowds kneel or fall beneath its shadow, then passed through as well. When it had disappeared into the monument, those who had not been crushed picked themselves up . . . and followed.

Vinnevra's fingers dug into my flesh. I pried them loose. We ran back to where Gamelpar was resting.

She composed herself and knelt beside her grandfather.

"We won't cross the chasm," she said. "We move inland—and west."

I realized Vinnevra was now using my words for directions. But that hardly seemed to matter. She did not mention the Captive. She wished to spare her grandfather that horror. But our expressions were too stricken, too obvious.

I could not avoid meeting his skeptical look.

"You've seen it, haven't you?" Gamelpar asked us. "The Beast. It's down there." His face crinkled with remembered terror. "That *is* a Palace of Pain, isn't it? And they're still being lured inside. . . ."

He could not finish.

Vinnevra curled up beside the old man and patted his shoulder as he sobbed. I could not stand that, the old man weeping like a child.

I wandered off to let them be, then sat and buried my head in my arms and knees.

NINE

B Y TREMENDOUS FORCE of will, Vinnevra ignored her compulsion and led us away from the chasm, back through the low dry hills and boulders to flat terrain— the direct opposite of where her *geas* was telling her to go. Gamelpar and I followed, walking in as straight a line as we could manage toward haphazard foothills like wrinkles in a blanket. Looking up along the low portion of the curve, I saw the foothills push against a sharp range of rocky mountains, all fading into the atmospheric haze about where the great body of water would be. Beyond the haze lay smooth Halo foundation lacking any artificial landscape, climbing for thousands of kilometers until it met a cloud-dotted line drawn perpendicular between the edge walls. Beyond that line, the Halo's false landscape appeared again, deep green and rich, tantalizing.

The wisdom of simply reversing course did not seem obvious to me, but Gamelpar did not object—and I could think of no reason not to put as much distance as possible between us and the Captive. The girl looked haunted.

Her geas, it seems, is not fixed. The Librarian seems to have programmed this wheel with the means to direct and protect her subjects. But who controls the beacons now?

I had no answer for the old spirit's obvious question.

Within a couple of hours, we were walking over irregular sheets of gray, flaky crust, overlaid with a powdery white char that tasted bitter on my tongue—bitter, burnt, nasty. What passed for natural landscape overlying the layer of bedrock, itself little more than a veneer, had been burned away, as if the Gods had decided to drop sheets of fire and destroy anything living.

Hundreds of meters ahead, blocking our path decisively, jagged sheets of blue-gray foundation material had peeled back, pushing aside the white char and crust and exposing a great gaping wound in the Halo itself.

Ruin laid over ruin.

We walked around the towering, curling, jagged edges of that hole, pausing once only to peer into a pit at least four or five kilometers across. None of us could speak, looking down through layer after penetrated layer of smashed, ruptured architecture and melted machinery—down many hundreds of meters, to be plugged at the bottom by shapeless black slag.

And yet—for the Halo, this was but a minor wound, not nearly as large as the great black smear we had seen high up on the sky bridge. Replacing our region of the wheel, our tile, was apparently not necessary. Not yet, at any rate.

The Lord of Admirals had no comment on this destruction, but I could feel a growing impatience and restlessness, his brooding, measuring intelligence gathering strength, waiting for the proper moment to make a difference. I did not know whether to be frightened of him. So many other fears loomed larger.

After a few hours, we climbed a rough scarp to reach a higher, relatively undisturbed stretch of level land—dirt, rocks, a ridge of granite populated by a few singed and drooping trees—and a small pond left over from the recent deluge. We paused. Gamelpar dipped his fingers into the pond and tasted the water, then nodded. Drinkable, he declared. But of animals, berries, any kind of food—nothing.

Again the shadow of night rushed down and we lay in the chill, shivering, half-starved. Gamelpar never once complained of cold or hunger. Vinnevra had said nothing for many hours.

Morning came, and listlessly we rose and washed ourselves. Then Vinnevra closed her eyes, turned slowly, hand out—and stopped. Her hand pointed back to the chasm.

With a convulsive shudder, she swung halfway around—reversing the direction her *geas* told her we should take.

When she looked at me, her eyes were bleak.

Her strength was impressive. Against all my instincts, I found myself admiring, then growing fond of this pair. Foolishness—it was Riser I needed to find, and once I found him, wouldn't we celebrate by shaking our feet and leaving all others behind?

I wondered now, however, whether I could guess what Riser would do. He had always surprised me.

We traveled onward, inland and west, through the rolling foothills toward the more sharply defined range. This path took us by the end of the day to the edge of what might have once been another city—a strange, shifting ruin, over which the ghosts of monuments flickered, as if struggling to return.

Vinnevra stood for a while on the broken boundary of a rounded, slagged causeway—raising her hands as if imploring, begging for relief or at least some sort of explanation.

"I need to go back!" she said to us. "Keep me, hold me! Stop me!"

Gamelpar and I gently held her arms and we all sat down as a sour wind blew through the rubble, moaning over hollows and whispering through shattered arches.

Just a few hundred paces over the waste, to the left of the causeway, lay half of a ship larger than the Didact's star boat—many hundreds of paces long, its rounded hull blackened and slumped. This boat's spacefaring days were over. It seemed to have been attacked and brought down through the Halo's atmosphere, to smash into this section of the great hoop.

These were not fresh ruins, and this place had never been a human city. Again, here was grim evidence that decades ago, Forerunners had fought Forerunners, and many had died.

The Lord of Admirals now decided to rise up and gloat.

Confusion to the enemy! Those who tyrannize humans have fought among themselves. Dissension in their ranks! Why should that not bring us joy?

The old spirit seemed to take control of my feet and legs, and for the moment, without making a conscious choice, I ceded my eyes and body to him. Beyond any plan, any stretch of my own experience, we strolled along the causeway, leaving Gamelpar and Vinnevra behind for the moment, feeling disappointment, sorrow, vindication—just as I had felt at the first awakening of horror and pride back on Charum Hakkor.

The causeway ascended at a gentle angle, and we walked up the slope, leaping away as the edges of jagged cracks squirmed and sparkled with a strange light—as if trying to rejoin, to begin repairs. But for this place, the will, the energy, the resources no longer existed. The command structure had long since been broken. That much seemed obvious—though I could not even begin to understand the underlying technology.

Again, I felt like bowing down and worshipping.

They are not gods, the old spirit reminded me with an air of disdain. But the ruins were too sad, and he no longer expressed any sense of triumph.

They are like us, in the great scheme of things, sometimes strong, too often foolish and weak, caught up in politics . . . and now at war. But why?

The Lord of Admirals walked me to the end of the causeway, and we looked out over the dead ship and the shattered, exploded skeletons of buildings that once had risen thousands of meters into the sky, but now lay across each other like so many dead on a field of battle—toppled, half-melted, yet neither entirely still nor silent.

I was distracted by the reappearance of walls and framework beams rising from the ruins perhaps five hundred meters away—rising and reassembling, much as the Didact's ship had built itself at the center of Djamonkin Crater. It seemed for a moment that it might succeed—took on almost a finished aspect—but that was an illusion.

The walls disappeared, the skeletal framework flickered, dropped away . . .

Vanished.

In mere seconds, the effort came to an end with a sigh and rush of wind, and the building's ghost was no more. Then—to the right of the causeway—another futile effort, another resurrection—another collapse and rush of wind.

The city was like a buffalo brought down by a pride of great cats, its flanks torn and throat slashed, bleeding out as the predators wait, tongues lolling, for its sharp black horns to cease swinging. . . . The buffalo struggles to regain its feet, but the hyenas scream and laugh, and the pride leader growls her hungry triumph.

I was being drawn into the old spirit's memories of the destruction of Charum Hakkor, the collapse of entire fleets of human ships. . . . The pain and sense of loss staggered me. The old presence, this spirit, this ancient *thing* within me, was as much a ghost as the ruins writhing and moaning all around.

Finally, neither the Lord of Admirals nor I could bear to watch. I could feel neither his words nor his emotions. He, too, had collapsed, retreated.

"*No more!*" I shouted, and covered my eyes, then stumbled back to the margins.

The girl looked to me as if for some explanation.

"We shouldn't cross this place," I said. "A bad, sad place. It doesn't know it's dead."

HALO: PRIMORDIUM

TEN

W E DECIDED ON a course around the ruins.

Another day of travel and Gamelpar's strength seemed to be flagging. We rested more hours than we traveled, but finally found a shallow rivulet of water and edible weeds—or so Gamelpar assured us. They were less obnoxious than the greasy berries, and with thirst quenched and stomach less empty, the old man seemed to revive. He waved his hand, then moved away on his stick.

Ahead the hills resumed. Here they were covered with dry grass and spotted with trees I wasn't familiar with, pleasantly shaped, of middle height, with black bark and gray-green leaves that splayed out like the fingers of cupped hands.

The sky was free of clouds, except far up the bridge, at the point where the bridge was as broad as my outstretched palm. I squinted and moved my hand, covering and uncovering the clouds, while Gamelpar watched without much interest. Beyond the sharp mountains we could now see the body of water very clearly. The shadows had grown long, the air was cooling, the sun was three fingers above the gray wall. Darkness was coming.

We rested.

In the shade of a black-trunked tree, I pried a stone out of caked dirt and looked it over, marveling at its simplicity. Simple—and false. Everything here had been manufactured by Forerunners. Or perhaps it had all been stripped away from a planet, transported here, and rearranged. Either way, this land and the ring itself was like the toy of a great, spoiled child that can have anything it wants, *make* anything it wants.

Yet humans had nearly defeated their fleets, ten thousand years ago.

"You have that look," Vinnevra said, kneeling beside me. "Like you're somebody else."

"I am, sometimes," I said.

She gazed through the deep twilight at where Gamelpar had rested with his back against the smooth trunk of a tree. "So is he." She scratched idly at the dirt. "No good here for insects."

I hefted the stone. "I could learn to throw rocks at birds."

We both smiled.

"But we'd starve before I got any good," I admitted.

Gamelpar was much tougher than either of us thought. He kept up with us beyond the foothills and into the mountains.

I lost count of the days.

ELEVEN

WHILE GAMELPAR AND Vinnevra rested near the base, I hiked to a granite outcrop at the top of the closest and lowest rocky peak. Along the slope I found a few bushes with small black berries that had a certain sweetness and did not upset my stomach. I nibbled, but gathered the rest into my shirt, saving them for my companions.

The wide streak of dark blue water was about thirty kilometers away, protected on this side by both the mountains and a dense region of nubbly forest. Looking inland and outward, this huge lake stretched across the band many thousands of kilometers. From where I stood, I guessed its breadth at about two or three hundred kilometers.

And where will we find a boat?

I shook my head in absent reply, then studied the lake intently as cloud shadows and dapples of light played over it. Clear enough even from this distance, the water was studded across most of its width and breadth by tall, narrow islands like pillars. About two or three kilometers from the near shore, some sort of growth or construction connected and lay over the pillars and islands—dwellings connected by bridges or just peculiar vegetation, I could not tell which.

If we were to follow the course established by getting the hell away from the ditch and the Beast, then we would have to cross that lake, but first, penetrate the surrounding forest.

Soon, with night bearing down, I descended the slope. The old man and the girl had moved a short distance from where I had left them, near a dry riverbed, and Vinnevra was patiently rubbing her grandfather's arms and legs. Both looked up as I approached.

"What's out there?" Gamelpar asked, patting his grand-daughter's shoulder. I delivered my berries and they ate, tipping their hands in thanks. Vinnevra's steady appraisal disturbed me.

Then she got up and walked away, and I felt a peculiar disappointment—for both of us.

The old man reached for his stick, as if prepared to move out right away, based on some report of danger. "What's out there?" he asked again.

"The big lake," I said. "Dense forest."

"I've seen that one many times from the old city," Gamelpar said. "I never expected to go visit it."

"We don't have to," I said.

"Where else is there?" he asked.

"She doesn't know," I said.

Vinnevra had hunkered miserably a few steps away, head bowed.

"We need purpose. We need direction." He followed this with a direct look that as much as said, *Without that, I, at least, will soon die. And what will become of the girl then?*

I shared more of my gleanings with the old man, then walked over to the girl, who again seemed to reappraise me, like some unexpected and unpleasant marvel, as she accepted the last spare handful and ate.

At that moment, I wondered—for the last time—what my chances would be if I just took off on my own. I could move faster. Out there, I'd likely be as knowledgeable about the conditions as either Vinnevra or Gamelpar, so far from their home. . . .

I had at least as much chance of finding Riser by leaving, I thought.

But of course there were larger problems to solve, and the old man still held, perhaps, some answers—particularly with regard to the Captive. The Primordial.

The Beast with the glittering eyes.

The morning came bright and clear, and once more we had a view of the red and gray orb, a waxing crescent now showing visible details—part of an animal face, like a wolf or a jackal.

"It's getting closer," Gamelpar said, performing his usual rather impressive stretches. The exercises hurt the old man, and their effect diminished through the day's journey, but they were essential. He would stand on his good leg, arms out, then rotate his body and hips around until balance became difficult—hop to recover, and stretch out again, leaning his head back as if to let out a silent howl.

Vinnevra stood with arms by her sides, waiting for us to make up our minds, she would follow wherever we went, that was her destiny, she deserved nothing more . . . and so on. All in slack posture and blank, staring eyes—staring away, away from us, away from everything.

"You both look gloomy," Gamelpar muttered as he finished. "What I would not give for a bunch of plump, cheerful shopkeepers."

"What would we do with them?" I asked.

"Make jokes. Dance in rings. Eat well." He smacked his lips. The old man's rare expressions of humor were almost as disconcerting as the girl's appraising silences.

We walked off, taking a long inland route around the mountain. I had seen gentle pastures with hummocky terrain and water-worn tablelands on that side of the peak, and beyond, more and more trees until another bare and arid strip that stretched right up to the dense, high forest.

Two days between.
Two dreadful, silent days.
And then, suddenly, Vinnevra was cheerful again.

———

She still did not say much, but she recovered a lightness in her step, a set to her eyes, a vibrant, swinging motion of her long arms and skinny legs that spoke eloquently that for her, at least, the worst of the disappointment was over, it was time to feel young again, to look around attentively and feel a glimmer of hope.

Her energy passed on to Gamelpar and we made better time. Here, winding through hummocks and eroded plateaus, Gamelpar became convinced we were now back in decent hunting territory. He showed us how to make a snare from stiff cane and plaited grass loops, and we worked for a time stretching them over one after another of a circle of fresh-looking burrows.

We carried stones to block off the open holes.

"Not rabbits," Gamelpar said as we stood aside to wait. "Probably good to eat, though."

He then took his stick a few meters away and dug a hole in the sandy soil. After a while, a muddy dampness seeped into the bottom of the hole, and we all took turns digging deeper. Soon there was water—muddy, far from sweet, but wet and essential. If we were patient, we could drink our fill.

Then the first of the snares bobbed and danced and we had a little brown animal, like a lump of fur with eyes, the size of two skinny fists. That last night before we reached the forest, we captured four, set a low, smoky fire with dry shrubs and scrap twigs, and ate the fatty, half-raw meat.

Does the Lifeshaper come to these poor beasts when they are born?

I ignored that blasphemy. The old spirit had no respect.

I slept well—no dreams. We were as far from the ditch and the Captive as we could take ourselves. Of course, who knew how fast it could travel on its grotesque floating plate?

But for the moment, neither terribly hungry nor terribly thirsty, I was able to watch the stars on both sides of the silver and pale brown sky bridge—as well as the crescent wolf-faced orb, now as wide as two thumbs.

Gamelpar remembered seeing a small wandering star of that color just after the brightness and the fires in the sky. Since, he had ignored its habits and routines—and while he allowed they might be one and the same, there was no way of telling. But my old spirit roused to suggest it was not a moon and could not possibly be in orbit around the wheel— that just wouldn't work—but was more likely a planet, and it was growing closer day by day.

I still had difficulty thinking of the sky as something other than a great spreading flatness, on which little glowing insects moved, and occasionally someone opened up a door to let in light from outside. . . .

Old teachings die hard.

TWELVE

THE WALL OF the forest was the most formidable living barrier we had encountered—to the point of being impassable. The great brown and green trunks—some as wide as the three of us stretched head to toe—rose up in implacable, sullen splendor, like pillars spaced along the wall of a fortress. Great gray thorns grew in from the trunks and met like meshed teeth in a tightly clamped jaw. Above the thorns, ten or twelve meters up, thin, wiry branches interlaced to form a tight canopy.

Vinnevra actually smiled at this. I thought she was taking comfort in the possibility that it didn't matter which way we walked, we were bound to meet up with something or other unpleasant and discouraging. But that was unfair. I was compensating for my growing attachment by casting aspersions.

How mature to see that.

"Oh, shut up," I grumbled.

We could climb to the canopy, but it leaned out a considerable distance—several meters—and I doubted we could all clamber up and over.

I studied and stroked the thorns' tough, thinly grooved surfaces, almost hard as stone—then pushed my finger in as far as I could between two of them. There was a bare minimum of flexure, of give—no more than a fingernail's thickness. Perhaps the trees would present less of a barrier if we could bend and break the thorns with sturdy poles—wherever would we find those! Gamelpar's stick was too flimsy.

But nothing we could do now would make much difference, and so we prepared through the slanting light of dusk to sleep out in the open yet again, with no idea where the next morning would take us.

———

From my uneven bed on the spiky dry grass, my eyes kept lifting above the tree-wall to the stars and the sky bridge. I drifted in and out of sleep, only half-caring that the dreams that moved behind a thin, translucent wall in my mind were not my own, nor mere fantasies, but ancient memories, with all the uneven detail of memories, made worse by being witnessed by an outsider.

Some, however, were remarkably vivid—lovemaking in a garden under a sky crisscrossed with Precursor architecture; the impassioned face of a female whose features differed from the women of this time, and especially from Vinnevra—so much variability in our kind!

But if these passing glimpses were at all indicative, humans had stayed remarkably true to their stock during our suppression and reevolution. We were all recognizably of the same kind, the same breed, and we did not grow up or get transformed into different physical castes like the Forerunners.

The dream-emotions conveyed by the Lord of Admirals felt sharp and raw, like the waft from a freshly slaughtered animal . . . strange juxtapositions of pain and pleasure, hidden fear and anticipation, a glowing spark of battle-rage kept from flaring—held in reserve.

For these dreams spoke of leave-taking and farewell, of the last night before a grand battle that would spread across a hundred thousand light-years to determine the fate of a thousand suns and twenty thousand worlds.

All dreams are young, my host, my friend. All dreams belong to youth, whether they be nightmares or idylls.

———

A snapping, clacking sound abruptly pulled me up out of this bizarre eavesdropping.

I started from my rustling pad of plucked grass and looked at the thorn-packed, forbidding wall of the forest. The thorns were withdrawing, pulling back into the trunks . . . opening wide, dark passages below the thick black canopy.

I crawled over to awaken Vinnevra, and she shook the old man's shoulder. He slept lightly if at all, came awake more alert than either of us, but he did not rise up. Instead, his eyes moved back and forth under the silver-ivory reflected light of the sky bridge.

"Dawn's a few hours off," he said.

Vinnevra bit her lip. "We need to pass through the forest," she said.

"Still the same direction?"

"If we are moving against . . . where I really want to go, yes."

"That's no guidance at all, really," I offered.

The girl and the old man got up, brushed themselves down, and stood staring into the dense blackness between the trunks.

"If that way leads us to the Primordial," the old man said, nodding back in the direction of the wall-hugging pillar, "then anything that leads us *away* . . ."

He was now using the same word for the Captive as my old spirit. He did not finish, and did not need to. We had already had a discussion about trying to walk back to the edge wall, around the forest, but that was a journey of at least two hundred kilometers, and possibly a thousand or more, depending on the convolutions . . . and there was no guarantee that the thorn-trunk trees, to either side, did not grow up flush against the wall, blocking passage everywhere.

On the other hand, if the thorns were everywhere dense within the forest, and we were caught between the trunks when they chose to thrust out again . . .

"We'll have to move quickly," I said, my breath coming up short. The combination of pitchy darkness, the threat of being pierced through, of basically being chewed to pieces by a strange forest . . .

Vinnevra and the old man seemed determined. But despite my complaints, I was no longer even thinking about separating from the only compass available to us on this wheel. No matter that it worked best in reverse.

I did not want to be alone out here. And these were my only friends, until we found Riser—if we ever found him.

"You'll know a straight line through?" I asked the girl.

"I think so," she said. "Yes. I still need to go back there." She pointed away from the forest.

"All right," I said. "You lead the way."

Gamelpar picked up his walking stick. Before I could object, or gather up my sleep-addled wits, we plunged between the trunks and vision was no longer our guide.

The journey might have been awful, but once committed, I felt a strange calmness. Oddly, it was the old man who suffered the most, groaning and flinching as we brushed past the wide trunks, or collided with them. I had heard such sounds from young boys and men lining up to fight in the narrow alleys of Marontik, but the terror he felt in this dark puzzled me, until the old spirit within offered a plangent observation:

Strange fears echo through both old man and warriors. Those near death know it too well.

But Gamelpar did not slow down, and we kept moving. I had no idea whether we were keeping to any sort of straight line, but not once did Vinnevra hesitate.

Perhaps an hour later, some vague indication of daylight oozed and dripped down from the canopy, emphasizing rather than relieving the gloom below. Our dark-adjusted eyes were befuddled by this promise of coming brightness, and we lost our growing sense of knowing where a trunk might be.

Our collisions became more frequent.

Then—it seemed to happen all at once—I saw long shafts of day up ahead, echoing in golden, almost blinding silhouettes through a dozen great trunks. Vinnevra pulled us all along at a run. Gamelpar swung his stick against the trees, grinning and laughing, holding on to the girl's other hand. . . .

We broke through. The dawn on the other side was just beginning, but after hours of struggling to see, we were like moles tugged up out of a burrow. I blinked, stumbled, let go of Vinnevra's hand, tried to find Gamelpar. But they had moved away to stare across a beach of great rounded boulders and smaller rocks, tumbling down to a deep blue body of water that seemed to stretch on forever.

At the first direct ray of light over the far edge wall, the trunks gave a deep, booming groan and the thorns pushed out again, meshing tight—closing off retreat.

Gamelpar, closest to the trunks and thorns, reached back with his stick and tapped them again, then gave me a mischievous glance—followed by a deep sigh of relief.

"We're stuck here," I said.

Vinnevra paced back and forth along the rocks, using both hands to shield her eyes against the morning glare. "I know that!" she said. "I'm using all my willpower not to just turn around and wait for the thorns to open again . . . just to go back *there* and become part of . . . *that*. It's getting stronger," she said. "If I can't stop myself . . . will you two tie me up and keep me with you, no matter what I say or do?"

I wondered what we could do if the impulse became so strong she decided to lie to us. For now, at least, it seemed clear that we had to cross the water, however we could. Walking along the inside perimeter of the forest, over these rocks, was no more a real option than walking around the outside.

I picked my steps carefully down to the lapping waves and looked out over the lake, deep blue, almost black. Kneeling, I dipped my hand into the cool wavelets and lifted it to my nose, smelled it—clean but different—then tasted it.

Instantly, I spat and wiped my mouth. "Salt!" I cried.

Vinnevra helped Gamelpar down to the shore and he also tasted the water, then agreed. Vinnevra tasted last and made a bitter face. None of us had ever tasted salt water before, it seemed. This provoked an observation from the old spirit.

You've never visited the great oceans, or seen a salt lake?

I admitted I had not. I knew of freshwater lakes like the one in Djamonkin Crater, and streams and rivers—sometimes freshets becoming floods—but all had been either fresh or filled with bitter minerals, never so salty.

Inland boy, the old spirit said.

"My best wife spoke of such water," Gamelpar said. "She called it *the sea.* Her parents lived on the shore when she was a small girl and netted fish from out in the deeps. Before the Forerunners took them away."

"Why salty?" I asked.

"The gods piss salt," Gamelpar said. "Because of that, some animals live better in salt water."

I did not want to ask him where freshwater came from.

"What about people . . . are we happier when we swim in salt water?" Vinnevra asked, balancing on a round boulder and stretching out her arms. Again, she looked like a carefree girl, as the worry and fear seemed to slip away from her face, replaced only by curiosity. So changeable!

So adaptable. Her People are survivors.

"Perhaps," Gamelpar said, after giving her theory due consideration. "Are we going to swim?"

"I don't know how," Vinnevra admitted.

"I'm not going to try." The Librarian was fond of strange and exotic beasts and plants. I thought of the irritable merse in Djamonkin Crater. What kind of creatures would she stock in a great, wide sea like this? How big, and how hungry?

"Look out there," Vinnevra said, pointing to our left—inland. "There's something hanging from those big towers."

The light was at such an angle now that we saw dark strands stretched between a collection of stone pillars—bridges, I guessed, looking from this distance like hanging strings wrapped around posts. They might have been four or five kilometers inland and a kilometer or so out in the water. The longer I looked, the more it seemed there was quite a dark mass arranged between and on top of the pillars, whether made by People, or some sort of vegetation—an outgrowth of the thorny trees—I could not tell.

But I could just as easily imagine webs, traps, nasty things awaiting the curious.

"We should go there," Gamelpar said.

I studied the rocky margin around the water with a skeptical look, but the old man raised his stick.

Litter from the great wall of trees had fallen on the rocks. Wind and waves had pushed the branches and bark up against the trunk wall, where they formed a thick mat. I investigated. The litter was several hand-spans deep, like a tough, woody crust. I stepped up on it. The path was irregular at best, but supported my weight—and I was the heaviest.

"Let's go," Gamelpar said. We helped him onto the path. He raised his stick high as if in salute to the trees, and started off.

Vinnevra shivered again, then leaned over and whispered to me, "It's bad. It hurts. I need to . . ."

She took hold of my hand, raised it to her lips, then kissed my palm, eyes desperate, beseeching. "Kill me, if you have to," she said. "Gamelpar won't. He can't. But I don't want to go anywhere near the Palace of Pain."

My heart sank and tears started up in my eyes. I could no more kill this girl than her grandfather could. I still remembered her smell when she first leaned over me, welcoming me back to the living. She was not my idea of beautiful, but I felt for her, and not just because of what we had already shared.

"Promise me!" she whispered, giving my hand a painful squeeze.

"It won't happen," I said. "I won't let it happen. But I can't make that sort of promise."

She dropped my hand, spun about, and climbed up on the matted litter, then glanced back, face pinched, disappointed, even angry. I could not imagine what she was feeling.

Imagine. The old spirit again burned within me, his rage threatening to break through. *Imagine the worst. It is all we can expect from Forerunners, all we can ever expect.*

"But the Lifeshaper . . ."

Just another Forerunner.

"Without her, I'd be . . . free, but ignorant, empty of all but myself. And you'd be dead."

The Lord of Admirals retreated, but not before his bitter miasma tainted my thoughts.

I kicked at the litter and performed another thrashing dance of frustration—well aware how stupid I looked, how desperately foolish and trapped.

How I wished I could talk to Riser and hear what he thought!

I followed after the girl and the old man.

THIRTEEN

THE SMELL REACHED us from some distance away, but Gamelpar gave a grunt and pushed on. The shore was littered with decaying bodies. We made out gray and green shapes slumped over the rocks . . . and then we were upon the first, and my worst fears were banished—but not by much.

These were Forerunners, not humans. By their size and build they had been Warrior-Servants, fully mature. One of them could be Bornstellar, I thought—larger after receiving the Didact's imprint. But they were far too decayed to make out individual features.

Vinnevra hung back, holding her hand over her nose

and mouth. "What happened here?" Gamelpar asked, his voice quavering.

"Another battle," I said. "They're not wearing armor."

"Every Forerunner wears armor. Why would they take it off?"

Then I remembered and understood. My armor had stopped functioning, of course, but so had the armor of my Forerunner escorts—either jammed up by the metal fleas, or just stopped working. "Something killed all the armor," I said.

"What, the Beast?"

"I don't know. Part of the war, maybe."

"And here they fought hand to hand?" Gamelpar asked.

The bodies were badly decomposed. Slash marks with puffy, swollen edges crossed what remained of their faces and torsos. A few puckered holes seeped inner decay.

I looked out at the rock pillars and the rope-bridge and platform-town—isolated from the shore, accessible only by water and so more defensible, but against what, I could not know. Forerunners of course could have flown out there, and would not have built such a primitive structure. Likely this was a human town.

On Erde-Tyrene, I had heard of villages built on lakes, usually out in the great north, but had never seen one. "There was a battle in the town," I theorized, "and when they died, they fell into the water and drifted to shore. What does *your* old spirit think?"

Gamelpar made a face. "Sad, even for Forerunners. Is the whole wheel dying?"

We were too small, too trivial to know such things.

Vinnevra had walked up the shoreline to get away from the smell. "There's a boat over there, behind the rocks," she said. "I think it's made from one of those trees. It has thorns on its sides."

We walked along the matted path. She pointed behind a pair of boulders draped with wrack like thinning hair over gray heads. It was indeed a boat, and not a bad one, either.

How convenient. The gods piss salt water but leave us a boat.

Sometimes I found my old spirit to be a real prig.

Vinnevra stood between us, eyes fixed on mine. "We can use pieces of bark for oars, and row across the water," she said. That seemed like an incomplete plan at best. "Gamelpar needs the rest, and we'll do the rowing," she added, eyes still piercing.

I shrugged. "Water is the only path," I said, then set to inspecting the boat. It was about four meters long, blunt bow and stern, carved as she had suggested, no doubt, from one of the great trunks. The sides were indeed lined with formidable thorns. "Protection or ornament?" I wondered, feeling a sharp point with my thumb.

She tried to push the boat out into the water. It was jammed tight. Together, we pried up one end, then slid it out over the rocks, and with a grumbling, thumping scrape, pushed it into the water. Vinnevra held it while I helped the old man across the rocks and then lifted him up bodily, at which he snorted and made an unpleasant scowl.

I lowered him into the bow.

"Find some pieces of bark," Vinnevra ordered, her face damp with sweat. She sounded excited and looked even happier. Perhaps we were passing out of range of the beacon signal.

Finding proper pieces of bark, fortunately, was not difficult. The trees shed in long, tough strips varying from a hand's width to two or three. With a little vigorous bending and tearing, the strips made decent oars. I picked up several more and piled them into the boat.

Soon we were rowing across the water.

"We go to the town first," Gamelpar insisted.

"Why?" Vinnevra said, her face clouding. "Let's just row across and leave *that* be."

"Looks quiet," the old man said. "There might still be living People out there. Or food."

"Or stinking bodies," Vinnevra said.

I rowed, she rowed, and finally we rowed together so that the boat did not go in circles but toward the pillars, the drooping bridges, and at the center, the suspended village. It took us the better part of the day to row against a steady, lapping tide. Then, without reason, the tide reversed and rushed us in minutes toward the pillars, so that we had to back water vigorously to avoid being thrust between two adjacent pillars. We clumsily managed to make our way to a wide wooden dock in the crossing shadows of a network of bridges.

On top of many of the pillars, individual huts perched like storks' nests. The bridges at that end could be raised or lowered to provide access, with platforms between that might be used by all. Here, I counted four layers of bridges, houses, platforms—denser and denser toward the center of the village, where, finally, the dwellings merged.

In the gloom beneath, stairs, ladders, and ropes descended to other docks. I saw no bodies, no evidence of fighting—but also heard no voices nor any of the sounds of a living town. Just the regular lapping of the salty waves.

Then Vinnevra gasped. Something long and pale passed beneath us, a wide, greenish cloud like smoke in the dark water. She scrambled up onto the dock and I quickly followed, hauling Gamelpar with me. This time I caused him pain and he cried out, then pushed away, balancing on one leg, while I reached down and snatched his stick from the boat. The boat drifted, so I kneeled, groaning at the thought of leaning out over the water, and grabbed one side. "We need some way to tie it up."

"I'll stay here and tend to it," Vinnevra said, glancing calmly enough into the water—once again clear and dark through its depths. She preferred whatever had passed below, or its companions, to what we might find up above.

"Not a good idea," I said. "You'll come with us."

My concern was twofold. I worried about her safety, but I also worried that she might give in to her compulsion and leave us stranded out here. I didn't trust her change in mood—or whatever might be causing it.

Fortunately, on the opposite side of the dock, a wooden bracket was hung with several ropes left to dangle in the water. Gamelpar pulled one up with his stick and soon we had the boat secured, then all of us climbed the steep steps to a hatch in the lowermost platform.

Gamelpar, I learned, was quite capable of scaling such steps, as long as he took the climb slowly, braced his stick on the treads, and used it for balance.

Through the hatch, we emerged on a wide, railed platform about twenty meters across, connected to other platforms and a few enclosed shacks—for at this level, still in the shadows, they were little more than that: places to store things or dwellings for the poor.

I crossed several bridges, looking into the shacks, and found emptiness—neither inhabitants nor food.

"They were all taken away," Vinnevra said.

Had the humans here been worth fighting over? I wondered. What else could cause Forerunners to battle each other in such an insignificant place?

Surely the humans hadn't killed them!

We climbed still higher, ladder and stairs and more ladders, until we reached a narrow round turret atop a central stone pillar, slender and, I thought, naturally six-sided rather than hewn—if anything could be natural here.

Gamelpar watched from below.

Wind blew through Vinnevra's tight orange-brown curls as we walked around the turret together. From here, we could see out over the entire complex.

"You don't need to worry about me," she said. "It's fading."

"What's fading?"

"My sense of direction. Something's changed again—back there, *out* there. But I just wanted to say—I really don't like it here."

"Not a warning from your *geas*?"

"No. I hardly feel anything about that. I don't even see the Lady." She shook her head. "I'm of little use now to anybody."

"Nonsense," I said. "We know where to go, because of you."

"You know where *not* to go," she corrected.

"Just as useful, don't you think?"

She pointed toward the largest building, a peaked pentagram supported by five roughly equidistant pillars, each about twenty meters apart. Their blunt tips poked through the perimeter of the roofline, forming a truly impressive central hall—or the dwelling of some powerful leader.

"Over there?" she asked.

I traced and mapped the bridges with a darting finger. "Maybe," I said.

"You might actually learn what happened here," she said, her voice low.

"What do you sense?"

"Nothing good," she said. "Can you hear it? Above the waves and the wind."

I cupped my hands over my ears and directed them toward the pentagram hall. For a moment, I heard nothing—and then, something heavy slammed inside the building, making the bridges sway. We held on to the turret rail and

kept very still, like hunted animals, but nothing so loud followed.

I looked down and saw Gamelpar frozen in place just
like us, facing the direction of that hall.

Then I heard—or imagined I heard—other, softer sounds
coming from within the plank walls. Sounds not unlike the
lapping of the waves, but more prolonged, and only slightly
less *liquid*.

Vinnevra pushed back from the rail. "Something's in
there," she said. "Something odd and very unhappy."

I had been around this girl—no longer really a girl in my
eyes—for long enough to feel the hair on my neck and arms
bristle. I descended from the turret, Vinnevra close behind.

"Do we go and look?" I asked him.

Gamelpar said, "We've come this far. We're obviously
none of us here for our health."

Somehow, that also struck me as blasphemous. But these
deep emotions were being challenged both by fear and by
the unspoken attitudes of the Lord of Admirals—who had
no such sentimental perspective about the Lifeshaper.

We followed several bridges, moving in a broken spiral to
the central hall. Finally, we gathered on a walkway that ran
completely around the hall, and circled the perimeter until
we came to a broad, high double door. The frame of the
door was ornamented with blocky, simple carvings of leering
faces, fruits, animals—and what looked like wolves or dogs.

At the peak of the door frame, one very convincing ape
looked down upon us—like those great black beasts said to

be found in the northern highlands back on Erde-Tyrene, half a dream's distance from Marontik.

I studied this oddly peaceful-looking visage. Had it been carved from life?

Gamelpar nudged my leg with his stick, and I pushed one side of the door. It swung in with a mournful groan.

The smell that came out of that hall was indescribable, not the smell of death—not rot and decay—but a thickened stench of endless fear and life gone desperately wrong. The door's creaking opening was followed by more fluid-slopping sounds from deep inside, curiously muffled as if by thick curtains.

Vinnevra and Gamelpar were driven back by the smell—and perhaps by the sound. Gamelpar held out his stick and gently pushed Vinnevra farther away, giving me a look that said with no uncertainty, only you and I will enter that place. My daughter of daughters will stay here.

"Gamelpar—," she began, and I heard in her tone fear of being alone out here, of having no one to keep her from her compulsion, should it return, no one to cross the wide salty water with her . . . no one left on this broken wheel that she knew and trusted or loved.

But the old man would not be dissuaded. "You will stay here," he said. He nudged my shoulder with his hand. "You first," he said.

This was neither a joke nor any sign of cowardice. We were entering the kind of place, perhaps, where things were more likely to come upon one from behind. Things not

truly alive . . . failed gods from old times, bitter and dusty;
the ghosts of our ancestral enemies, outside human emotion, simply wound up to hunt and gibber along through the
darkness . . .

Why I thought of these things I do not know, but I was
reasonably certain Gamelpar was thinking the same things.
We were both far beyond any personal experience of what
lies behind the apparently solid and real.

I had hoped the Lord of Admirals would provide some
helpful comment, some guiding memory, but he seemed to
have retreated completely, as a snail draws in its horns at the
shadow of a great, pecking bird. . . .

A snail that knows its death is near.

We entered the hall.

FOURTEEN

AT SUCH MOMENTS, the day is never long enough, and there is no time to regret prior delays, dawdling, not paddling fast enough, or taking so long to pick out the proper pieces of bark for the job.

Light still filtered through gaps and chinks in the roof and walls, revealing a series of open cells, some round, some square, all visible two or three meters below where we stood, at the top of a flight of curved stairs. But that light was rapidly dimming. The long shadow of the edge wall was coming, even here, many kilometers inland—and soon Halo night would be upon us.

"A few minutes of light left," I whispered to Gamelpar.

"Quick in, quick out," he said.

We descended the steps. These cells might have once been places of sleep, or drinking, or eating—or just places where tinkers performed their duties. They were too close-packed to be any sort of reasonable collection of market stalls.

And wrapped in deeper gloom at the center of the hall stood a large cage, five or six meters high, and twice as wide. Somehow, I did not believe humans had made such a cage—even in the darkness, there was a regularity, a craftsmanship, to the vertical wall of bars, as well as bluish tint. Keeping close, we followed a narrow, sinuous corridor toward the cage.

I glanced into several of the cells and saw chairs, small tables, shelves—tools and piled supplies of bark, wood, leather. The craftsmen were not in evidence, nor was there any sign—other than the leering faces on the door frame—what sort of humans these might have been.

In a few dreadful minutes, we were close to the cage, and the failing light only hinted at what waited within: a great lump of shadow, big as ten or twelve men piled upon each other—a pile of corpses, then? Some of the inhabitants, taken here, left behind, forgotten?

But the smell had not been of death.

Tiny glints of phosphorescence seemed to flit around the mass, like fireflies on a hot grassland evening—provoking a shiver, a hint of slow, uncertain motion.

"One of the lake creatures," I said softly. "A great fish, or something else, dragged up and left here!"

Gamelpar kept his eyes fixed on the mass, through the bars, and neither responded to my theory, nor moved in any way. He had become still as a statue.

Then his eye shifted the barest degree, and met mine, and something passed between our old spirits—nothing complex.

Simple recognition.

The Lord of Admirals had seen such a thing before.

It's a Gravemind, he told me, and illustrated that enigmatic description with a quick series of memories I could only half-interpret.

Before either of us—Gamelpar or me—had a chance to understand, the mass made a sudden, spasmodic movement, and its entire surface became a net of orange and green fire—crawling veins of light, literally veins! Like glowing, burning blood vessels on the body of a flayed beast—and yet not one beast, not one animal flayed and arranged in this mass, but many, many—dozens! And not human, too large of limb and torso to be human.

Not the mashed-together, former inhabitants of this water-locked village . . .

Instead, we were seeing a mass of Forerunners—Warrior-Servants or others of that kind, I thought, but there was no way to know for sure. They had been gathered up as if by some monstrous sculptor and molded and melted into each other like living clay, but more horrible yet—some still had heads, torsos, faces, and some of those faces could look outward, through the bars, and were watching us with faintly glowing eyes.

The mass flinched again, making the entire building shudder beneath our feet.

Then came the voices, soft at first, gradually coalescing, many voices in one, but the words poorly coordinated, spread out and blurred into an awful, cacophonic lament.

I could only understand some of what the voices were trying to say.

They wanted to be free.

They wanted to die.

They could not decide which.

Then the mass pushed up against something we had not noticed before—a transparent wall or field, very like the bubble in which I had been swept away from the San'Shyuum system. A cage within a cage. Forerunners had wrapped this thing, this mass, this Gravemind and then had left it here—or had died defending it and this place, died before they could reclaim their fellows and cure them of this atrocity.

If they have a cure, which I doubt very much.

I could not stand any more. I grabbed Gamelpar, lifted him up, and carried him back down the corridor, as the last light in the hall, from outside, faded, and the only glow that remained came from the excited mass within, still crying out in false hope, pain, despair.

FIFTEEN

IN OUR PANIC, we could not quickly find our way back to the small boat, moored somewhere below us. And in our flight, all three of us, blundering through the twilight cast by the sky bridge, kept coming across more corpses—more decay.

More dead Forerunners, lying on decks, bridges, walkways, or within dwellings.

Hundreds of them. And no humans.

Yet there were no signs of explosions or fire, only of sharp blades—perhaps fishing tools, likely human-made—or improvised clubs, and of course none wore protective armor.

Something had compelled them to square off against

each other in this most unlikely of places, and they had fought until all had died—down to the very last Forerunner, I guessed, and the Lord of Admirals supported me on that much.

But why?

They fought for a prize—or to prevent that prize from falling into the wrong hands.

"What prize?" I cried out as I ran, Vinnevra close behind, Gamelpar not within sight.

Realizing that, we both stopped, until I saw him, half-dead with exhaustion and pain, stumping and crutching along a far bridge.

"You . . . two . . . *children!*" he shouted. "It's back that way. You missed it." We backtracked to join him. He led us back to the ladder, the hatch—all in deeper darkness, until we could only feel with our feet the last flight of steep stairs down to the docks, and hear the lapping of the waves against the dock and the pillars all around.

In the deepest shadow of all, we managed to crawl into the boat, cast off the line, pick up our oars, and push out from beneath the suspended village.

While above, not nearly far enough above, the mass thumped and writhed again and again and the whole village shook, dropping grit and dirt and who could guess what else down on our heads and necks and shoulders.

Out under the stars and the sky bridge, we picked at each other, tossing away the fallen bits, then took turns diving into the water, quickly sluicing, climbing back into the boat—all the while watching for whatever might swim in these waters, fearing, right now, not sea creatures—but other things entirely.

I held Gamelpar while he swung his arms and legs in the water, then pulled him back into the boat, wide-eyed and shivering with the cold.

"What did you see?" Vinnevra kept asking. "What was it?" Neither Gamelpar nor I had the heart to tell her.

We were many kilometers out in the lake, away from the village, away from the shore, in the gently rolling currents taking us now toward the west, inland, away from the horror, when we saw we no longer needed to row.

We collapsed in the bottom of the boat and slept.

SIXTEEN

THE CURRENT MOVED us slowly, slowly, across the salt
sea, while night came and day followed, and always the
sweep of the great wheel overhead and the stars.

"My old spirit seems to know where we are," Gamelpar
said from one end of the boat, where he lay facing up at the
panoply. "He's been studying the stars for years now."

"Where are we, then?"

"A hiding place. A refuge." He pointed at three bright stars,
arranged in a looping formation with four dimmer ones and
a scatter of those barely visible. The dim stars were greenish,
the bright stars, red and intensely blue. "That is the Greater
Tiger. See"—he drew with his finger in the air—"there's the

tail, dimmer than the eyes and teeth. Human forces retreated here after Charum Hakkor. This was our last front—forty prime cruisers, ten first-rate tuned platforms—"

Vinnevra reached out to shush him with her finger, then looked at me resentfully. Gamelpar chuckled and shook his head.

"They're not real," she told both of us.

"Neither is your sense of direction," I said.

"No," she admitted. "I don't even feel it now. The farther we drift . . ."

"Why bring the wheel to this place?" I asked Gamelpar.

"Because all the worlds here are slagged ruins, polluted for millions of years by weapons our forces—human forces— unleashed when they saw defeat was inevitable. No Fore-runner has a need to visit here—and all subject species are warned to stay away."

I had not heard of subject species before. "Subject species . . . who are they?" I asked. "Like us?"

"No. We were the defeated. There were also subservient allies. Some were used to gather and imprison humans after the defeat." His face worked in disgust.

"A place no one visits . . . why here?" I asked Gamelpar.

Because it is stolen. Let the two of us old spirits rise and talk directly.

I shook my head stubbornly. Gamelpar watched me closely and gave the slightest nod, as if approving. Neither of us wanted to be out here on the strange salt sea under the control of dead warriors from long, long ago.

"They're strong," I whispered, not to disturb Vinnevra, lying down now with eyes closed.

"They are *we*," he said. "It's only a matter of time before they are harvested. And we might die when that happens. My old spirit speaks sometimes of something he thinks they called the Composer—Forerunner or machine, I don't know which. But the Composer was once used for such purposes, in the past."

I didn't want to understand what this meant, so I shook my head, lay back beside Vinnevra, and shut my eyes.

———

Just as light crossed over the sea, the boat's rocking woke me from a dream that was entirely my own, a dream of the grasslands outside Marontik, where I hid by the side of a rutted wagon path, stalking well-to-do merchants. . . .

Obviously, before Riser took me under his tutelage.

I blinked and looked around. The boat continued to rock in a gentle swell. We were now far from either shore, out in the middle of the sea, and yet swift, steady ripples were touching us, orienting the boat parallel with their troughs— something disturbing the water not far away. The ripples began to subside but were then met with new ripples coming from the opposite direction.

Vinnevra woke next—Gamelpar slept like a stone and it took a rather rough shaking to rouse him. We looked both directions, trying to see what might be causing the disturbances. "They're just waves," she concluded, but I could tell the difference. The longer, straighter waves were not the same—larger, wider, they were reflections from the uneven shoreline. Their rhythm had lulled us to sleep. These new ones had awakened us.

Something gray and gleaming humped the water a dozen meters away, then withdrew, starting another round of slickly perfect undulations. Then the surface was all confused as a downdraft of cool air fell around our boat and created a wide roughening.

"Merse," I said. "The lake is full of merse. The Lifeshaper loves them."

Vinnevra and Gamelpar didn't understand what merse were. I started to explain, but then a great, greenish black fin rose up just beside our boat, touching the side, spinning us around gently enough—and sinking again, like the tip of a huge knife.

I grasped the side and darted looks in all directions.

"Crocodile," I suggested next, but I had never heard of crocodiles with fins. Only fish and river dolphins, and this was much bigger than anything I had ever seen in a river. It did not take long for another hump to rise nearby, also slick and green. The fin seemed to flow under the water to join that smoothness—then, all together, the huge shape slid beneath our boat.

"My best wife spoke of sea creatures big as villages," Gamelpar said. "The Lady could have brought them here. She brought *us* here, didn't she?"

The rounded shape and a pair of long fins roiled the

water about a hundred meters off, departing rapidly. . . . And that made me peer down through the clear water, down and down—to see another paleness, like the one that had approached us under the suspended town, the same color but even larger, not so far beneath us and stretching to all sides like an island trying to rise.

The others saw it as well, and held on to each other. The paleness broke water on both sides of us—but what it was precisely that broke the water, I could not tell. I immediately feared the worst—that something like the mashed-together lump in the Forerunner cage had somehow gotten loose and occupied this sea, filling it everywhere, collecting everything that lived but still hungrily seeking more creatures to add, until it rose up as high as the edge wall itself.

But as I studied the paleness, I saw it had its own nature, its own original strangeness, and I knew, somehow, it was no product of the Shaping Sickness. To my right, a rounded, lobe-edged appendage, purple and blue in color, emerged from the water in a slow roll, sweeping up and around. At the end of each lobe protruded a finer series of lobes, and at the end of each of those lobes, the same, until the outermost seemed to be covered with fuzz.

On the other side of our boat rose another.

The flesh that made these lobes was like milky glass shot through with bubbles . . . yet not bubbles, for they seemed to contain gently shining rolling jewels, like little sacs of treasure.

These manifestations were beautiful beyond my ability to describe them, even now.

For hours, as we drifted, these shapes and a bewildering number of variations swept up and down, perhaps observing us, perhaps ushering us along, who could tell? But never did they try to reach out and snatch us from the boat, nor did they ever come close to capsizing us.

"What are they?" Vinnevra asked.

"The sea is rich," Gamelpar said when he had recovered his speech, after our fear had departed, leaving only numb wonder. Neither of us had any answer—nor did the old spirits within us. The reach of the Forerunners, it seemed, had so far exceeded that of humans that we could cross this wheel and climb up the sky bridge, and back down again, and never see an end to the Lady's collections, her accumulated wonders. Why had she gone to such lengths?

"They—or it—have been gathered by the Lifeshaper," I said. "She keeps some of her favorites here."

"More favored than you and me?" Gamelpar asked.

If this was the Master Builder's wheel, this great weapon that was also a zoo, a refuge for humans—then had the Lifeshaper partnered with him as well as with the Didact? Did she serve two masters?

Or did they all serve her?

The water had calmed, the lobed fans had disappeared, the water beneath was black into its depths.

———

The next afternoon, we slowly drifted past something I thought we should have certainly seen from a considerable distance—a great, cone-shaped structure, dark gray, rising from the calm salt sea perhaps three or four hundred meters. Smooth but not shiny, it had no apparent texture or detail; it was disturbingly perfect, even for a Forerunner object. Water lapped around its broad base, and a twisting streamer of cloud lazed around its pinnacle.

The currents swept our little boat around it and the great gray cone gradually receded, until, abruptly, it was no longer there—blink, and it was gone.

More Forerunner magic.

"The wheel is looking for its soul," Gamelpar concluded. "It's waking up again and deciding what it wants to be."

That got me thinking. The cone might have been a quick sketch for a Forerunner power station. I had seen one of those back on Erde-Tyrene, smaller but roughly the same shape. The wheel, the Halo, could be imagining itself fully repaired and ready to live again—just as Gamelpar said. It was drawing up plans that soon enough it would finalize and make solid.

Vinnevra kept glancing at the sky. The wolf-faced orb was now so large it illuminated the entire shoreline, adding to the sky bridge's reflected glow. Dark sky—and hence any good view of the stars—was going to be rare from now on.

Hours later, we approached the far shore and saw beneath thick, lowering clouds mountains of medium height, cool and deep green and wet.

Following the first edge of day, our boat bumped up on another rocky beach. We abandoned it and began to trek into the dense, rolling jungle, traveling no particular direction, following no *geas*. We were lost children, nothing more.

Even Gamelpar.

SEVENTEEN

FRUIT THAT TASTED like soft-boiled eggs hung in bunches from the thick-bunched trees, but out of caution, we ate sparingly at first—the only satisfying food we had had since Gamelpar's snares caught the fist-fur rodents. Other edible plants that both Gamelpar and Vinnevra seemed to know would taste good grew around or between the twisted, twining trunks, vines, and creepers—and so we settled down, full and peaceful, not caring for once where we were or what might happen next.

But walking was what we did, so we did not stay more than a day.

Though we had eaten well, Gamelpar seemed to be losing

both strength and enthusiasm. He walked more slowly and we rested often. The forest cast a twilight over us even during the day, and at night the pale light of the wolf-orb and the sky bridge filtered down, only slightly less helpful. We might have covered a half kilometer during the next daylight hour, keeping to the winding, open patches between the greater trees, pushing through soft, leafy vines that seemed to grow even as we watched.

There was food. There was quiet. The old spirits did not bother us.

It could not last, of course.

We had risen with the brighter twilight of day and were now sharing a reddish, melonlike fruit that tasted both sour-bitter and sweet, and cut both thirst and hunger.

Biting flies and mosquitoes haunted the shadows. They were enjoying us as we enjoyed the fruits of the forest. I swatted, examined bloody remains on my palm, finished my portion of the melon, and was about to toss aside the rind when my eyes froze on the near forest.

What might have been an odd gap between the trees—shaped like the great figure of a man, broad-shouldered, with an immense head—had appeared to our left, fewer than ten paces away. I reached for Vinnevra's shoulder and gave it a light squeeze. She had seen it, too.

The shadow moved—we both jumped. The air hung still and damp in the morning gloom. I could hear the rustle of leaves, branches, ground-creeping vines. A vine near my foot tightened as the shape stepped on it.

From across the small clearing, Gamelpar let out a whistle. Vinnevra did not dare respond.

The great shoulders of the shadow rotated and shoved aside thick branches, pulling at clinging vines until they snapped and swung up. I thought for a moment that this was the Didact, returned to gather me up—but no, the shadow was larger even than the Didact, and furthermore walked on both arms and legs. Its long, dark-furred arms shoved down like pillars into the matted, overgrown floor of the forest.

With a snort and a deep-chested grumble, the shadow swung about and rose up against the canopy. Vinnevra went to ground like a fawn—still as a statue, perched lightly on the balls of her feet, ready to bolt. Our eyes followed the shadow's slow, stately approach.

A great black-furred arm dropped within reach. At the end of that arm flexed a huge hand—four or five times broader than my own. A massive face leaned over us—and such a face! Deep-set eyes framed in a wide fringe of reddish fur, a flat, broad nose with immense nostrils—jowls reaching almost to its shoulders—and yellow-white teeth glinting between thick, purple-brown lips.

The great green eyes looked down on me, unafraid, curious—casually and calmly blinking. Then the eyes looked aside, no more afraid of me than I would be of a small bird.

In the corner of my vision, a yellow light came flickering through the trees, tiny as a glowing fingertip. The great dark face abruptly pulled up and away, and we smelled grassy, fruity breath.

Silence again. How could something so large move so quietly? But I did not have time to think on this, for the light appeared from behind a wide tree trunk. It was like the flame of a clay lamp, but held in a Forerunner's hand. Often with seven lithe fingers, purple-gray skin with pink underside— and above lamp and hand, a slender, questing face, glancing at where the great shadow had been, then back at me, as if acknowledging that we had both seen something, and that we were now seeing each other—and all of it was real.

The Forerunner brought the lamp flame closer. Vinnevra had a glazed look. She could not flee. She did not want to flee. I, on the other hand, had no wish to be carried off to the Palace of Pain. I leaped up and tried to run—straight into a wall of black fur.

Huge hands closed around me. One hand clutched my ribs and another took hold of my flailing arm. Off to the side, soft voices rose from the forest. The hand around my torso let go and the other lifted me by my arm from the dirt and leaves. I dangled, feebly kicking, while the lamp flame came still closer.

The Forerunner was neither like Bornstellar nor like the Didact. But it did bear a sort of resemblance to another that lingered in my dreams—the Lifeshaper, the Librarian. The Lady. This one was not female, however—at least, not the same sort of female. Of that I was sure.

But very likely a Lifeworker.

As I hung, the huge hand rotated me, allowing me to see, outlined by the glow of the flickering flame, three or four other figures. These looked human, male and female—but not like me and not like Gamelpar and Vinnevra.

As for what it was that dangled me like a child—

"Ah, finally!" the Forerunner said in a thin, musical voice, light as a breeze. "We'd feared you were lost for good." Then he addressed my captor in a gruffer, darker tone, ending with a chuff and a clack of teeth, and the clutching hand lowered me to the floor—gently enough, though my wrist, fingers, and shoulder hurt.

"Your name is Chakas, true?" the Forerunner asked, waving the flame near my face.

Why fire? Why not—

I stood up, stretching and massaging my sore arm, surrounded by extraordinary figures. The humans were not any variety I had seen before, but more like me than the Forerunner, and certainly more like me than the looming, black-furred shape.

I answered that was my name.

"He is not from here." Vinnevra shoved through the circle and stood in front of me, arms extended, as if to protect me. I tried to push her off, to get her to leave—I did not want to be responsible for anything that might happen here—but she would not budge.

"Indeed he is not," the Forerunner agreed, stretching out his hand and spreading those long, slender fingers. "His coming was anticipated. He was to be the Master Builder's

prize. Do not fear us," he added, more for Vinnevra's bene-
fit than mine. "No one will be taken to the Palace of Pain.
That time is soon finished, and there is no need for punishment or vengeance. The Master Builder's doom and the
fate of his forces is worse than humans can imagine."

MONITOR INTRUSION ALERT.

Ship's data accessed: Historical/Anthropological Files, re:
Earth Africa/Asia. Source determined to be Forerunner
Monitor.

CAUTIONARY NOTICE FROM STRATEGIC
COMMANDER: "Any further break-ins to ship's data
and I'll toss that damned thing into space. I don't give
a flying fortune cookie how much you're learning! It's
a menace! Make it get to the point!"

RESPONSE FROM SCIENCE TEAM *DELETED FOR
BREVITY*

AI RECALIBRATION

FIREWALLS PUSHED TO ^INFINITE RANDOM MAZE^
MONITOR STREAM NUMBER THREE (Nonrepeating)

In the morning light, we followed in the train of the
Forerunner, taking a winding vine-covered path to higher
ground. The foothills to the mountains were also thick with
jungle. The mountains themselves trapped the cloudy
masses of moist air that echoed back and forth across the
span of the Halo and forced them to drop their moisture

nearly every night, and so the false rocks and ridges ran with cascades of foaming water, drawing silver-white streaks over the green and black. Those probably emptied into the sea behind us, but there was no way of knowing.

The air too was wet, and the ground beneath us warmer, steaming, as if great vents of hot water laced through the foundation (and perhaps they did).

Once, on Earth, there were many types of hominids, hominoids, and anthropoids who no doubt also thought of themselves as People. I was closest in form to those who now interrogate me; Riser was smaller, of a different species. Gamelpar and Vinnevra I suspect most closely resembled those you call Aborigines, from the ancient continent of Australia.

The humans who accompanied this lone Forerunner bore some resemblance to those you now refer to as Denisovans. They were taller than me, chocolate brown, with spare bodies, reddish hair, and square heads. The males had copious facial hair.

The huge black shadow with long arms—a great ape like a gorilla, but not a gorilla—I believe is known to you only through a few fossil molars of impressive size. You call it *Gigantopithecus*, the largest anthropoid ever seen on Earth, almost three meters at the shoulders and crest, even taller standing up.

And this one was a female. According to your records, the males could have been larger.

Frightening in countenance but gentle in behavior, the great shadow-ape seemed to have taken a liking to Gamelpar and Vinnevra and carried them for a time on her shoulders. Great bristling wings of gray-tipped dark red fur framed her broad, sloping face. Huge lips pouched down around squat, thick incisors large enough to chew through wood and crush bone—but in our presence she ate mostly leaves and fruits.

Gamelpar, riding high over us, clutched the dense fur on the ape's shoulder and smiled all the while. Vinnevra looked happier than I had yet seen her. Several times she looked down upon me, walking among the Denisovans—three males and two females, laconic and moody—and said to me, each time, "It's coming back to me now. This is my true *geas*. This is what I *should* have seen."

Eventually, the ape's loping gait and frequent passage under low-hanging branches forced Vinnevra and Gamelpar to the ground to walk on their own.

The Denisovans, who appeared to find Gamelpar's age intriguing, studied his weariness with sympathetic sighs, then used vines to tie together a litter, and for a while he rode that way, Vinnevra walking by his side.

The old man's lips drew back in a broad smile. "Much better," he said.

There was something about this process—the regular way the litter swung, the smoothness with which it was carried—that caught my eye; but I dismissed my concerns, for now.

We climbed higher. The canopy thinned. We could see much of the sky. By the time the sun brushed the middle of the darkling band of the sky bridge, and shadow was equidistant from us to either side—"noon"—we arrived at a plateau.

The Forerunner called forth several hovering, round, blue-eyed machines, which met us at the thinning margin of the jungle. He addressed them with finger-signs, and the machines moved among us, paying particular attention to Vinnevra and Gamelpar—then to me.

The Denisovans did not find these floating balls remarkable. "They're called monitors," the tallest of the males said to me. He had chunky, ruddy features, a very large nose, and thin lips. "They serve the Lady . . . mostly."

The old man leaned on his side in the litter while one of the machines passed a blue band of light over his skinny frame. The machine then did the same to me, and spun around to face the Forerunner, who accepted some communication we could not hear and seemed satisfied.

We had traveled some distance. The ape had found a little food suitable to the rest of us—fruit, mostly: strange green tubes with pointed ends and round, pulpy masses encased in reddish skins—but we were still thirsty. Worse, more insects had taken a liking to our blood and buzzed around us in annoying clouds.

"Why does the Lady allow such nuisances?" Vinnevra asked me in an aside while the machine was examining her grandfather.

I shook my head and swatted.

"This is a special reserve," the tall Denisovan said. "We feed the flies, the flies feed the bats and birds and the fish. It is the Lady's way." But I noticed the insects ignored them and focused on us.

Vinnevra was not impressed. She swung and slapped and murmured, "It was better back in the city."

"Back in the city, you were under the rule of the Master Builder," the tall Denisovan said, as if that explained anything. "Was it better to be taken to the Palace of Pain?"

Vinnevra shuddered. "We are the *People!*" she said defensively, giving that last word the peculiar emphasis that denoted superiority.

"No doubt," the tall Denisovan said with an understanding smile.

Vinnevra wrinkled her nose, took a deep whiff, and glared at me, but I was in no mood for her theatrics.

———

We stood on the edge of the plateau. For a moment, a breeze came up and scattered the insects, then—a profound stillness. I looked around at the others.

"What's your name?" I asked the tall Denisovan.

"Kirimt," he responded with a sweep of his hand. In turn he introduced the females, partners to the other males. One of the males did not seem to have a female in this group.

Vinnevra received these introductions with a haughty expression, unwilling as yet to admit any of them to her protected inner circle.

During all this I kept my eye on the Forerunner, and now he returned his attention to me. His focused interest made me uncomfortable; he seemed to look right through me. Then, his facial muscles altered slightly, his eyes crinkled up, and he bowed his head.

I had learned, during my time with Bornstellar, to pick up on some of the expressions Forerunners used, however strange and stiff their faces, and I thought I detected a hint of relief and something like pride. But this one was stiffer than usual, stiffer even than the Didact.

"With this group, the Librarian may have enough," he said—or some word like "enough," more technical.

Gamelpar held up his hand and climbed off the litter. He drew himself up straight, then took back his stick from Kirimt, who had carried it for him.

"Our capabilities are much reduced," the Forerunner continued. "The Master Builder's security has suffered a great setback, but we who serve the Librarian have yet to regain our strength."

The ape reclined on the grassy ground. Vinnevra and Gamelpar knelt down next to her, then leaned back on her great round belly and rested. The ape cocked her head, as if capable both of listening and understanding.

"What's your name?" I asked the Forerunner.

"I am Genemender Folder of Fortune," he said, blinking eloquently. Something about his eyes—the smoothness of that quick motion of the eyelids—disturbed me.

"Are you going to set us free and return us to Erde-Tyrene?"

I asked. The question just popped out of me, and it reminded me that despite all I had experienced, I was still young and more than a little brash.

"I wish that were possible," he said. "Communication has broken down and many of our facilities have been damaged. Power stations everywhere have been sabotaged. There are only a few damaged stations left to supply the needs of the entire wheel. They are not enough—yet."

The breeze had slowed and the insects returned. The Forerunner waved his long fingers, and suddenly they all moved off to hover in a ball several meters away. "I advise you to stay here with us until stability returns. There is food, shelter, and an explanation I hope will satisfy all as to our intentions."

After a few minutes' rest, the Denisovans and the Forerunner urged us to get moving again. The Denisovans took the lead, skirting the humming ball of frustrated insects and walking in a loose line toward the middle of the plateau.

"Will you ever allow us freedom?" I asked Genemender. "Or are we like those insects?"

A quick flick of expression—embarrassment?

"Not our choosing," he said.

We pushed through the edge of the jungle and saw a clearing ahead, a flat expanse of short-cut green grass. Huts raised on stilts surrounded the clearing on three sides but not where we entered.

"Come with us," Kirimt said. "This is where we live."

The air at the center of the clearing shimmered and a

silvery blue blob appeared, surrounded by a wall of tree trunks. From where we stood, it was hard to determine just how large the blob actually was—its rounded contours were perfectly reflecting, in a distorted way, everything around it. Perhaps the blob concealed something else—perhaps it was what Bornstellar had called a Dazzler.

The shadow-ape stood back for a moment with Vinnevra, but she supported Gamelpar, who now refused the litter. As he walked past me, arm over her shoulder, he said, "There is no other place to be. But *we* hear you." And he gave me a direct gaze, one old soldier to another—neither exactly present.

Kirimt swung up his arm and jerked his head, let's go, and I realized there was nothing more to say or do for the moment but comply.

The Denisovans escorted us over the lush grass to the huts. An empty hut waited in the middle. All the huts were accessible through steps or ladders, but the shadow-ape lifted Gamelpar up and over the rail onto the porch. He stood there, gripping the bamboo rail, while Vinnevra and I climbed the rough-cut steps. From the porch we had a broad view of the clearing and of the Denisovans gathered below.

"Clean up, rest, and then we will share supper," Kirimt said.

Vinnevra wrapped herself in her arms and stooped to pass through the low door into the hut's interior. Gamelpar seemed content to watch the shadows lengthen across the jungle and the clearing.

175

The ape reached out, gently nudged the old man's hip with a thick-nailed finger, *whuffed*, then moved around to the left and vanished in the trees.

Vinnevra returned and took a stand beside Gamelpar. "This is my *geas*," she said, "more than any other place, but something's still not right. We cannot stay here."

"Not to your taste?" I asked, nodding at the hut.

"It's very comfortable," she said with a shake of her shoulders, though there were few insects at the moment. "That Forerunner—I do not smell him. I do not smell the others, either. I only smell the ape."

I had noticed the same thing but did not know what it meant. I hardly knew what anything around here meant.

"My nose is old," Gamelpar said. "I barely smell the ape."

The hut's interior was made of bamboo and wood slats. There were leafy beds, a small rough table, and three chairs. A basin of stone supplied water that poured out of a bamboo pipe when it was lowered. I studied this mechanism with idle curiosity, drank some of the water, splashed it about my face, and took a leaf cup to the old man. He drank sparingly, then lay back on one of the beds, and was almost immediately asleep.

Vinnevra remained on the porch, where she knelt with her forearms on the rail. I saw her through the low door, silhouetted by glowing clouds.

Just after dark, Kirimt called us to our supper.

EIGHTEEN

WE CROSSED A dirt path to a larger log hall at the corner between two lines of huts. Thunder echoed across the mountains and we barely made it inside the hall before rain began to pour down.

The hall was almost fifty meters long and twenty wide. Tables had been set up in four long rows under a high arching roof woven from branches and vines. The drum of rain on the roof was almost deafening. The heat had gotten more intense and the air seemed wet enough to swim through. Still, Gamelpar shivered as if with chill, enough so that Kirimt and one of the female Denisovans—I had a difficult time telling them apart—provided him with a roughly woven blanket.

Four more females carried in a pallet and offloaded food onto a head table. I watched them with real curiosity, for they were not Denisovans, nor like Vinnevra and Gamelpar, and not at all like me. Their heads were long, their jaws prominent but chinless, and they walked with a graceful lope. In some respects they reminded me of Riser, but larger.

When they were done, having delivered two pallets, the table was piled high with bowls of cooked grains, fruit, and a thick paste that tasted of salt and meat, but was not meat—not any meat I knew, at any rate. A flagon of cool water and another flagon of what tasted like honey mead, but was purple, completed the repast.

We filled wooden plates, then gathered at a corner table to eat. Gamelpar sat sidewise, his sore leg sticking out and swollen tight at the ankle. Yet he was not being tended to. Were we to be left to our ailments, as well as biting insects? Was there some greater Lifeshaper plan at work here, requiring that we suffer more?

For the moment, after the food-bearing females departed, we three and the Denisovans were the only ones present—eight of us sitting in a space that could hold many more. The shadow-ape had not accompanied us.

But slowly others strolled in singly and in groups and took their places. The hall was finally half-filled by at least a hundred humans. My eye was far from expert but I judged they came in seven or eight varieties. They seemed to have no prejudices against each other and no problems either serving or mingling, as if out of long habit.

Vinnevra chuffed again, still unimpressed. "How many of *our* People are here?" she asked Gamelpar, looking around with a pinched expression.

"Just us," he said. I had always wondered about Vinnevra's prejudice, the quick ease with which it rose up, the difficulty she had in tamping it back down—even in my case.

In the cities, someone divided humans against each other to control them.

I paused, wooden spoon lifted to my lips, listening to the inner voice.

This Forerunner is unlike the Master Builder. He fosters unity, not division. He may be strange and weak, but he is not cruel. Perhaps he alone of his kind remains and all the others are dead.

We had certainly seen enough dead Forerunners—and no other live ones.

Across the table, I met Gamelpar's look when he peered at me, as if hearing similar words in his own thoughts. Again I wondered how the two of us could ever bring our ancient experiences, knowledge, and personalities together, without losing our own souls in the bargain.

Genemender entered with the last stragglers. For reasons I could not articulate, and not just the lack of smell, my queasiness only grew stronger.

"I see two of you have the Librarian's mark, but one does not," said Genemender, standing behind me. I craned my neck to keep him in sight. "Chakas, you clearly remember Erde-Tyrene, do you not?"

I felt my flesh creep at the steady gaze of so many faces—so many kinds of faces. "Yes," I said. "I would go back there if I could."

"I believe the Librarian would have us all return," Genemender said. "That is not yet possible. Eat, be strong . . . rest. There is much to be done here, and little time."

NINETEEN

SOMEBODY POKED ME in the shoulder.

I came awake in the middle of the darkness. My sleep had been heavy, dreamless—my weary body lulled by the warmth of the ground and the hot, moist air.

I rolled over, the cot rustling under me, and saw—

A small, gray-furred face peering down at me, almost close enough to kiss—which I nearly did. Riser!

I reached out for him but with a lip-pouching frown, he held up his hand—quiet!—and withdrew into the hut's shadows.

"Are you living here, too?" I whispered, loudly enough to make Vinnevra roll over, but not to wake her.

Riser's silhouette did not respond.

"I didn't see any other Florians. . . ."

The silhouette waggled an arm as if in warning, and I felt a tingling chill—perhaps Riser had died after all, and this was his lost and wandering ghost!

But I caught the figure's meaning and stopped talking.

He approached again and touched my face with his long fingers, showing how glad he was to see me. He leaned in as if to nuzzle my ear and spoke softly: "Dangerous here. Weapons and ships gone, broken. The one who hates the Didact, and his fighters . . . still here, still moving humans around like cattle. This place, right here . . . not real! Full of dead! You and me—"

Came a creaking as someone climbed the steps to the porch outside. Riser made another frantic gesture—do not reveal me!—then pulled back, hiding behind a chair. I still hardly believed I had seen him, heard him—could a ghost accuse others of being ghosts?

The Forerunner peered into our hut through the low door, carrying that ridiculous candle-lamp in his spidery hand. "It's fortunate you and the old one made your way here and not to any of the other stations," he said in a low voice, not to wake the others. "Please come with me—outside."

Somehow, I had lost all fear—Riser's return, even if only as a transient spirit, had reawakened a perverse sense of adventure. With a quick glance at the chair, I pushed through the low door and climbed down the ladder.

Genemender waited for me on the grass.

"Why are we so fortunate?" I asked.

"The girl responded to your presence with her own imprinted instructions," he said, walking ahead of me toward the glistening shape a hundred meters away. The rain and clouds had passed and the trees and huts shone silvery and clear under the night stars and the sharp-cut arc of the sky bridge.

I jerked at a sound from nearby. The ape had returned sometime after we left the dining hall to lie down under tree-cover near our hut. She watched us with almond-shaped eyes, full lips pressed together. Her nose wrinkled and twitched, sniffing the air, and she raised her arm, then waved her hand, as if dismissing something—or trying to warn me. Perhaps she had seen Riser as well.

"Does the Lifeshaper know everything that's going to happen?" I asked, trotting to keep up with Genemender's long stride.

"Not all," he said. "At least, I doubt it. But she has a remarkable way of moving us about—humans and Forerunners."

I could not disagree.

"Your young female saw a human wearing Forerunner armor, having fallen from the sky in a rescue pod. . . . Not at all normal or what one would expect, even here. Her people were long ago imprinted with the need to bring such curiosities to a station where we might evaluate them."

"She almost led us to the—" I stopped myself. To reveal important facts is to share trust. Before I shared, I wanted to learn more from this peculiar host. "This wheel is a wreck, cities are destroyed—broken star boats everywhere," I said. "How could she know where to go, with everything changing?"

"Yet you are here," Genemender said. "Beacons send signals, and the signals are updated as circumstances change."

I shrugged. No sense arguing. Beacons across the wheel, sending out conflicting signals . . . Not impossible.

"You've fed us and let us rest," I said. "What do you intend to do with us? Add us to your specimens?"

Genemender regarded me steadily. I almost felt my thoughts and memories projected like shadows on a tight-stretched skin—nothing could be hidden from this one.

"You've come upon evidence of the Shaping Sickness," he said. "That's what humans called it."

"The Flood? My old spirit certainly thinks so," I said—then wondered if I had revealed too much. But Genemender was not surprised in the least.

"Indeed. Your old spirit, as you call it, one of the archived warriors stored in your genetic material . . . How many of them have come awake within you?"

Genemender paused, listening closely for my answer.

We had walked to within a few meters of the smoothly reflective mass suspended above the wall of tree trunks and branches.

"One, I think," I said.

"No more?"

"I might have felt others at first . . . now, there's just one. What use are such things to Forerunners—or to the Master Builder?"

"Let us begin with Erde-Tyrene," he said. "A young Manipular was led to your birth-world by his ancilla."

"The blue lady," I said.

"Yes. When you met Bornstellar, part of your own imprint, given to you by the Librarian, was activated. You and the small Florian named Riser led the Manipular to Djamonkin Crater."

I wasn't about to tell him the Florian was here. I still wasn't convinced myself.

"A deeper imprint was germinated when you met the Didact, and flowered when he took you to Charum Hakkor. There, the imprint took on a distinct shape—a personality was revived. A species is not just the record of how to make a male and a female. History and culture are also part of the whole. The greatness of humanity has been stored within you, and so very little is actually lost. Brilliant!"

His admiration bothered me. I was allowed to feel, to worship, on the Librarian's behalf, but for a Forerunner to share those deep-held opinions—to look upon me as a marvelous bit of craft, simply fulfilling my design—I found that disturbing, even disgusting.

Genemender stepped through the branches and trunks— not between, but through. I tried to follow but came up short, convinced I would be bruised or poked in the eye.

"Come along," he called. "It's safe."

I closed my eyes and walked through, feeling just a suggestion of hard bark and twigs.

"The great anthropoid could not do what you just did," he informed me. We stood under a high, round ceiling, at the origin point of radiating corridors lined with tall, twisted cylinders. The cylinders had an odd, translucent quality that came and went, sometimes foggy and shifting—sometimes solid. I followed him down the middle aisle. A steady glow accompanied us.

"I've never seen an ape as big as that one," I said, talking just to hide my worry. I wondered if these cylinders were containers, instruments—or perhaps some kind of ceremonial sculpture. I did not know whether Forerunners engaged in that kind of art.

"The last of her kind," Genemender said. "She once lived on Erde-Tyrene, not so far from where you were born. Even at their pinnacle, her people seldom numbered more than a thousand. When the Lifeshaper came to Erde-Tyrene to gather what could be saved, she found only five. Now, unfortunately, the others are dead."

I could not bring myself to ask how they had died. Perhaps in the Palace of Pain? "Are you not in the habit of wearing armor?"

"All armor and ancillas on this installation have been corrupted. Not even the monitors are completely trustworthy, but those that remain are essential to maintaining the reserve."

"What corrupted them? The machine with the green eye? Or—the Captive?"

There—I had blurted it out.

Genemender made a strange face—half-stiff, half-concealing. My flesh crawled. He did not have a smell and he did not know how to react to certain questions.

Incapable of telling a lie, but unwilling to reveal all? This is no Forerunner!

I still reserved judgment—but I was definitely unhappy in Genemender's presence, however much he seemed to want to keep me calm.

"In good time," he said. "Let us begin at the beginning. Halos were the primary weapons in the Master Builder's proposed defense against the Flood, which was already ravaging parts of the Forerunner realm. These Halo installations, constructed on great Arks outside the margins of our galaxy, were designed to destroy life in millions or even billions of star systems, should the Flood spread out of control.

"The Didact opposed their construction and planned instead a very different campaign of containment and isolation by building and positioning Shield Worlds—even more massive and in some respects more powerful than Halos, but capable of carrying out more selective campaigns of destruction."

Star-hopping, the Lord of Admirals said within me, and I was distracted by a sudden vivid burst of charts and maps showing the rippling membranes and expanding spheres of an interstellar war. *It was his way to isolate, besiege, and lay low, at the most opportune moments, only those points of greatest strategic importance, and ignore the rest.*

"The Master Builder convinced the Council that the emergency was already too extreme," Genemender continued, "and that the Didact's Shield Worlds were not the answer. The Didact's plan was denied. In protest, and to avoid serving the Master Builder, he went into exile, entering his Cryptum, where you and Bornstellar found him a thousand years later. The Halos were built, to the great profit of the Master Builder and his kind.

"But after concealing her husband's location, the Librarian went to the Council and invoked the Mantle—the fundamental duty of Forerunners to nurture and protect life. The Council forced a bargain with the Master Builder and decreed that Halos would also serve as sanctuaries for species from across the galaxy, to preserve them against almost universal destruction, should the installations be forced to carry out their mission.

"The Librarian has always favored humans, much to the dismay of the Didact. As part of the Council's agreement, the Librarian was given space on several of the Master Builder's installations. Humans were brought to this one—over one hundred and twenty varieties, many hundreds of thousands of individuals. Others were placed on the great Arks where Halos are built and restored. All were designated as reserve populations, not to be tampered with. But the population of imprinted humans on Erde-Tyrene were not made part of that plan. No humans from your planet were brought here—until recently."

Not even the Librarian would risk my presence on such a weapon!

I objected, "But Gamelpar, the old one—and me—"

"The Master Builder altered the Librarian's plans."

How like gods and devils everywhere—Forerunners scheming, lying, denying their firmly held principles. My head reeled.

Very human, actually. Makes you wonder, no?

"Why?"

"Back then, the Flood was known to some Forerunners, but kept secret until its nature and extent could no longer be concealed. Almost immediately after the Forerunner victory over the humans, many of their captured records were translated, and Forerunners learned that humans had already encountered this strange life-form, and that with the arrival of the so-called Shaping Sickness from outside the galaxy, humans had essentially fought on two fronts. That may have hastened their defeat.

"But before that defeat, humans apparently discovered ways to both prevent and treat the disease. They had orchestrated a program of research that depended in part upon massive sacrifice—including deliberate infection. Humans, it seems, had their own Palaces of Pain. Methods of containment and even prevention were discovered and implemented. Their battle commanders were trained in these methods. Fully a third of all human colonies were destroyed during this purge."

Some among us had hoped to carry the Shaping Sickness to the Forerunners and infect them. But those who believed in this strategy were denied. It seemed some would face defeat rather than perpetuate such an atrocity, even on our worst enemies.

Now I became very uncomfortable, wondering just who or what was within me: human, monster—or human monster?

It makes no difference in war.

"Upon learning of this, the Librarian's imprinted humans suddenly acquired immense value. The latent memories of those ancient warriors likely carried the secrets that could save us all. But not all humans carry the necessary imprints—the proper *old spirits*, as you say. And so a search was begun by both the Master Builder and the Librarian, while Forerunner research on the Flood continued."

So much the Lord of Admirals had already conveyed. I still had difficulty sorting out the complexities.

"But then, the Master Builder reneged on his agreements with the Librarian. Over the last few hundred years, reckoning by the years you know, the Master Builder's forces took command of the installation's human specimens. Lifeworkers lost control of most of the reserves. In contradiction to specific instructions from both the Librarian and the Council, beginning just over a century ago, humans from the Librarian's special population were transported here from Erde-Tyrene. New and isolated communities were created. That was when the Master Builder began his own experiments. Many humans were subjected to excruciating tests to see if they were truly immune to the Flood. Some were. Others were not."

"The Palace of Pain."

"Yes. But the essential differences still could not be discovered. Some Lifeworkers acquiesced to the hierarchy and carried out the Master Builder's plan. Still others—selected for their courage and discipline—did their best to keep the Librarian's preserves intact. They made what you might call 'a devil's bargain.' Warrior-Servants, at the bottom of the hierarchy, were forcibly recruited to serve and defend the installation.

"Then—the installation was moved to Charum Hakkor for its first major test. The Master Builder did not foresee the results."

"The Captive," I said.

"Yes. The Captive, as you call it, was accidentally released from its timelock. Builder Security then transported it to the Halo. The Master Builder ordered Lifeworkers, under pain of disgrace and death, to study and, if possible, interrogate the Captive. Some believed the Captive and the Flood were somehow connected. Others did not. The Halo was moved again, to prepare for what the Master Builder believed would be his crowning triumph—when he would reveal his solution to the Flood.

"In extremis, the Didact planned to put all Forerunner defenses under the command of a metarch-level ancilla. That ancilla kept a primary extension on this installation, as on all Halos. But it was not allowed to assume command except in dire emergency. The Master Builder, however, found another use for it—unauthorized, as usual.

"The Master Builder did not trust Lifeworkers. He ordered this ancilla, the supreme intellect on the installation, to take over the Captive's interrogation. That questioning took forty-three years.

"At the end of that time, the Master Builder sent this Halo to a quarantined system, which held the last of the San'Shyuum. Against all Council instructions, he then used this most hideous weapon to suppress a mere rebellion."

And then he had ordered the destruction of the Didact's star boat, the capture of the Didact and Bornstellar, and of Riser and myself.

"The San'Shyuum system was stripped of all life. The Master Builder, in command of a weapon capable of destroying all life, had violated the deepest precepts of the Mantle. Many Lifeworkers and Warrior-Servants on this installation went into open rebellion against the Builder and his loyal forces. They were suppressed.

"Then—a political crisis occurred in the capital system. The Master Builder was indicted for his breaches by the Council. There is strong evidence that the Master Builder's ancilla was subverted by its long discourse with the Captive. Yet this was unknown to the Council. With the arrest of the Master Builder, and with the class of Warrior-Servants in disarray, this ancilla, subverting all of its corresponding parts, took charge of all the installations gathering in the capital system. This Halo, and the others, then attempted to carry out the greatest betrayal of all—destruction of the Council and the capital.

"I do not know the extent of the damage they caused. But in defense, all of the installations were fiercely attacked, some were destroyed, and this Halo barely escaped through a portal—to be brought here and placed in hiding.

"The battle between the subverted ancilla, Builder Security, and Lifeworkers continued—continues, some say, to this day. But I am not kept informed. Mistakes were made, no doubt. Hideous mistakes."

"So what is this wheel, now?"

"A ruin. But still—a laboratory."

"Whose laboratory?"

We had reached a gap in the rows of cylinders, within which had been arranged a circle of smaller, more intricate machines.

"In good time. First, I need to retrieve your awakened imprint, to better understand what the Librarian intended for you." He walked around me, activating the monitors, some of which rose from the floor and approached, eager to begin the procedure. I did not relish the prospect, but I certainly did not want to show fear.

So I continued to talk. "We owe our lives to the Lifeshaper, all of us, whatever has happened since."

"That is so."

"But now we are caught in a fight *between* Forerunners—and some sort of mad machine."

"That is so," Genemender said.

I put aside these confirming facts—and decided to move on to other matters, testing how far this Forerunner was willing to be truthful, or how much he knew after all.

"What happened to the Captive? Is it still here?"

Genemender's whole demeanor altered. He squared his shoulders. "We will not speak of *that one*," he said. "We should begin scanning now."

Time to flee!

I backed away from Genemender and the hovering monitors. "Not yet. I need to know about the Captive."

Hesitation—then, "It claims to be the last Precursor."

"What are Precursors?"

"Creators of all life in our galaxy. The originals. They made Forerunners. They made humans. They made thousands of other species—and erased them when they felt the need. Long ago, when it became apparent that the Precursors were about to erase Forerunners, there was a war, and Forerunners erased *them*."

Genemender moved his arm again, and I was surrounded by machines. No way between them!

"The ones who met us in the jungle, who filled the hall—why don't they have any smell?" I asked.

The Lifeworker again gave me that familiar, stiff look.

"They're not flesh, are they?" I asked. "What are they?"

"Spirit, you might say. They are all kept here," Genemender said, pointing to the cylinders.

"Frozen inside?"

"No. Scanned, protected—neutralized. They will not be abused by the Master Builder, or anything else."

"They're not here physically?"

He agreed, and my heart sank further. "Then the ones outside . . ."

"Periodically, I rotate the records and refresh their experiences with projected walks around the compound, where they can interact."

"You let them out?"

"I give them that impression," Genemender said. "The only actual physical presence here is the female ape. She, too, enjoys company."

"Where are their bodies?"

"Not essential. Scans are sufficient, and easier to control."

"You killed them."

"They are no longer active, and no longer a danger."

"They were all from Erde-Tyrene?" Suddenly all became clear.

The machines tightened their circle.

"Yes."

They do not look strong, those machines. They were made for science, not fighting.

"It was the last command of the Librarian, conveyed to this installation when it returned to the capital," Genemender said. "There was a good reason humans from Erde-Tyrene were not brought to the Halo installations. They contain the memories and life experiences of ancient warriors. That makes them dangerous, and on such a weapon as this—"

Move.

The old spirit rose up with furious strength and took charge of my arms and legs. I kicked and flailed at the machines. They backed away, and I launched myself at the Forerunner, screaming with a rage so old it might have been kindled on Charum Hakkor itself, in those last days.

Then—a startling thing happened. For a moment, the Forerunner was not standing before me. My blows did not land. I flew into empty air, to strike the floor beyond and roll to my feet.

The machines now kept their distance.

Then, the Forerunner reappeared, off to one side—but while his body took a shimmering shape, I saw something else through the shimmer: a monitor with a single dull blue eye.

Then, Genemender was back, as solid as ever, regarding me with what might have been perplexity, or sadness.

"You're dead, too, aren't you?" I said.

No answer.

"Did you die to defend the preserve?"

No answer.

"You've explained everything to me. Why?"

Still no answer. I jumped toward the image again, but it swiftly shifted away, flickering uncertainly.

"You can't lie," I said. "You're just a machine—an ancilla."

The same steady, sad gaze. "Once, I was a Lifeworker. I chose this fate rather than serve the Master Builder."

"But you can't actually *do* anything to me without my permission, can you?"

"I offer peace. I offer an end to questions that cannot be answered. And I am bound to carry out the Librarian's final instructions."

But the machines still did not move in.

"How do you know the instructions came from the Librarian?"

Again the shimmer.

"There's not much power left, is there? All the power stations have been sabotaged. The beacons have been corrupted. That girl out there—was it the Librarian's signal that sent her toward the Captive? Who commands *you*, really?"

"I am sure of my instructions." But the stiff expression remained.

"There are dead machines, dead Forerunners, everywhere," I said. "This Halo is *dead*."

"Would that it were. You refuse the honor of being archived?"

"I refuse."

"You wish to leave?"

That did not seem to require an answer.

"Do you know what awaits you out there?"

"No."

"It is beyond my comprehension, and so it is likely beyond yours. Evil so vast . . . an awful misuse of all that Forerunners know and have created. Misuse of the Composer, designed once to save us all. . . . Destruction of the

Mantle, and such knowledge of history that it rots a Forerunner's soul. Yet we must serve the Librarian's will. Even you. You owe her your very existence."

"Not anymore," I said, in sudden equal partnership with the Lord of Admirals. "I'm going to leave now. Can you stop me?"

No answer, but the shimmer increased. Then there was no Genemender—only that rather small monitor, its single blue eye dimming as I watched.

It moved back among the other machines.

I was alone, and the space with its rows of twisty cylinders filled with a silence and gloom more profound than I could bear. I spun about—and heard, from far outside, a woman screaming. It was Vinnevra, I was sure of it—accompanied by a throaty, deep roar that I immediately knew was the ape.

I had to get out of this place! I ran back along the corridor and again found a thicket of branches barring my way—branches that poked and creaked as I grabbed and pushed and pulled, but would not yield.

Again, Vinnevra screamed.

I felt someone behind me—swiveled about, hands raised in defense—and saw Genemender lost in apparent melancholy. "I am unable to resolve these contradictions," he said. "Time is short. The old human is very ill. He needs immediate scanning or his imprint will be lost."

He walked through the barricade.

The thicket let me pass as well.

We left the atrium of cylinders. I had no intention of allowing the monitor to do anything to Gamelpar.

Vinnevra had fallen to her knees in front of the hut. Gamelpar squatted on the porch, leaning against a post. The shadow-ape was moving in circles around Vinnevra, looking left and right, swinging one arm—protecting both of them.

Vinnevra shouted, "I woke up and saw the little one—I could smell him! I touched him! But the others—I know why they don't smell—they're ghosts! They just vanished!"

Genemender regarded me sorrowfully. "It is difficult maintaining appearances," he said. "Our beautiful ape will be sad without the others. It is our duty to keep her contented, and to welcome visitors—especially those traveling under the Librarian's imprint."

This machine is both mad—and weak.

"You're not real!" I said.

"I am equal to my responsibilities."

More madness! Yet it obeys!

I ran over the last few meters of grass, pulled up short when the ape rushed me—but stood my ground. She broke her charge, fell back on her haunches, gave another mournful, howling growl, then shook her giant fist at the sky.

Gamelpar did not appear at all well. Leaning against a bamboo post and clutching one forearm, he looked down from the porch through rheumy, discouraged eyes.

Vinnevra had seen and touched Riser—and smelled him. He wasn't an illusion, wasn't stored here in the twisted cylinders with all the others. But where was he, then? Did he even want to be associated with me?

That was too disturbing a thought, so I switched problems and tried to think through the motivations of this machine. It was a follower of the Librarian—or so it claimed. And so had I been—until now, perhaps.

"You are here to support the integrity of the Librarian's specimens," I said.

"And to prevent those of you from Erde-Tyrene from taking over this installation."

"Does that seem at all possible? Is there anything left to take over?"

The monitor hummed again.

"All that's left is our integrity and our survival," I persisted. "To make any decision about where we might best survive, where it's best for us to go—to fulfill the wishes of the Librarian—we need to know what's real and what isn't." For a moment, I almost felt like my old self, persuading the gullible back in Marontik to part with their meager wealth.

The monitor continued to hum, no doubt hampered by its declining power. Finally, it rose slightly and said, "That is a reasonable request. There is no contrary evidence, nor any recent instruction to prevent compliance."

A shimmering veil seemed to rise from the field and the jungle around us. The entire compound suddenly became ragged and ill-used. The huts—even the one in which we had stayed—were revealed as shabby and poorly maintained.

The grassy field was overgrown—which explained the feeling of damp up my calves.

"It is good to be of real use," the monitor said. "Are we useful?"

"Yes," I said, distracted by the condition of the compound. "For now."

Then, for a moment—a few seconds only—the compound returned to its former state. Many people emerged from the tree line, from the circle of huts—the Denisovans, the long-headed females who had served us food, the many, many varieties that had given me a strange glimmer of hope that all was not lost for humans on this broken wheel.

They seemed to want to gather, to apologize, to explain—

But the power was weak at best. The veil rose again, and just as dawn light caught the wispy clouds above, they all faded. The huts were revealed again as ruins, the jungle as an ominous wall of trees and advancing creepers, working hard to reclaim the field.

I thought of the blue lady in my armor, of the services that ancillas supplied to their masters, of the strange presences within the war sphinxes that had taken us across the inner lake of Djamonkin Crater to the Didact's growing star boat. . . .

And then, of the ghost or ghosts inside me. For a sudden dizzying moment, I feared that my body would twist up in a knot like some forlorn haunt—that I myself would turn out to be long dead, had died in the custody of the Master

Builder around the San'Shyuum quarantine world—perhaps even as far back as on Charum Hakkor, on the parapet over-looking the pit where the Captive had once been held in a timelock. . . .

Perhaps I had already been stored away by the Forerun-ners and was no more real or solid than Genemender or the Denisovans.

But I would not just let my soul fling itself about in my skull and then fly apart. I could not accept that I was part of this awful deception—this awful, necessary, *caring* decep-tion mounted to serve the Librarian.

The great, gentle shadow-ape, who had immediately taken a shine to Gamelpar and Vinnevra, and even now was protecting them, must have known all along. The deception had never fooled her. It had not fooled Vinnevra. And I had thought she was just exhibiting prejudice!

It had not fooled Riser.

Only I had been taken in. I had to start thinking more clearly. Everything on this wheel was deception, and what-ever the Librarian had wanted for us had been perverted, turned deadly—or worse.

You still believe in the Librarian, deep inside. You are still afraid to be alone, without family or friends. . . . And yet that is your natural condition, no? A thief. A con artist. What if being alone is the only way you can survive?

I slapped the side of my head until my jaw stung. I wanted to reach inside my head and pluck out that misera-ble, ancient voice.

"I can never be alone with you here, can I?" I murmured, then looked back at the blue-eyed monitor, trying to decide what to believe, of all the information I had been fed, and what to throw aside. "The real Forerunners are gone, aren't they?" I asked it.

"I know nothing of their present plans. The communications have stopped, since the last message that warned us to look for you, to expect you."

"And are you sure that message was sent by the Librarian?"

"Not now. No."

"But you complied because you had no other instructions."

"Correct."

The Librarian's servants had tried to do their best, but for how long? And now, even that had failed, leaving only this monitor and a few others, no longer in evidence—occupying the almost deserted plateau—and the shadow-ape.

"We have to leave," I said, my voice choking.

"Where will you go?"

"Anywhere but here."

"That is not wise. All your efforts on behalf of the Librarian will be doomed—"

"I serve no Forerunner," I insisted, knowing how much of a lie that still was. The conflict was sharply painful. "Will you try to stop us?"

"The old one is too sick to travel. All of you need to be scanned."

I looked up on the porch at Gamelpar.

"You can make him healthy again," I said. "Forerunners can work miracles!"

"We preserve, we protect, but we do not extend. The way of the Librarian is followed in all aspects. We will scan him and archive him, but that is all we can do."

"No!" the old man cried out, struggling to push himself to his feet. "I will die free. Do not let them do this to me! I must leave this place forever."

Vinnevra clambered up the steps and knelt beside Gamelpar, while the shadow-ape rose to her full height and stood between them and the monitor. The old man accepted Vinnevra's embrace with a pained expression, then pushed her gently aside. His eyes looked down between the bamboo poles. He could barely see me, so I stepped closer.

"Do not let them have my ghosts," he said.

"I won't. I promise."

"It has been good to travel with you," he said. "My old spirit will be disappointed not to join forces with yours. But what do we know? Perhaps we carry all the old spirits, like the great First Human, whose forefinger was tall as a tree, and who held the souls of all his children, for all generations to come, within that finger."

This was the first I had heard of such a being. Yet how was that different from what we had found here? "You must come away, come with us," I insisted, but it was more for me than for the old man that I pleaded.

"No," he said, looking off at the trees. "When I am still, it will take only a short while before I am safely fled. Keep the machines away until then, but leave my body here, for it is nothing after that."

"How do you *know*?" Vinnevra cried, clasping his shoulder, the sinews of her forearm as tense as drawn bowstrings.

"It is true," the monitor said. "If we do not scan while he lives, the imprint will be lost."

The Composer. Ask it about the Composer!

I shook my head, unwilling to listen to anyone or anything else. I had to follow my own instincts. I had to believe I was truly alone.

But I could not just run away from a dying old man. The sacred farewells had to be made. I drew close to him, touched his knee—was startled by how cool it felt in my fingers.

"Abada will scare off the hyenas," I said, "and the crocodile will rise from the shore of the western waters and snap at the buzzards. The Elephant will nudge your bones from the dirt, and you will finish your travels whole and sound, while the families of our ancestors await you on the far shore. *For so I have seen in the sacred caves.*"

Gamelpar's eyes suddenly turned warm and damp. He pushed gently again at Vinnevra. "It is not seemly for an unmarried woman to see an old man die," he murmured. "Daughter of my daughter, say good-bye to me now, lead the poor giant away from here, and let the boy speak to me alone.

We will all join up again, by and by. You, young man, will stay for a time. I need to hear these things you say, for they are old and true."

Vinnevra shook all over and her face was slick with tears, but she could not disobey, and so she kissed the old man on the top of his head, climbed down the steps, and led the shadow-ape away by her great hand.

Both looked back several times before they vanished into the ragged jungle.

I climbed the steps and squatted beside Gamelpar, whose name means Old Father. I recalled as much as I could of the paintings in the narrow, winding caves a day's journey outside Marontik, and of what they meant.

"She is all I have," he said, interrupting the flow of ritual. "She is willful but loyal. If I leave her to you, will you watch over her, and guide her away from this place? Take her to where she can be safe?"

Trapped! I trembled at the contradictions within and without. A vow made to a dying man had to be kept—there was no way out. And I could not let this one die in shame and disappointment.

"You will not leave her behind and go off on your own, will you?"

"No," I said, hating myself, not knowing whether that was a lie or not.

"Her true name . . . known only to her mate, her life partner . . . or to her sworn guardian . . ."

And he whispered it in my ear.

I resumed the ritual storytelling, only vaguely aware of the blue-eyed machine still hovering over the long grass.

Just as I finished, I saw that the old man's eyes were mostly closed and had fallen back the tiniest bit, unmoving, within his skull. I stayed by him, listening to the last tick of his breath, watching the last twitch of his limbs. . . .

It did not take long before I knew he had crossed safely over the western waters. He had suffered much already, and the Elephant and Abada are kind. Still, I wept and felt the sadness of the old spirit inside me.

We never shared. . . . Whom have we lost yet again?

Then I saw that the machine with the blue eye was slowly dropping into the grass, and the eye was dimming, turning black.

There was nothing left for Genemender to do, and no power left to do it, anyway.

———

I angrily gathered up a few scraps of clothing from the old huts. Some at least of the food had been real—a final feast produced within the pavilion of cylinders—and I packed up what I could.

None of the monitors moved. Their eyes stayed dark.

I walked into the jungle a few hundred meters and joined Vinnevra and the ape at the start of a nearly overgrown trail, little more than a winding gap between the towering trees. I could not meet her look, and when she asked me if he had died well, in tune with *daowa-maadthu*, I simply nodded.

I felt barren inside. No Riser, no old man, and even the voice within was quiet. I had no notion where we might go from here, and neither did Vinnevra. But we started down the trail, anyway, to the far side of the plateau. After her question about Gamelpar's passing, she did not speak for hours. It was her way of mourning.

The station where Gamelpar had died was several kilometers behind us and the jungle was thinning when she asked me to tell her the old stories, just as I had told them to her grandfather.

And she in turn would speak the stories Gamelpar had told her, including the story about the First Human's soul-finger.

It was then that Riser chose to rejoin us.

TWENTY

WE WERE WALKING along the trail, picking our way over the creepers—or in the ape's case, plowing and swinging through them—and watching through the broken canopy of branches and leaves the perhaps not so endless progress of shadow and light on the sky bridge. The skies had cleared for a time since midmorning and the air was moist, but the trail—dead leaves overlying stones and bits of wood—was drying and firm enough underfoot.

All illusion. How could I know anything was actually solid? Perhaps this was an amusement being enjoyed somewhere by jaded Forerunners. If I did not amuse, then at any moment my story, my life, might be crumpled up and thrown away. . . .

Our tales spun on while we walked. I told Vinnevra the ancient story of Shalimanda, the heaven-snake, who one night swallowed the original shining, jewel-encrusted stream of worlds, and the next night exploded, showering the sky with all the darker, earthy orbs on which humans would grow. As long as I heard us speaking, our voices soft and hollow in the jungle, I seemed more tightly bound to what was real, to all that I could smell and see and feel.

The girl—the young woman, for she was no longer a girl—was a comfort to me. More knives in my head as I tried to resist.

But I continued to listen and to speak in turn. I knew her real name. Perhaps that is not something you feel much about, one way or another, but for anyone tuned to *daowa-maadthu*, the old man's confidence was terribly important. I could not just leave her behind, not now, any more than I could abandon a sister . . . or a wife.

The ape listened to us and occasionally threw in her own commentary, low rumbles and occasional sighs. If she used words, I could not understand them—perhaps they were hidden in her grunts.

Something made a small crunching sound off to our left and silenced us. Vinnevra cocked her head to listen, then threw it back and sniffed. "It's your friend," she whispered. "The little one."

Riser came out of the jungle, climbing over two embracing tree roots, then stopped several paces in front of me, stood straight, and folded his arms. He looked me up and down, as if to satisfy himself I was not another ghost.

His small, wry face was as hard and serious as a stone.

I was still numb at the loss of the old man and the loss of my freedom. I wanted to reach out and touch my friend but didn't dare. Then, Riser began to silently weep. He wiped his eyes with one long-fingered hand and turned to Vinnevra.

"You knew first," he said, and then, to me, "The woman is smarter than you. No surprise."

"Why did you follow us and not show yourself?" Vinnevra asked him, as if chiding an old friend. Riser had that way with some people.

"The ape is smarter than both of you put together," he said. "She smelled me and she knew I was following, didn't you?"

The ape pushed away creepers and branches, showering dead leaves over the trail. Standing tall in a shaft of afternoon sun, her white-fringed jowl and cheek fur forming a nimbus around her nearly black face, she withdrew her lips, showing strong, square teeth, and shook out her arms, softly guttling. She was glad to see the little one.

My tension broke. I could not help but laugh. Even now, Riser could befuddle me. He looked me over critically, walking around me and poking my ribs, my back, determined I was sound, then snorted at the ape. She snorted back.

"Cha*manush* once knew Sha*kyanunsho*—her people. So she says. She even speaks a language I understand, a little, so it must be so. She says her lending name is Mara."

"You were there all along, but you didn't trust me," I said.

"Forerunners make ghosts," Riser said, eyelids flicking white. I got down on my knees before the Florian, held out my arms, and he fell into them like a child—though he was easily ten times my age. We hugged for a moment, then became aware that Vinnevra was watching with a needful expression. So Riser wriggled loose, stepped over to her, grabbed her around the hips, and hugged her as well.

"Sister or wife?" he asked me, looking back.

"Neither!" Vinnevra said.

"You like this boy," Riser said. "No?"

"No!" Vinnevra said, but glanced at me.

The shadow-ape squatted, pushing aside several saplings, and watched us contentedly while combing fingers through the fur on her arms.

Insects had found us again, and so we moved on. "How long have you been here?" I asked Riser. "Tell me how you got here. You fell from the sky?"

"Long story. Tell soon."

"I want to hear it now."

"So do I," Vinnevra said.

"First, make a wide look around," he said.

Riser ran ahead of us, up a gentle slope to a small clearing above the tree line, set with three giant rock pillars. We made a circuit around the rocks and joined him to survey the landscape below.

We had come to the lower edge of the plateau and now faced wildly hummocked terrain, many mounds and low hills, while off to our right, mountains rose steep and forbidding, folded around their skirts by more jungle, above that a barren belt, and finally, patches of snow.

I sighed. "I have no idea where we need to go," I said.

"My *geas* says nothing," Vinnevra confessed.

"I fell into a bad, bad place," Riser said. "We won't go there. Everyone dead. Ugly."

"War?"

He pushed out his lips. "Maybe. I walked from far over that way." He pointed away from the mountains, at a sharp angle inland. In that direction, many hundreds of kilometers away, the hummocky terrain blued out in thick atmosphere and clouds. Beyond the clouds, naked foundation stretched all the way across the band, marked with geometric details—the usual Forerunner imponderables. Foundation material stretched up that side of the wheel for perhaps four or five thousand kilometers, then ended in a turbulent roil of perpetual cloud.

Within that mass of cloud, lightning flashed every few seconds—brilliant but silent.

"You mean, your ship—the ship that carried you here—crashed out there?"

He tapped his shoulder once, yes. And that also indicated he wanted to use the mix of cha*manush* signs and chirps and grunts he had taught me back on Erde-Tyrene, a patois we had never shared with Bornstellar or used in front of any Forerunner. He settled on his haunches and picked at a patch of moss, then pulled out a tuft and sniffed it philosophically. "I tell it, and when I finish," he said, "you tell them."

As if Mara would understand! But perhaps she understood more than I suspected.

And so Riser began. When he spoke this way, his halting speech and mannerisms seemed to drop away and he became positively elegant—but only with difficulty can I convey the flowery style, with so many inflections and declensions. Florians used nouns, adjective-like phrases, and verb tenses that recognize thirteen different genders and four directions of time. So I simplify.

Pity. When inspired, or when bragging, Riser was quite the poet.

RISER'S STORY

F I WERE happy I would sing this for all time, but there is much sadness, not of our doing, and so this can only be a tale told by slaves.

"The first part you know. We were there. Then Forerunners put me away like sugar-fruit in a pot. You, too, I think.

"Later, I woke up on a dying star boat, falling through noise and heat. The boat became bent and broken with parts and things glowing, not fire, like the spirit of the boat trying to come together again or just find home and die. The boat fell apart when it became too tired to keep trying. And we spilled out onto a graveyard-desert, below those clouds, way over there.

"*We* means three Forerunners and me.

"All of us wore armor at first. One of the Forerunners, his armor was all locked up so he could not move. The other two were making sure he did not move. He must have fallen out of favor with those two.

"My armor was not much good, no blue lady, so I climbed out, but it was no use trying to run away. I did not know where I was. This place—very strange, and the graveyard-desert, *terrible*.

"So I stayed with the Forerunners. They did not seem to know anything about me or care much at first, but then the locked-away Forerunner, very angry, told them a story. I only understood a little. He said I was important and they could use me later to become rich. I was treasure. You like that, huh, maybe you sell me to Bornstellar, huh?

"It was enough. They paid more attention and tried to protect me.

"This locked-up one said a monster had come to the wheel, where we had crashed, and that the monster spoke long years to the machine that bossed this place under orders from the Master Builder, you remember that one— the arrogant bad one who opposed the Didact, another arrogant bad one, I think, but I do not judge him forever, that one, yet.

"Still, he did not like you and me, did he?

"Anyway, they talked some more and their armor spoke to me in words I understood, like cha*manune* speech, and I heard this story, which is probably not far wrong.

"A thousand years ago, the Master Builder made this big hoop-world, and then shared it with the Lifeshaper because other Forerunners who had power told him to, and so the Lifeshaper put many humans here of all types. Why she favors humans I do not know, but I still say hello to her in my dreams.

"And the Didact is her husband, how is that possible? Never mind. I'm talking here.

"The Master Builder learned by stealing knowledge from the Lifeshaper that some of us humans could stand up to the Shaping Sickness, and survive. I did not know what the Shaping Sickness was, but someone inside me did. You look at me now, we looked at each other back on the Didact's star boat—we both felt old memories rising up, put there by the Librarian. You still have them, don't you? So do I. Not what I would choose.

"Now this monster over so many years persuaded the boss machine to turn on the Forerunners and try to destroy them; that is what monsters do, they cause trouble.

"And this monster is a very old monster, mother and father of all troubles.

"But that is a story I do not know. I think it is big and maybe important.

"We have fallen in an awful place. None of them are curious, and now we have to leave. I said it was a graveyard-desert. I have no other sign/sound for it. I wonder if maybe lava erupted and grew up over everything, trees, mountains, humans . . . cities filled with Forerunners. The whole land is made of frozen, painted-over dead people and the places they once worked and lived. I don't have sounds/signs for those places, but they are much bigger than the power stations back on Erde-Tyrene.

"But the lava that coats the people and all the things that once lived is not rock. It is dead or dying powder, more like ash than lava. This desert stretches for a long ways. I don't see how we can escape.

"But the two Forerunners pick me up and carry me and the other Forerunner who can't walk because his armor is locked. They move fast, even carrying us—jumping, running, leaping. I wish I had known armor could do that, I would have tried rough stuff on the Didact. But probably the blue lady would have stopped me, too bad.

"I have a hard time breathing. The Forerunners talk to each other and their armor does not tell me what they are saying, but I understand a little. They are scared but hope someone will come rescue us, because (they say this without happiness) I am important, not them; I am more important than they are.

"I don't know why. Do you? No? Then be quiet. I am talking here.

"The Forerunners move fast, but slowly things change and their armor doesn't like them and then it tries to kill them. The Forerunner who is a prisoner is crushed by his armor—it just squeezes him to death, like a bug who squashes itself.

"The other two shed their armor and it writhes all over,

kicking up ashy dust, but it still tries to reach out and kill them, kill me—but they grab me up fast and carry me away.

"Now we are really in trouble. Things like mountains, but big and round, are exploding off in the direction of the night that comes like a running shadow. I ask if these mountains are volcanoes, but no; the Forerunners call them sporepeaks. Do you understand? No? You don't know. Then be quiet. I am talking here.

"The shadow runs over us. The Forerunners are having a hard, bad time. They cough and wheeze and slow down. But we try to keep walking, nowhere, I think; they don't know where to go. I have never seen Forerunners so frightened. It makes me sad, because I once thought they were all-powerful and now they are just people, not human, but people, naked and afraid.

"Finally they are too weak to carry me. I walk beside them, but they walk like their legs are made of rock. They are very sick.

"I see clouds cover up the stars, but by the smell—like mold off old fruit, dusty-green-sneezy, I know they are not just water-clouds. Soon it rains, and in each drop is the powder. The clouds have carried it from those exploding sporepeaks. It shrouds everything, clings to my skin—*moves* on my skin. The powder sits on top of puddles and moves there, too, so I lie down and cover my face with my hands.

"I am so tired and afraid. I cannot die now. Abada sometimes smells fear and does not come. The hyenas smell fear and laugh and grind up your soul. The Elephant never finds your bones because he turns away from the smell of fear. So we have seen in the sacred caves. So I showed you when you were young and tough. If I am going to die, better to die unafraid. The only way to escape this sort of fear is to sleep a big, deep sleep.

"And so I sleep now, too. Shh."

As if the strain of telling this story had taken its toll, Riser's eyelids drooped, his chin dipped, and he dropped off into a heavy doze, leaving us to sit there.

"Is he finished?" Vinnevra asked. Mara grumbled and drew her legs around the cha*manush* to protect him while he snored.

"I don't think so," I said.

She looked at me different now. I did not like that look and became very uncomfortable, even more uncomfortable when she moved closer to me. Mara reached out and nudged me toward her, and I glared at the ape, but she pouched out her lips and guttled.

Vinnevra settled in.

After a while, I told Vinnevra and Mara about the story devil who went from tribe to tribe and town to town, telling the very best stories ever, but whoever listened to him lost the power of speech and instead spoke useless babble. I did not know if the shadow-ape understood all that I was saying, but she listened close.

I finished with, "And even now, we find the descendants of those who heard his stories and all they talk is babble."

A lame fable, but all I had.

Vinnevra gave me a wry look. "Is *that* in your sacred caves?" she asked.

"No," I said. "Those are about life and death. This is just about how story devils confuse us."

"This monster the humans captured and the Master Builder released—was *that* a devil, too?"

"Maybe."

Mara grumbled and looked away, then shook her head. Perhaps she understood more than she let on.

"Is the Lady who touches us at birth a devil?" Vinnevra asked.

"No," I answered.

"Is our flesh her story?"

I shook my head, but the idea bothered me, flesh and story all tangled up. . . . *Maybe. Maybe so.*

We waited while Riser slept. Dusk drew over us and the insects became fierce. But we did not shake him, because he might be grumpy and stay quiet for a while if he did not sleep well, and we hoped he really did know something useful.

Finally, he opened his eyes, leaned and stretched on Mara's thigh, looked on Vinnevra and me with something like approval, and resumed.

"That was a good sleep," he said. "I remember more now. Swat some of these bugs for me."

We swatted some bugs until he was satisfied and resumed his telling.

"Day comes. I wake slowly. The land is dry, the powder is crusty and dead, not moving, just dead. It smells like old dung in deep caves. The Forerunners do not look the same as when I went to sleep. They are all clotted powder. They tried to grow together during the night, and now they are just lumps. Their flesh is gone, their bones are gone. They are dead. I am not dead.

"The powder falls off my skin.

"I am alone. It is never good to be so alone. In this graveyard-desert, it is worse. The spore-peaks will erupt again and more powder will come and I think maybe next time it will know how to dissolve my bones, too, or fill my nose and mouth forever.

"Six times the night sweeps over and there is more rain. I walk through the rain. Too much rain. Sometimes, when it is not raining, both night and day, I see shooting stars and think they are star boats. Once, I find many crashed star boats, smaller ones, scattered on the desert. They have spilled out broken machines, like the one back there, but their eyes are dark. I kick them and they don't fly away. There might have been Forerunners in the star boats but now they are only lumps of powder.

"It seems that Forerunners have been arguing and fighting, but also they are losing a fight with something else, something awful, and that tells me to wake my old memories. I have been ignoring the old spirit in me ever since Charum Hakkor, but now I let it loose, and it watches through my eyes.

"This hoop-world is like nothing known to the old spirit. It decides this must be one of their great machines, perhaps a fortress.

"Before the old spirit fought Forerunners, it once fought the Shaping Sickness. Even back then, it was spread by touch or by a fine powder and turned flesh into lumps. Sometimes it gathered the sick together—two people, four people joining up and speaking with one voice.

"It called this a Gravemind.

"But I have listened to the Didact and the Master Builder, and I know 'Shaping Sickness' is what they call the Flood. I am in the middle of a place blasted by the Flood, which old humans long ago fought and defeated, but now it has come back, and it has changed. Why? How did the sickness get here? I look to the spore-peaks, shooting up great clouds of fine powder, and the winds that carry it all over. That is the source. The Shaping Sickness infects Forerunners, and it is winning.

"But then—I learn a wonderful thing!" Riser's eyes flick rapidly and he looks up. "My old spirit was once a female. Better a female than a hoary old male who might argue and be offensive to me.

"The old female spirit asks me if the 'Primordial' was let loose. That's the name she uses. She shows me a memory of it, all grasping arms and an old man's fat body, but like a giant beetle curled up—and big, it would cover this mound— with a low, flat head, a mouth of many jaws, and dead jewel eyes. I have to tell her, I think that it was let loose, taken to this place, this hoop-world, and she says, *Ah, so it is, and now there is great danger.*

"You have seen it, too? Then it is real. Too bad.

"When I reach the low hills of the mountains, where the Shaping Sickness has not come, and see the small round machines going up and down the hills, searching, waiting, watching . . . I follow them quietly up to the plateau, and that is where I find you and all those ghosts that walk outside and try to act like people. But they have no smell." He raised his hands, palms up, and tapped one shoulder with three fingers. "That is what I know, but I know so little."

"You both saw where this devil was kept, didn't you?" Vinnevra asked us. "On the world where humans last fought the Forerunners and died."

"Charum Hakkor," I said.

"Yes," Riser said. "We both saw that place, but the monster was gone."

Within me, my own old spirit was rising from a long quiet.

I must speak with this little one!

Half-compelled, I gave the Lord of Admirals my voice and he spoke through my mouth. The effort racked my body. My muscles twitched and sweat beaded my brow. His words at first were clumsy and mumbled.

Then the shaky voice—not quite my voice—became more clear. But what I heard from my mouth was not what I heard in my head. The accent was different—the language, at first, imprecise. My mouth was used to forming words a certain way—not the way nor in the manner of this old spirit.

Vinnevra watched with furrowed brow, Riser with eyes wide, attentive, nostrils flexing nervously.

224

"Tell me . . . tell us your name," the Lord of Admirals said, addressing the spirit within Riser. "Tell me your *old* name."

Now it was Riser's turn to give up his mouth. For him, it seemed even harder. Riser's body was older than mine, more set in its ways.

"I am Yprin Yprikushma," his old spirit finally managed. Neither of us understood that strange name—but the Lord of Admirals seemed almost to burst into flame, a flame of anger, dismay, and disappointment.

But also, strangely, of exaltation! These old humans had different ways of mixing their emotions.

"You—!" he cried, then pulled back his anger, banked the fires—tried to swallow them. Still, they seemed to burn and gouge the insides of my head.

This type of anger I had never experienced before from the old spirit, and I could see by Riser's expression that he was feeling something similar.

We sat, Riser and I, in the shade of the great boulders on that promontory, experiencing a new relationship to one another—a relationship Gamelpar and I were never able to complete. Vinnevra looked between us with that same furrowed frown she used when Gamelpar and I had spoken about these things.

"And who are *you?*" Riser's old spirit asked.

"Forthencho—Lord of Admirals, supreme commander of the last fleets of Charum Hakkor."

"The one who lost the war to the Didact."

"Yes. Yprin Yprikushma—you saw what the Shaping

Sickness has done here," the Lord of Admirals said. "And that has brought you forward, out of guilt! Out of pride!"

"I am dead. You are dead." Riser's voice was almost unrecognizable.

We had become puppets, and I feared these spirits would never let us go.

———

The dialog between the old spirits went on for some time. I was not precisely present for all of it, so what I remember is shifting, dreamlike, but the facts—the larger facts—loom clearly enough, and if I wish—if I open many old doors—I can resuppose, reimagine the histories and emotions now being allowed to clash once again.

"And now, many more are dead," my old spirit resumed, "because you recovered and preserved the Primordial. From a place lost to the memory of all, including Forerunners, you brought it to Charum Hakkor. . . ."

"I have no disgrace. I had reasons to speak to the Primordial, and it is not known to this day whether the Primordial was responsible for the Shaping Sickness. Confined the way it was, *where* it was, and found long after the sickness began—how could it be?"

"By reaching out, ordering the movement of ships from beyond our galaxy, ships that brought the plague to Faun Hakkor—"

"How could it communicate? It was hidden naked and half-dead on a lost cinder of a world. And then—we froze it in a timelock! You are confused, Forthencho. Besides, the Primordial gave us information, and with it, we saved billions of human lives."

"That is far from the whole truth. Humans themselves discovered what needed to be done to preserve ourselves and our descendants against the Shaping Sickness."

"That has ever been in dispute between us," Riser's old spirit countered. "It may always be argued this way, or that. But *it is why we are here*. This knowledge, however acquired, is what forced the Forerunners to preserve remnants of those they defeated, rather than wipe us from the slate of history, as they had so many others before."

The Lord of Admirals responded with bitterness, "That may be so, but it only pulls thin curtains on your disgrace."

"Look around you! The Primordial is *here*. The Shaping Sickness is *here*! Forerunners are dying—but we live on! And that is what the Primordial promised!"

"It said no such thing to me."

And so it went for much of that night, back and forth, round and round. I tried to catch the important details, but they were too strange, too frightening—those visual impressions, like my nightmare of the Captive, what the old spirits called the Primordial—but stamped with a mark of authenticity. . . .

The threads of different ages tangled until I did not know who I was, who was feeling fear, who was feeling *any* emotion. . . .

My most lasting impression of that long night: Riser lying down on the ground and giving small cries of distress, but the voice within kept pushing out through his lips, expressing that ancient agony of knowing all those you love have either died or are about to die, in many strange ways— memories and knowledge overwhelming and incomprehensible even to these dead spirits, to the fundamental children that lie at the center of us all.

It is too much even now!

The Lord of Admirals is not testifying before the true Reclaimer.

I am Chakas. I am all that remains of Chakas, and still I am haunted!

I give up being Chakas. I withdraw! Please stop your recording, Reclaimer.

I am unstable.

Exquisitely painful.

I am breaking apart.

We are all dead, and even our bones are dust!

AI TRANSLATOR BREAK

Science Team Analysis: Monitor has shut itself down. Whether this is due to prior damage is not known. AI Translator reports that before the shutdown, twin streams of language appeared in the data stream, conflicting with or overriding each other. Monitor memory may be defective, or more than one stream of memory may be incompletely integrated. Repairs are still impossible. The monitor must recover on its own.

Resumption of response streams may be problematic.

Thirty-two hours elapse.

ONI COMMANDER: "I have to say, I'm having difficulty with all this information. 'Arks?' There's more than one?"

SCIENCE TEAM LEADER: "The Halo as described is also larger than any we've encountered. That could imply a larger Ark, right?"

ONI COMMANDER: "Hmmh. There's still a high probability that this machine is a decoy, and all of the information it's giving us is a ruse. However ancient, the Forerunners might have anticipated an eventual human resurgence, and possible rematch, and prepared for it. To the extent that this testimony could demoralize our troops, we may be playing right into their hands."

SCIENCE TEAM LEADER: "That would imply a truly astonishing level of prescience, given that Forerunners vanished from our galaxy a thousand centuries ago, and left us on Earth as little more than a bunch of wandering savages."

ONI COMMANDER: "Forerunners didn't vanish completely, did they?"

SCIENCE TEAM LEADER: "We disagree about the possibility of a ruse. Everything the monitor has related ties in with other Forerunner records we have discovered—including the Bornstellar Relation found on Onyx. There is no possibility of recent communication between those points. The data matches, and so it is almost certainly accurate."

POLITICAL TEAM LEADER: "The Commander's concerns have been noted. But all information gathered thus far with relation to the Forerunners has been sequestered and will have no effect upon team morale. The interest of the overall Halo/Shield Alliance in the facts and inferences these sessions have produced is sufficient to override all our lower-level concerns. Interrogation will continue."

ONI COMMANDER: "With all due respect, ma'am, we have already seen that this machine can breach our security with alarming ease."

POLITICAL TEAM LEADER: "Also noted, Commander."

Thirty-two hours elapse.

Monitor light resumes glowing.
AI Translator receives and converts a new response stream.
AI TRANSLATOR COMMENT: What follows is a multilevel, noncontiguous and ambiguous narrative.

Some phrases, perhaps many, may not be translated accurately.

INTERROGATION RESUMES WITH:
RESPONSE STREAM #1352 [DATE REDACTED] 1270 hours
(Repeated every 64 seconds.)

What am I, really?

A long time ago, I was a living, breathing human being. Then, I went mad. I served my enemies. They became my only friends.

Since then, I've traveled back and forth across this galaxy, and out to the spaces between galaxies—a greater reach than any human before me.

You have asked me to tell you about that time. Since you are the true Reclaimer, I must obey. Are you recording? Good. Because my memory is broken and covered with thorns. I doubt I'll be able to finish the story.

Once, I was Forthencho, Lord of Admirals.

RESPONSE STREAM #14485 [DATE REDACTED] 1124
hours (nonrepeating)

TWENTY-ONE

WITH DELIGHT I felt the moving muscles and living body of the one I inhabited, in whom I was slowly being reborn. . . .

My memories seemed to rise from scattered pieces, like a building blown to pieces and dropped into a deep well of thick fluid . . . then sucking in reverse from that awful mire and reconstructing itself chunk by chunk, year by year, emotion by emotion.

How could I be here? How could I live again, through what miracle, or—more likely—what awful Forerunner technology?

The Composer! So many possibilities and capabilities

tied up in that strange name. . . . A Composer of minds and souls!

But because of its talents, used by the Librarian, I was here.

I did not feel guilt. To this young human, so lambent in emotions, so confused in thought and action, I felt both gratitude and irritation, because he was strong, and I was weak. He was young, and I was . . .

Dead.

The emergence that became *me* seemed so delicate at first, capable only of brief interruptions, wry comments, like a flea hiding in an elephant's ear. A strange sensation indeed, nudged along by strangely familiar observations, stimuli forcing me up and out, like iron bars prying up stones in a field: Forerunner ships, the Didact himself, the arena where the Primordial had once been stored—and then released!

How *could* the Forerunners have been so stupid? Was it deliberate?

So strange, the familiarity of this boy's emotions—recognizably *human*—and yet separated from my existence, I learn, by ten thousand years of history.

———

I remember those last hours in Citadel Charum.

The Librarian walked slowly, reverently, among the captured, the wounded, the dying, the last survivors of Charum Hakkor. She was accompanied by other Lifeworkers as well as many hovering machines.

One by one, as we were laid out under the shell of the Citadel—rows upon hundreds of rows, stretching off to the limits of my blurred vision—the Librarian paused, bent over, knelt beside us, spoke to us. Strange indeed that such a simple and elegant face can appear so compellingly beautiful, so filled with empathy.

She expressed sadness at our condition, and her servants administered relief for my pain.

Perhaps it was an illusion, like the absurd belief in this boy that the Librarian touches us all at birth. Still, I do not deny this memory.

Beside her stood the Didact, a great, hulking presence, my sworn enemy for fifty-three years of continuous battle. Yet he had not aged. Forerunners live so very long; human lives are like candle flames flickering and guttering before their steady torches.

Even though we had stripped off our uniforms, doing our best to erase all evidence of our identities and ranks, the Didact found *me*, the Lord of Admirals, who had opposed him longer and more successfully than any other. He bent beside me, hands clasped as if he were a supplicant before a shrine. And this is what he said to me:

"My finest opponent, the Mantle accepts all who live fiercely, who defend their young, who build and struggle and grow, and even those who dominate—as humans have dominated, cruelly and without wisdom.

"But to all of us there is a time like this, when the Domain seeks to confirm our essences, and for you, that time is

now. Know this, relentless enemy, killer of our children, Lord of Admirals: soon we will face the enemy you have faced and defeated. I can see that challenge coming to the Forerunners, and so do many others. . . . And we are afraid.

"That is why you, and many thousands of your people who may contain knowledge of how humans defended themselves against the Flood, will not pass cleanly and forever, as I would wish for a fellow warrior, but will be extracted and steeped down into the genetic code of many new humans.

"This is not my wish nor my will. It arises from the skill and the will of my life-mate, my wife, the Librarian, who sees much farther than I do down the twining streams of Living Time.

"So this additional indignity will be inflicted upon you. It means, I believe, that humans will not end here, but may rise again—fight again. Humans are always warriors.

"But what and whom they will fight, I do not know. For I fear the time of the Forerunners is drawing to a close. In this, the Librarian and I find agreement. Take satisfaction, warrior, in that possibility."

It gave me no satisfaction. If I were to rise again, fight again, I wished only to once more match myself against the Didact! But the Didact and the Librarian passed on, moving down the endless rows of our defeated. The Lifeworker machines—through the strange, ever-changing, multiformed presence of the Composer, a machine? a being? I never saw it clearly—sent patterns of blue and red light over our broken bodies, and one by one, we relaxed, breathed no more. . . . Set free our immortal wills.

I lost all time—all sense.

Yet now I was alive again, in the body of a boy on an unknown Forerunner fortress—a weapon of immense power.

For a time, I had hoped there would be an ally within the old one called Gamelpar, who had the beautiful dark skin of my own people—but he died before any connection could be made. The girl, Vinnevra, his granddaughter, did not seem to carry ghosts.

But the final irony—the one who had befriended this boy, my host, for so very long—the little human with the wrinkled face and white-lidded eyes—contained the last impression of my most despised *human* opponent, whom I blamed for everything that had happened, including the defeat at Charum Hakkor. How had we been brought together? How could Yprin Yprikushma have found her way into this little, narrow-wristed monkey-man?

And yet, she at least was someone I knew, someone from my time in history, my own age. The dead do not have the luxury of hate. The ties to past emotions are slender and frail.

We warily put aside our past differences and spoke with each other for as long as we could, before our hosts rose up and deposed us, and this much I remember even now:

Forty years before the last of the human-Forerunner wars, it was Yprin Yprikushma who had been summoned to the murky boundaries of the galaxy, upon the discovery of the small planetoid within which some intelligences, long

HALO: PRIMORDIUM

ago—perhaps the earliest Forerunners themselves—had imprisoned the Primordial.

And it was Yprin who had excavated that planetoid, found the Primordial preserved in viscous hibernation in an ancient capsule—barely alive even in the sense in which it lives. She it was who recognized the Primordial as a major curiosity, the most ancient biological artifact we had yet encountered, and transported it to Charum Hakkor.

Charum Hakkor! The greatest repository of Precursor antiquities, an entire world covered with the artifacts and structures of that enigmatic race. Inspired by these indestructible ruins, humans had centuries before made this world the center of human progress and advancement.

It was here on Charum Hakkor that Yprin and her team of researchers discovered how to revive the Precursor, and then constructed the timelock to subdue its baleful power. It was here where she conducted her first interrogations of that ancient and deadly being now held prisoner within.

At that time, we did not know—though some of us suspected—that the Primordial was itself one of the Precursors, perhaps the *last* Precursor. . . .

The answers given by the Primordial during those interrogations began the demoralization of our culture. It was the leaking of those extraordinary answers that began our ultimate downfall.

Following on that brilliantly successful effort—that mindbending transmission of a devastating message—all Yprin's prior accomplishments were besmirched, *tainted*.

And yet—it was Yprin who prepared our forces for combat with the far more advanced Forerunners. And she who encouraged our scientists and robotic intelligences to take what we learned in our early conflicts with the Forerunners, anticipating their technology, and thus making so many technological advances.

Her efforts gave us a few extra decades of triumph and hope.

————

Ironically, it was Erde-Tyrene that fell first, a tremendous loss both in strategy and morale, for it was the most likely to have been the birth-planet of all humans. We had lost those records and memories during the dark ages, before we encountered the Forerunners, but our own historians, scientists, and archaeologists had done their work, analyzed the makeup and physiology of the humans spread across that sector of the rim and inward, and decided Erda was the genetic focus of all human activity—the planetary navel of our races.

Completing that survey, that analysis, encouraged her to believe she completely understood human psychology and culture. Yprin had advanced to Political and Morale Commander of all human forces.

I disagreed with that advancement, her rise to power. I had severe doubts that Erda was our planet of origin. Other worlds in other systems seemed more likely. I had been to many of them and had viewed their ancient ruins.

And I had seen evidence that Forerunners had also visited these worlds, were also interested in human origins—not just the Librarian and her Lifeworkers, but the Didact himself.

———

We defended Charum Hakkor against the Forerunner assaults—which came in an unending sequence, one after another—for three years.

My own ships swept back and forth hundreds of times across the star system, pushing back pinpoint orbital incursions before they could establish corridors of least energy dominance.

In all such battles, within the vast reaches of a stellar system, hyperspacial technologies give only a slight advantage; tactics in such close quarters depend on stable positions established near planetary objectives, where triangulations of fire can focus on mass-delivery portals and turn them into logjams of debris and destruction.

Occupation of vast reaches of space means nothing. It is control of population centers and essential resources that determines victory or defeat.

But our ships were depleted month by month, our battle positions worn down year by year, as Forerunner ships ranging in scale from fortress-class behemoths to squadrons of swift and powerful dreadnoughts opened brief entry points and attacked from brilliantly surprising angles, with sweeping, erratic arcs that reminded me of the scribblings of madmen—brilliant madmen.

The hand of the Didact himself drew those reckless and daring entries and orbits.

Forerunner dominance of the advanced technology of reconciliation—repairing the causal and chronological paradoxes of faster-than-light travel, so crucial to journeys across interstellar distances—slowed and even blocked our own slipspace channels and interfered with the arrival of reinforcements.

The crushing blow, long anticipated, even inevitable, was agonizingly slow to arrive. The final Forerunner assault was staged from seven portals opened at one-hour intervals to disgorge the massive fleet of the Didact himself, along with his finest commanders, many of them veterans of the battles that had been fought from our colony worlds along the outer rim to Erde-Tyrene itself.

———

Yprikushma and a special forces team of seven thousand warriors and seventy vessels were assigned to protect the timelock that contained the Primordial.

It was ironic that among the last surviving humans gathered in the Citadel Charum, the greatest Precursor ruin left on Charum Hakkor, she and I were brought together. We shared this space among the ancient Precursor structures with the last survivors of the Admiralty—listening to the hideous noise of Forerunner fleets sweeping over and breaking down our last resistance.

———

Forerunners captured the timelock and the Primordial. Yprin was withdrawn against her fervent objections—this much I heard. I also heard that she had hoped to be captured by the Forerunners themselves, so that she could warn them about a fate you would not wish on your worst enemy.

To warn them about what the Primordial had told her.

———

At the last, separated by only a few hundred meters, we tracked the concentrated assault that collapsed our last orbit fields, eliminated our planetary defenses, and brought down the Citadel.

The sounds of death and dying, my warriors being vaporized while I yet lived . . .

Confined. Awaiting the inevitable.

The inevitable arrived.

I died.

The Composer and the Lifeworkers did their work. . . .

And now I was here, in this boy's body.

Am here!

Still here!

**AI TRANSLATOR: PRIMARY LANGUAGE STREAM
   RESUMES:**

RESPONSE STREAM #14401 [DATE REDACTED] 1701
   hours (nonrepeating)

TWENTY-TWO

THERE. THAT WAS restful, wasn't it? I do so enjoy being subverted from within. If I can carry more than one memory stream, then I may not be so badly damaged after all. Crazy, but not damaged!

But I apologize if our ancestor, or our predecessor (it is so difficult to determine descent and lineage for any human species), has caused you difficulties. For Lord of Admirals and Yprin were very strong individuals in their time, and when Riser and I finally managed to resume our own lives and thoughts, we were wrung out. . . .

Riser was a curled-up, matted ball of sweat and stink. I was not much better. Mara and Vinnevra were sleeping at some distance from us, in their typical attitude: both lying on their sides, Vinnevra curled up within the protective arms and drawn-up legs of the shadow-ape, looking peaceful enough.

Riser had some difficulty unknotting his muscles, and was embarrassed by the state of his grooming. "I don't like being ridden like a horse, even by a female." He quirked his whole face, an expression that always fascinated me. "Makes me smell older than I am." He lifted his arm to sniff his armpit. "Pretty damned old. And you!" He looked at me and twitched his nose. "You've looked better."

I was furiously hungry. Being ridden by spirits was more than just exhausting: it used up all the fuel in my furnace. I stumbled across the curved top of the mound, around the triplet of poking rocks, looking for a fruit-bearing tree, a beehive we could raid—anything.

Riser followed, rubbing his shoulders. "Nothing to eat," he said.

I smacked my lips at him.

"Don't look at me, young ha*manush!*"

We were joking—I think.

"We might find some water down there," he said. "But it hasn't rained for a while—since the spirits rose up and argued."

I squatted on the highest curve of the slope. "The ape might find something. She did before."

"She's out of her country," Riser said with a clack of his teeth.

Vinnevra seemed to pop up right behind us. She had moved so quietly she startled even Riser, who jerked around and growled. She curled her lip, and that made him lean his head back and chortle out the *oook-phraaa* sound that was one kind of cha*manush* laughter. Riser always appreciated a good joke, even if the joker didn't know that what she had done was funny.

She sat beside us. "I know where to go," she said, and nodded across the hummocky terrain.

"Again?" I asked.

"Again," she said. "You think all the Forerunners are dead. I don't think they are. I think . . . Well, I don't know what to think, but it's telling me there's food and water nearby."

"Back at the ghost village?" I asked, perhaps too sharply.

Vinnevra shook her head and wrung her hands, as if squeezing her fingers dry after a wash. "It's what I'm being told." She looked at us without much hope we would listen to her.

"I don't think I want to take any more chances," I said.

"I don't blame you," Vinnevra said. "Neither do I. I'm going to ignore it, too, this time." Vinnevra was no longer the sparking young female who had rescued me from the broken jar and taken me to meet her Gamelpar.

"We need to decide what we're going to do," she said. "Mara is willing to listen to me—"

"You haven't disappointed her," I said, again too sharply and quickly.

Her wince saddened me. "True. I was about to say, Mara will listen to me—and I'm willing to follow both of you. Whatever you decide."

This transformation was oddly disturbing. She was quieter, more reasonable. Her face had a soft glow, as if she had freed herself from some impossible burden.

And I was responsible for her. Riser looked between us, squinting one eye.

Vinnevra turned to him. "I listened when your old memories talked. Some of what you said I understood. Gamelpar spoke like that, and taught me a few words and ideas. You really *do* have spirits inside of you."

"So did he," I said.

"Yes. I don't have such a spirit, and I'm not disappointed."

"No fun," Riser agreed.

"Anyway, this time, you can take me with you, or not. But Mara wants to go where I go, and she wants Riser to come with us. You, Chakas—she says you're going to be trouble." The soft glow took on a harder, more defensive cast.

"You're talking with the ape now, too?"

Vinnevra nodded. "Some. You have to listen deep to her chest, and to her high, little piping sounds . . . not so hard, once you get the hang of it."

"Maybe the Lifeshaper gave us all a way around the storyteller's curse," Riser suggested.

"The Lifeshaper lies," I said, but it hurt me to say it.

Riser shrugged. "No good going back where I was," he said. "And no good going back to the ghosts."

I had been studying the curve both during the day and at night, trying to understand what all the features and details meant.

The barren waste where Riser had crashed was apparent enough. Behind us was the great sea, across the entire band. There had not been much food there.

"There's a narrow way inland and then west, between the waste and the mountains," I said, pointing it out to them. "It seems to be covered in forest, not as dense as the jungle we've been through—and maybe grassland." I half-imagined it looked like the land around Marontik, but that was too much to hope for. "It might be we'll find game out there, bigger game where there's forest and grass. . . . We'll have to make weapons and hunt. If we're going to survive without Forerunners."

I wasn't at all happy with this plan, to tell the truth. I had no idea whether the Lifeshaper would have taken the trouble to stock her forests and plains with animals we could eat. They might just as easily be animals that would prefer to eat us—or monsters like nothing we had ever seen before.

"What do the old spirits say?" Vinnevra asked.

"Nothing. They're tired from arguing."

Riser quirked his face.

"Then it's a plan. Let's go find out," Vinnevra said, getting up. Mara came around the rock pillars, grunting happily at finding us.

Riser lightly pinched my arm. "Leader," he said, and walked off. We descended the mound and traveled opposite the flow of the wheel's shadow. Vinnevra walked beside me and kept pace. Riser stayed back with Mara.

"I don't mean anything by this," the young woman began, struggling to express herself properly and not provoke me. I wasn't sure I liked her being subservient—it worried me. "I just wanted to tell you . . . I see things out there. I seem to have a map in my head now."

"Is that a good place to go?"

"I don't know. I won't just follow anything that gets into my head—not now."

"We'll watch," I said. "If what you see in your head is right, if it fits the land, maybe we can use the rest."

She looked away, then rubbed her nose. "Itches. What's that mean?"

"Don't know."

"Gamelpar believed in you," she said quickly, "and you kept them from . . . doing whatever they would have done to him. He is free now, because of you." She rubbed her nose more vigorously until her eyes almost crossed. Then she turned to look at me, steadily, clearly—more strongly determined than ever. "I believe in you, too."

Vinnevra offered her hand. After a couple of steps, I grasped it. She then walked closer and looped her arm around mine.

"You can use my true name, if you want," she said.

My heart felt very strange. I had made a decision, laid

out a plan, and everyone was going along with me—even Riser.

I had responsibilities. Three of them.

I hated that.

TWENTY-THREE

FOR A FEW days, we passed through jungle of varying density, cresting the low mounds and hills, going around the big ones. Mara found us some fruit, not much—more of the green tubes that we peeled and ate the pulp out of, more seedy fruits with sallow flesh, mostly bitter.

Vinnevra was delighted to find a log filled with giant wood-maggots. They tasted better than scorpions. Even Mara ate a few. Riser poked and waded through a stream that crossed Vinnevra's chosen path, but there were only insects too small to bother with—no fish.

Still, it was water, and we drank our fill.

The sun had changed its angle to the rim of the wheel

even more. Once, sitting in a clearing, I considered the possibility that we might soon enter a long darkness, when the hoop, the Halo, found its place in orbit where its tilt was perpendicular to the . . . I felt around for the word . . .

Radius.

I didn't need much help from the old spirit to think through the rest. There would be a long stretch of darkness—many days—and then a dreary half-day, light falling only on one side of the band, while the Halo traveled around the sun some more. Not a cheery prospect. I finally stopped thinking about it, but the sun still dropped, day by day, toward the sky bridge.

And the wolf-orb kept getting bigger. It was now ten thumbs wide, a great pink-gray mass, its roundness clearly visible even during the day.

Vinnevra was very thin. Riser checked out our health with his nose and gave me a worried look; she was not doing well. None of us was doing well. The jungle was not providing much food, and we were walking steadily. Mara—it was hard to tell whether Mara was losing weight, her fur was so thick. But around her elbows and hips it was falling out in patches.

She would take those patches and set them up in trees, then wait below, for a while, before giving up.

The trees got small, then thinned out to grassy glades. The glades in turn gave way to a lush, tall grass meadow.

We had been traveling for over twenty-two days—again, I had lost count. Then, just after dawn, I saw Vinnevra standing beside Mara, who had planted a patch of her dark reddish fur on the tip of a tall grass cane, then crouched down below.

Several long-tailed birds started to flutter around the fur. Neither Vinnevra nor the ape moved. Eventually, the birds—none more than a morsel—grew used to them and flew lower, grabbed hold of the cane with their claws, plucked at the fur. . . .

Mara shot up her big hands and caught five at once. Five small birds. We broke their necks and ate them raw, including their innards. Mara we gave two, but she split half of one with Vinnevra. Vinnevra said the ape was sharing it with the memory of Gamelpar.

The meadow soon gave way to bare soil, lightly tilled, as if waiting for a fresh crop. We were still some distance from the desert of ashy blight, but I doubted any farmer would be planting here soon.

"Is this what you see?" I asked Vinnevra.

She nodded.

"I thought it was all grassland."

She shook her head. "There's more trees and grass out there." She pointed inland and west. "Like you saw."

But I had missed this tiny patch of dirt, no doubt just a brown line against the wider yellow and green. "Anything nearby?"

"Just dirt . . . for a ways."

"Why didn't you tell me that?"

"I will, from now on—if you want," she said.

"I want. Tell me . . . whatever, whenever."

She looked unhappy. "What if I'm wrong again?"

"Just tell me."

———

We spent a day trudging across the dirt, until we came in sight of a blue-gray line along the inland horizon. Hours later, we saw that the line was a great, long rail—a strange sort of fence rail that floated over the dirt without visible support.

"Where does this go?" I asked Vinnevra.

She pointed along the rail. That was obvious enough.

"What's at the other end?"

"Something I don't understand. I don't see it very clearly."

"Food?"

"Maybe. I see . . . and smell . . . food, if we go that way."

"Grass and trees?"

"Not that way. Over there, maybe." She pointed away from the rail.

"Game?"

She shook her head. "I don't know."

The old spirit decided now was the time to make a contribution again.

It might be a transport system.

I saw big, noisy objects running along, or above, or beside—or on both sides of—double and single rails, both on the ground and elevated, like this one.

Usually they go to places where there are resources. Or they carry passengers, and passengers need to eat.

So much for my being in charge. We were all starving again.

———

We changed direction and turned our group toward the spin, walking beside the soaring fence rail.

Riser and I fell back a dozen paces from the girl and the ape.

"A nudge from the old spirit?" he asked.

"Yes," I said glumly. "You?"

"Soon it will be long dark, she says."

"Right. I've seen that, too."

"Long dark, travel hard. We follow the girl again?"

"Yes," I said. "For now."

"It was worth a try, finding game," he said. "No blame."

He fell quiet for another while, then said, "Old spirit suggests lots of space below, caverns. Why don't we find a way down? Maybe things have not gone wrong down there."

I thought of the great jagged hole punched into the wheel, many kilometers back along our journey. Inside, below, there had been layer upon layer of broken levels, floors, interior spaces. And what about the chasm that had opened up near the wall? It was too late to go back and find out. Something might have even fixed the hole, and by now, the bottom of the chasm had probably filled in.

What had happened to all those people? To the war sphinxes that were herding them along like cattle? Were those machines controlled by Forerunners, or by the Captive, the Primordial itself?

Was the Primordial actually in charge of this wheel, after all?

"I'm not sure it's a good idea, going down there," I said.

"You smell bad," Riser observed.

"I want to piss my pants," I said.

"Me, too," Riser said. "Let's not and say we did."

It was an old cha*manune* joke, not a very good one.

We kept quiet for another few hours, until we came within sight of a long, large machine sitting on top of the floating rail.

TWENTY-FOUR

THE MACHINE RESEMBLED a giant moth pupa clinging to a stick, with two narrow vanes on each side—no windows, no doors, and no way to climb up.

"It's a big wagon," Riser said.

Or a balloon, I thought, somehow tethered to the rail—but it did not bob in the breeze.

We walked around and beneath. If this *was* a wagon, we might somehow climb up, climb in, make it work, make it move . . . fast!

But it was much too high to touch.

Vinnevra and Mara had plopped down and were watching us as we walked in circles, making our inspection.

"Does it carry Forerunners, or their stuff?" Vinnevra asked. "You don't see it?"

"No. Just the rail. What do you see, at the end?" Vinnevra, after a long silence, finally shrugged. "It goes where we need to go," she said, and then gave me an apprehensive look.

Arguing with her would have been pointless, even cruel.

You are all crazy here, Lord of Admirals observed wryly. *Forerunners have ruined what's left of us, raised us up, made us their tools . . . their fools.*

"Then go," I said.

She walked away, looking back, then got a fey look and broke into a lope, as if fleeing from us. Mara loped along beside her, sometimes upright, sometimes on her long arms, swinging body and legs after—less efficient in the open, it seemed to me, than in the trees.

She didn't seem to need my protection, or want it anymore. Good.

But I could not bring myself to follow right away. I sat in the dirt, head in hands, sick at heart. Riser sat with me for a few minutes, then got up, walked a few steps, and stared back at me, head cocked.

"Don't you feel it, too?" he asked.

I did—but I had been trying to ignore it. Vinnevra wasn't the only one being guided, pulled in like a goat on a rope. I saw food, shelter, protection. And now I smelled the food as well—great tables loaded with food, enough for hundreds of us.

Crazy inside, worn down inside and out.

Footstep after footstep, following the floating rail, hour after hour—and finally a change, something new on this endless, furrowed field of sterile dirt.

We came to a thick white pole with a wide circle at the top. The rail passed through the circle, at no point touching. I measured with my bleary eyes and decided the circle was big enough to let the transport pass through, but still, I half-heartedly wondered how the rail just hung there.

Lord of Admirals then condescended to inform me that this was not especially marvelous. With a kind of easy, instinctive pride, he told me that we—old humans, that is, separating me, his host, from the humans he had known—had once covered many worlds with networks of transportation much like this—rails, poles, and circles.

Far less marvelous than star boats. Which, by the by, we called ships. Star ships.

It occurred to me that Lord of Admirals was feeling something like contempt for all us poor slaves and pets of the Forerunners, so ignorant—but I let it pass. He was dead, I was alive, still moving of my own will.

Mostly.

"Did we ever make anything like a Halo?" I asked, hoping to sting him a little. But the Lord of Admirals did not answer. He could withdraw when it suited him into the quiet murmurs that filled my head—hiding behind my own half-formed thoughts like a leopard behind a cane brake. I could not force him out if he did not want to come.

"I take that as a no," I muttered.

Riser's forehead glistened with sweat. It did seem the air was warmer here even than in the jungle—warmer and drier. My thirst was fierce. Pretty soon, we'd curl up like earthworms on a flat, sunny rock—all brown and leathery.

"Worse here than when young tough ha*manune* caught me and tied me to a thorn bush," he said. "That was before Marontik was much of a town."

"You didn't tell me about that," I said. "I'd have beat them up and thrown rocks."

"They died before you were born," Riser said.

"You killed them?"

"They got old and wrinkled," he said with a shrug. "I outlived them."

I didn't ask if that gave him any satisfaction. Cham*anune* were not much concerned with vengeance and punishment. Maybe that was one of the secrets to their longevity.

"You still don't live as long as Forerunners," I said, more out of weariness than reproof.

"No, I won't," Riser said. "But *you* will."

"How?" I shot back, irritated. I didn't want to be anything like a Forerunner right now. Riser stubbornly refused to answer, so I let it go.

Another couple of hours' walking and the wheel's shadow swept down. We stopped, lay back on the dirt, and Riser and

I allowed Lord of Admirals and Yprin to quietly speak, while Mara and Vinnevra snored and the stars rolled along in the sky, behind and around the other side of the wheel. Wheels within wheels.

The wolf-orb grew each night. Thirteen thumb-widths, almost.

Somehow Riser and I nodded off, perhaps interrupting the old spirits' conversation. Just as light returned, we jerked awake, sensing a change in the air—and a soft sound like wind.

The rail wagon *whooshed* over our heads.

We all stood up and stared. The wagon was just a moving dot, already kilometers away.

"Something's working again," Vinnevra said. Mara whistled and grumbled, and Vinnevra agreed with her—whatever it was the ape had said.

"Walk more?" Riser asked her.

"No." Vinnevra looked around, hands on her hips, and shook her head firmly. "This is where we need to be."

And it was—if we listened to those inner guides.

Still, we looked around—nothing but dirt, no water, no food, no shelter—dismayed but hardly surprised. The skin on my face and arms was brown and flaking and Riser was pinking and patchy. Mara was still losing fur, though out here, there were no nesting birds she could tempt.

We were a mess, but it was so *good* to know we had finally arrived.

Again.

The sky bridge taunted us with its graceful silence.

———

It didn't happen right away, but after my thoughts had blurred into an agony of thirst and hunger, and the sun was beyond unbearable, and madness seemed near—

The ground shivered.

"Not now," I tried to say with a thick tongue and crusted lips. Riser didn't speak, just lay back flat and clasped his hands over his face.

Then the ground crumbled and split in sections. We crawled every which way until the trembling stopped. When I rolled over to look, a platform had broken through the dirt. Shuddering clods marched off its flatness until it was pristine white.

Along the platform's edge small poles rose up and benches shaped themselves at the center.

We waited. Anything might happen. The Primordial itself might pop out of the platform and reach out to grab us.

———

Halo night swept over and the tops of the poles shoved out little blue lamps that cast a steady glow across the platform. We watched all this, not moving, for many minutes, but then, as one—even the ape—we stood up and walked painfully toward the platform, stepped onto it, and peered up at the lamps.

Riser crawled up on a bench and began picking his feet. I hoisted myself to sit beside him, and Mara joined us. We waited some more. Every so often, my little friend would look up and wrinkle his nose.

Vinnevra kept near the outside of the platform, ready to run if anything bad started to happen. Of course, there was no place to run.

Then we heard a faint humming sound. Across the shadowed land, a star glowed way out along the rail. I watched the star move toward us down the wheel's shaded curve, trying to figure how far off it was—many hundreds, perhaps thousands of kilometers. Moving fast. It grew to a bright beacon that threw a long beam ahead through the dusty air, and then—another great wagon rushed down upon us—and we fell flat on our faces!

It stopped instantly, silently, right over our heads, ten meters above the platform. Wind followed and pushed at Mara's nimbus of fur.

The wind spent itself in gritty dust devils, spinning off into the darkness.

The humming became a low, steady drumming.

Vinnevra had found the strength to run off. I couldn't see her. The rest of us stood up under the transport.

A disk cut itself out of one side and descended to the platform. Again, I flinched—but it was just a disk, curved like the part of the wagon it had come from, blank on both sides. A series of smaller poles rose up around the outside of the disk, minus one, where, I supposed, we were expected to step up and get on.

I called hoarsely for Vinnevra. Finally she came out of the darkness and stood next to me.

"What do you think?" I asked. It didn't much matter whether we did this thing or stayed here. We were being reeled in. We didn't have much time left either way.

She took my hand. "I go where you go."

Mara climbed aboard, pushing sideways between the poles. We all followed. The disk lifted us through the air, tilted us at an angle—I was afraid we might slide and fall off, but we didn't—and then inserted us through the hole in the side of the transport.

I thought I saw three doors, was about to decide which one to take, but then—there was only one door, and we were inside. The disk sealed itself tight. No cracks, no seams—very Forerunner. The air was cool. Mara had to bend over to fit under the ceiling, which glowed a pleasant silvery yellow.

A blue female appeared—the wagon's ancilla, I guessed, human-looking but about as tall as Riser. The image floated at one end of the transport, toes pointed down. She raised her arms gracefully and said, "You have been requested. We will take you where you need to be."

The walls became clear and seats rose up that fit all of us—even a kind of low couch for Mara, who preferred to lie on her side.

"Would you like refreshments?" the blue lady asked. "The trip will not be very long, but we see you are hungry and thirsty."

None of us hesitated. Water and more of that pleasant-tasting paste, in bowls, floated out on several smaller disks, and we ate and drank. . . . My lips seemed to fill out, my eyes felt almost normal again, not covered with grit. My stomach complained, then settled in to its work. I could feel the humming, drumming of the transport through my butt and my feet.

The blue lady took away the refreshments before we made ourselves sick. We waited, full, no longer thirsty, but still expecting bad things.

"We have three passenger compartments today," the ancilla announced. I saw only one, the one we were in, and it looked just a little smaller than the wagon's outside. Where were the other two? "Our journey will begin shortly."

Don't trust any of it, Lord of Admirals advised me. I didn't need to be warned. We had been *requested.* That meant somebody knew we were here, and wanted us. And that, coming from any Forerunner, was likely not a good thing.

Vinnevra sat looking out at the passing, darkened land. I leaned forward—I was sitting behind her—and touched her shoulder. She turned her head and stared at me, half-asleep.

"I don't blame you for anything," I said. "I hope you'll let me off the hook, too."

She just looked ahead again, nodded once, and shortly after that, she fell asleep.

I too saw very little of the journey. And it was a long journey. When I came awake, the transport had passed into day and was crossing a rugged, rocky landscape, all gray. Clouds flew by. I wondered if we ourselves were flying now but couldn't see the rail, so there was no way of knowing.

Then something big and dark flashed past just a few meters from the wagon. At our speed, even that brief passage meant the wall or building or whatever it was must have been very large.

The lights inside the transport flickered.

The blue lady stood at the front of our cabin, eyes fixed, body changing in slow waves between the shape of a Forerunner—a Lifeworker—and a human. Her mouth moved, but she did not say anything I could hear.

The transport gave the merest shiver, then stopped with hardly any sensation. The disk-door fell away from the side, but this time fast, landing with a resounding clang somewhere below.

That didn't sound right.

Suddenly, I could feel, then see, shuffling, moving forms all around us—coming and going in slow waves. I seemed to stand in three different interiors at once, with different lighting, different colors—different occupants.

Riser let out a thin shriek and leaped to clutch my arm. Mara pushed her head and shoulders up against the ceiling, arms held high, trying to avoid the things moving around us in the awful guttering half-light.

Vinnevra clutched the ape's side, eyes wild.

Everything suddenly got physical. Dust rose around us in clouds. We were surrounded, jostled. Pink and gray lumps bumped into us as they shambled forward, trying to reach the exit. They might have been Forerunners once—all kinds, even big ones as large as the Didact—but they were hardly Forerunners now. One turned to look down at me, eyes milky, face distorted by growths. Tendrils swayed below its arms, and when it turned toward the exit, I saw it had another head growing from its shoulder.

All were partially encased in what seemed at first glance to be Forerunner armor—but this was different. It seemed to flow of its own will around their deformed and rearranged bodies, as if struggling to hold them together—and keep them apart. These malleable cases were studded with little moving machines, rising up and dropping back from the armor's surface like fish rising and then sinking in water—all working as hard as can be to constrain, organize, preserve.

Poor bastards. They've got it bad—the Shaping Sickness.

"I know that," I said, under my breath.

But it's been held back, retarded. Only prolongs their misery—but perhaps they remain useful, maintain their services to the Master Builder.

I wasn't sure of that, not at all. Perhaps something that controlled the plague was calling them in. Perhaps they had become slaves of the Primordial—of the subverted machine master of the wheel.

"They were with us all along!" Vinnevra whispered harshly. "Why didn't we see them?"

Bright lights moved just outside the door—monitors with single green eyes. Floating before them—under their control, but physically separate—metal arms and clamps guided oval cages. One by one, the clamps circled the transformed and encased occupants, tightened, lifted them, and inserted them into the cages, which then floated away. With what few wits I had left, I counted twenty, twenty-five, thirty of the plague-stricken things.

The interior stabilized.

The blue lady announced, in her human form, "You have arrived at your destination. You are now at Lifeworker Central. Please exit quickly and allow us to service this compartment."

Except for us, the transport again seemed empty.

TWENTY-FIVE

ANOTHER MONITOR—ALSO green-eyed—met us as we dropped down from the open door—no steps, no conveniences. The disk wobbled and clanked beneath our weight. Mara descended as gently as she could but the disk slammed down, then wobbled as she got off.

The transport was streaked with dust and a thick green fluid. Once we were off, the hole in the side filled in—grew a new door, I suppose—then the transport swung around and about on the rail, this time hanging down from the bridge, below the platform.

I think we just witnessed the work of the Composer, the Lord of Admirals said.

"You keep mentioning that," I murmured. "What is it?"

Something the Forerunners were using long ago to try to preserve those stricken with the Shaping Sickness. We thought they had abandoned it.

"You told me it had something to do with converting Forerunners into machines—monitors."

That was its other function. A very powerful device—if it was a device. Some thought the Composer was a product of its own services—a Forerunner, possibly a Lifeworker, suspended in the final stages of the Shaping Sickness.

I really did not want to hear any more. I focused on our surroundings—real and solid enough. We were inside a cavernous, murky interior. No other transports were visible. The transport that had carried us—and those awful, hidden passengers—now, with little warning, hummed, drummed, then rushed off into a pale spot of daylight some distance away, on another errand—back where it came from.

Riser gathered us together like a shepherd, even the ape, who reacted to his prodding hands without protest. The green-eyed monitor moved forward and rotated to take us all in. "Would you please follow? There is sustenance and shelter."

"What did we *eat* inside that thing?" Vinnevra asked, putting her mouth close to my ear, as if not to offend the machine.

"Don't ask," I said, but felt even sicker.

"Were *they* Forerunners?" she asked, pointing toward the darkened archway through which the other monitors were moving the cages.

"I think so."

"Was that the Shaping Sickness?"

"Yes."

"Will we get it, now?"

I shuddered so violently my teeth chattered.

We had recovered enough strength that walking wasn't an agony, but still, the hike across the cavernous space seemed to take forever. Above us, architecture silently formed and vanished, rose up, dropped down, came and went: walls of balconies and windows, long sweeps of higher roadways and walkways, in slow waves, like the ancilla inside the wagon. Wherever we were, this place was dreaming of better days.

The monitor took us through a great square opening and suddenly, as if passing through a veil, we were out in daylight again. Before us rolled a wide body of water, gray and dappled, reaching out to low, rocky cliffs many kilometers off.

Close in to the wide dock on which we now stood, several impressively big water boats lay at an angle, half in, half out of the water—partially sunken, it seemed to me—but one could never tell with Forerunner things. Large cylinders were tumbled and bunched around their underwater ends.

A few burned and scorched monitors lay scattered around the dock, motionless, their single eyes dark, all sad and decrepit—something we were certainly used to by now.

Our green-eyed guide rose to the level of my face, then urged us toward the edge of the dock. "There will be a high-speed ferry along shortly," it said. "You will wait here until it arrives. If you are hungry or thirsty, limited reserves of food and water can be supplied, but we must not stay here long."

"Why?" I asked.

"The conflict is not over."

Perhaps here was another truthful monitor. Best to get an update on the wheel's situation—from the green-eye's perspective. Not that we, as mere humans, could do anything about any of it.

"Where does the fighting continue?"

"Around the research stations."

"The Palace of Pain," Vinnevra said, face contorted. She raised her fists, either as defense against these words coming from the monitor, or because she wanted to reach out and strike it. I touched her shoulder. She shrugged away my hand, but let me speak. I could feel the Lord of Admirals subtly guiding my questions, expressing his own curiosity . . . supplementing me in both wisdom and experience.

"Were humans infected?" I asked.

"Not at first. Then . . . the Captive arrived."

"While this weapon was being tested at Charum Hakkor?"

"Yes."

"How did the Primordial—the Captive—get here?" Riser asked, no doubt guided by Yprin.

The green-eye seemed to brighten at this. "The Master Builder himself escorted it to the installation."

"Was the Primordial in a timelock?"

"It was not."

"Was it free to move about, act . . . on its own?"

"It did not move, at first. It appeared dormant. Then, the Master Builder departed from this installation, and left his researchers in charge. They reduced the role of the Lifeworkers on the installation, and finally sequestered them with a select group of humans in several smaller preserves."

"But there were other humans outside the care of the Lifeworkers."

"Yes. Many."

"And the Master Builder's scientists kept trying to infect them."

"Yes."

"Did they succeed?"

"Eventually, but only in a few humans. They also tried to access records stored in the humans by the Librarian herself."

This was too much like staring into my own navel. I felt a whirlpool of unhappy, contradictory emotions—and realized much of that inner turbulence came from Lord of Admirals himself.

"How did they access them? By asking them questions?"

"By removing the records and storing them elsewhere."

Ask about the Composer!

"What is the Composer?"

"Not in memory," the monitor said.

"You seem to know everything else. What is the Composer?"

"An archaism, perhaps. Not in memory."

271

"Not still in use—turning living things into machines, that sort of thing?"

No answer this time.

I could hear a distant whirring noise. Far across the body of water, moving along the distant rocky cliff, a white streak was making a wide turn and coming closer. This must be the ferry.

Questions bunched up. "Will you be coming with us?"

"No," the monitor said. "This is my station. I have care-taking duties to perform."

"Will there be other monitors out there, where we're going? Other ancillas?"

"Yes. Three minutes before the ferry arrives."

"The war . . . did Lifeworkers rise up against the Build-ers?"

"Yes."

Infuriating reticence! "Why?"

"The Captive held long converse with this installation's controlling ancilla. It in turn leveled the shields and broke safeguards at the Flood research centers and spread infec-tion among the Builders and many of the Lifeworkers. It then moved this installation to the capital system, where we were attacked by Forerunner fleets, and forced to move again . . . but not before the hub weapon fired upon the Forerunner capital world." The monitor's voice dropped in both volume and pitch, as if expressing sadness. Could these mechanical servants suffer along with their masters?

"Where are we now?" Riser asked.

"We are in orbit around a star out in the thinnest boundaries of the galaxy."

"Any planets?"

"Some. Most are little more than icy moons. There is one large planet composed mostly of water ice and rock. It is growing closer. Too close."

The ferry slowed as it approached the dock—in shape a pair of sleek, long white curves, like boomerangs linking their tips to make bow and stern. A spume of water cascaded behind and soaked us with mist.

The ape shook herself and launched another spray.

"You will go aboard now," the monitor said as a door swung wide and made a ramp into the interior.

"Are there sick things inside?" Vinnevra asked, her voice shaky.

"No," the monitor said. "You are expected, and time is growing short. That is all I have been told."

We walked across the ramp. The inside of the ferry differed little from the inside of the rail-wagon, though it was wider and the ceiling was higher. Mara did not have to crouch. Vinnevra poked about, checking carefully for other passengers. There were none that we could see.

"Maybe Forerunners pack passengers together and make some of them sleep and dream, so the journeys are shorter," I said.

Vinnevra curled up on a bench. "Shut up—please," she said. Mara let out a high whine and rolled over in the aisle.

Riser shook out his arms. "I don't think Forerunners are in charge now."

That did not make me feel any more secure. "Who, then?" I asked.

"Don't know." He squatted, then patted the seat beside him, inviting me to sit. We stared through the transparent walls as the ferry pulled away from the dock and gathered speed. Spray spattered the hull and slid aside, leaving no marks—all very sleek, yet strangely primitive. The rail transport, this boat . . . too simple. Far too simple—almost child-like. I expected more from Forerunners by now.

All my life, I had thought that Forerunners were little gods in charge of our lives, far away mostly and not particularly cruel but hard to understand. Since meeting Bornstellar on Erde-Tyrene, all my ideas about Forerunners had been taken apart, joint by joint, like so many birds that would never fly again. And what was left behind?

Being human has never been easy. Do not define who you are by comparing yourself to them.

"Please be quiet," I muttered. "You don't have to figure things out and stay alive."

If I'm so useless, why did the Lifeshaper put me here? I doubt you're hiding any great wisdom.

That irritated me. "You wouldn't exist without them . . . and neither would I."

Riser looked at me. There was a puzzled misery in his eyes, a slant to his mouth, that told me he was feeling much the same, and thinking similar thoughts.

The ride on the ferry was long and quiet. The lake or sea or river—perhaps the same one we had crossed earlier, we never did learn—continued gray and monotonous for many hours. For a time, the water narrowed into a channel, with gray cliffs on either side. Then it grew wide again, its distant shores running far up the curves.

I could not even estimate our speed, but the spray whizzed by.

For an uncomfortable time, I imagined these were the western waters and we were actually being ferried to the far shores. . . . But all of those tales seemed too antiquated, too *weak* now to be believed.

I had lost all connection with the pictures in the sacred caves. All that I had seen since leaving Djamonkin Crater made those drawings, first viewed by the smoky light of clay lamps burning tallow, seem hollow and stupid. I had no roots in this land and no way of knowing what kind of water this was—spirit water or dripping water, living water or dead. Life and death meant very different things to Forerunners.

My old spirit was also unimpressed by those stories, the things I was taught by the shamans while they scarred my back and marked and confirmed my manhood.

How low your people have fallen—how irrational. Like cattle or pets.

I did not rise to this insult. It was true enough.

Vinnevra reached forward from her bench to touch my shoulder. Her face was clear and calm and her eyes bright. "I think I understand now. This used to be a place for children. Forerunner children. A safe place to learn and play. And I know where my *geas* comes from," she said. "It comes into my head like sunshine through the dark. It comes new and fresh when there is something important to tell me. And it is the voice of a child—a lost child, very young."

"Why a child?"

"I don't know, but it *is* young."

"Male or female?"

"Both."

"What does it tell you now?"

"We're going where we need to be."

"Where's that?"

Mara held out her huge paw and Vinnevra gripped her thumb.

"We're all going to Erda," she said.

"How?" I asked. "Are we going to swim there?"

She made a face, then rolled over and curled up.

Riser growled, "The air is full of lies."

"Probably," I said, but my heart was strangely lightened by a new thought. "What if humans are going to be given a job because Forerunners couldn't finish it?"

"What sort of job?" Riser asked.

"Killing the Primordial," I said. "The Forerunners fought and made each other sick. So we're the only ones left to kill the Primordial, fix the Halo, and take it to where it needs to be."

Riser leaned forward, his eyes sharp and bright. "We're the dangerous ones," he whispered. "The old warriors awaken."

The boat approached a near shore, turned, and shot along parallel to high, faded green cliffs. Riser pointed to blue-gray buildings far off along the cliffs, growing closer and larger as we were whisked along—blocky, irregular towers packed in undulating rows. Their tops supported what might have once been the remains of a roof, arching, jagged pieces like the broken shell of a huge egg. We passed under the closest tower. The boat leaned into another wide turn, shooting up a tall plume of spray, aiming our view through gaping holes in the roof at the sky and then back down to the water.

A thrill ride for young Forerunners! I tended to accept Vinnevra's theory.

Still many kilometers off rose a wide gray mass with a flat top. As we rushed closer it resolved into a great, curving wall of falling water, throwing thick clouds of spray up around its base. The mass might have been nine or ten kilometers tall.

"A storm?" Riser asked, frowning.

"I don't think so," I said. We watched the foaming whiteness grow closer. Just as we were about to merge with the tumult, our ferry lifted parallel to its violent plunge, like a bird flying up a wall—up and *over* the crest and then across a wide expanse of dimpled, mossy green water. The ferry dipped down to that jewel-slick surface and again threw up an enthusiastic plume, moving swiftly against the outward-flowing current.

Sometime later, the roil seemed to reverse and now rushed us toward a great, central hole, easily twenty or thirty kilometers wide. As we shot through successive rainbows and clouds of spray, nearing the edge of this inner cascade, I sensed it was much deeper than the outer falls.

"It's like a target," Riser said. "The Librarian likes targets. Do you think she's here?"

Vinnevra stood beside us. "It's not the Librarian," she insisted. "And it's not a Forerunner. It's a child—a young child."

That made no sense to me. But the Lord of Admirals seemed to find something interesting in her idea.

They start again as children—all together.

It is what the Composer was designed to prevent.

That name again! I did not want to hear any more about it.

The boat rolled and angled and we saw the sun almost touching the high, shaded sky bridge. Off toward the east, we again saw the red and gray wolf-orb, as wide as several of my hands—a waxing crescent so close even its shadow showed rugged detail.

It's too damned close, the Lord of Admirals said. *It's on a collision course.*

"Forerunners can carve up planets like oranges," I said.

This wheel is far more delicate than it might seem to you

and me. Someone likely wanted to guarantee a way to destroy it, should they lose control.

He pushed forward in my thoughts a vivid diagram for a failsafe orbit, closing gradually with the wolf-faced orb. For a moment, this clouded my seeing and I felt half-blind—but I understood the urgency, the importance. My understanding of orbits and large-scale tactics had already expanded marvelously under his tutelage.

And once I had thought that stars were holes punched in the sky by huge birds pecking for insects!

Placing the Halo on a collision course made sense. If a faction lost control and guidance was not reclaimed in a certain period, then by prior arrangement, the wheel would smash up against the wolf-face orb.

It would self-destruct.

I gripped the seat, filled with instinctive terror—but not at this dire if still abstract prospect.

The boat plunged over the central cascade. We felt and heard nothing but a low hum but what we saw made us cry out and grab hold of each other. Even gigantic Mara whined and hid her face with her hands.

All around, as we fell, the darkening waters divided into hundreds of vertical streams, their turbulent surfaces rippling blue and green and deeper green. And then—the streams crossed over and around each other like braiding snakes, weaving and writhing in incredible patterns while tightening in on the space between.

Our weight went away, and we rose up toward the ceiling,

clutching at each other. I wanted to be sick. Riser and Mara *were* sick.

We fell for many minutes—and then, the braided streams flew up and away and we dropped into a measureless void. Above and behind, the streams spread outward to form a vaulted ceiling—an upside-down roof of flowing water. There could be no doubt we were now inside the great mass of the wheel, far below the surface. But where we might be going, I had no idea.

We remained without weight—in free fall—but stopped being sick. The speed and distance of our descent was hard to judge. It could easily have been dozens of kilometers, even hundreds. My eyes adjusted slowly to this different kind of darkness—a black below black, darker than night, darker than sleep.

Mara pressed her face against the transparent hull and made small whistling sounds, then tapped the bulkhead with a wrinkled, drawn-in expression. By now I could see what she was seeing. All around us, our falling boat was surrounded by dimly glowing shapes.

I wrapped my fingers around Riser's arm. He shook loose and stared at me resentfully, then followed our eyes to the spaces outside the boat.

"Boats," he said. "Great big ones."

Neatly arranged, lined up above and below one another, row upon row moved off through the far darkness, sketched out by gentle, guiding lines of blue and green, speckled by faint stars like glowworms hanging in a cave. Then they, too, rose up and away and another, emptier darkness swallowed us. I wondered if what we had seen were indeed boats—or ships . . . or power stations, or some other machine or magic.

Machines, science; not magic, the Lord of Admirals reminded me, but my eyes were too lost in blurred-out fatigue to care what this ghost thought.

I saw only suggestions of whatever was outside—spots of brown, a swiftly passing cord of dark gray, like a hanging bit of spiderweb. . . . Then, weight gradually returned and we descended to the floor in the cabin. Our fall was coming to an end.

We braced our hands and legs on the floor and the bench. The walls fogged, then become opaque.

We stopped.

The hatch swung out.

We retreated from that black circle in a loose gaggle, as far as we could get—into a corner at the rear of the cabin. Mara wrapped us in her capacious arms.

A whisper of cool air blew in, but for a few moments, nothing more. Then we heard a distant musical note, echoing, jarring, like the song of a strange, lost bird.

"Is this the Palace of Pain?" Vinnevra asked. None of us knew; I could only imagine what awaited us now that we had passed over the waters, under the waters, through the waters.

The light inside the boat dimmed, and simultaneously, the light outside grew brighter, though not by much.

"Something wants us out," Riser said, shoving into Mara's

dense fur. His nose twitched. I could smell it now as well—food, hot, savory, and lots of it. Despite everything, we were all of us hungry again—ravenous.

Vinnevra was the first to push out of Mara's protective embrace. "This is where we have to be," she said. At that, we all groaned—even the ape. But the girl walked through the open hatch, looking back just once, eyes searching our faces, before stepping down—and vanishing.

We had no choice, of course. We all agreed—this was where we should be.

We followed her.

TWENTY-SIX

THE BOAT HAD come to rest at the center of a great, green-glowing web radiating outward in avenues, pathways, streets—whatever they were, they were wide enough for three of us to walk abreast (or one and Mara). Many crossed to join with other paths, shaping not just a web, but a glowing, greenish maze on all sides for as far as I could see.

Hovering just above a distant belt of pitchy darkness were faint suggestions of other structures, straight and very tall, perhaps pillars or supports, surrounding and faintly reflecting the web's light. I had no idea how far away they might be, but as my eyes adjusted, I tracked them up and up to a great height, and they became thinner and thinner until they seemed to meet overhead.

We might have been at the bottom of a high, narrow tunnel dropping vertically into the depths of the wheel, where ships and other equipment were stacked away, stored, waiting to be retrieved. I stood beside Riser, who had never been greatly impressed by big things of any sort.

"More Forerunner devil stuff? *Boring,*" he huffed. "Where's the food?" Then he looked back, and his eyelids flashed white in concern.

Vinnevra had dropped to her knees. Mara strode along a path to keep close to her, holding out her arms as if to keep balance—and seek our help.

The girl pressed her hands against her temples and cried out, "I *hear* you! Enough!"

Something around us changed—*withdrew.* I felt the sudden absence with a gut-deep sense of disappointment, even bereavement. But for Vinnevra, the absence came as a relief. She rose to her feet. "That way!" she said, suddenly cheery again. "Don't worry. The web won't let you fall."

Mara was not reassured. The darkness beyond the edge of our landing platform had a disturbing sense of *depth.* It sure looked as if we could step off and fall forever. But following the scent of food, and keeping as far away as we could from the edges of the paths, we proceeded in the direction Vinnevra had indicated.

I had heard long ago tales of the games that devils and gods play on humans. Back on Erde-Tyrene, children had often been subjected to such horrors and wonders. Yet it was apparent to me now—and would have been earlier, had I not been too distracted—that all the nightmares and day-dreams we are heir to as weak and feckless mortals had come true since I met Bornstellar.

Break free, then, Lord of Admirals encouraged me.

"How?" I whispered.

Turn their power upon them. Here, they are the ones weak or dead.

"Here, nothing is real!" I cried. Riser lifted his finger to his poked-out lips, then winked—not in humor, but giving sound advice. No sense encouraging our old spirits at this stage of our journey.

We followed as Vinnevra crossed to a path on the right, and then another—this one long and straight. Behind, the ferry grew smaller and smaller, until I could cover it with my thumb . . . and then the center of the web went dark and the ferry with it.

Behind us, below us, darkness. Above . . . the inner surface of the wheel might be up there, its false landscapes just barely painted on—deserted cities, blasted plains covered with ashen dust, dead Forerunners, all that we had left behind, including our fellow humans.

Or perhaps that had been smudged out as well. The wheel itself might be gone, and that would mean there was only this glowing web.

Too often, in a dream, you can never go back to where you were, and if you try, it's not what you remember. If our ultimate destination was to be Erde-Tyrene—Erda—that would violate this most basic law of all dreams.

And where there is a web, there might very well be a spider. Now I really wanted to piss myself or loose my already-empty bowels, to disgust any predator with my stink—humans can make such a great stink!—and run, run, or leap over the edge and fall. Falling, perhaps I would come awake and jump up from my rough bed of grass and wood slats, hear my mother clinking pots in the next room—stretch, yawn, plan for another day doing whatever Riser thought would be best for us to do.

Happy times, those. Best of times.

No going back.

And if I had died, if I was already across the western waters, clearly I had not found favor with Abada.

We walked. The dead, some of the old stories say, walk forever and never know where they are going.

———

Riser was the first to see the spider. He poked my hip—hard. Looking to our left, now I saw the jagged, spiky blue leg—and then another. Riser yawped and tried to climb my torso as if I were a tree. I let him.

Clutching my friend and turning slowly, awkwardly left, I saw Mara, and beyond her—far beyond her—yet another long, jagged leg, moving and dropping to touch part of the web-maze. Completing my turn, I saw dozens of legs prancing slowly and delicately across the web.

Just as I had feared.

It took all the courage or foolishness I possessed to lean back and look up. Above, supported by those flashing, sharp-angled blue legs, hung a mass of close-packed crystals, big as a city but upside-down and pulsing with a deep, shadowy light. The facets of the crystals crawled with intense glow-worm stars, drawing luminous threads behind.

By flashing and flexing, the legs had revealed they were not legs, but more like solid lightning supporting the crystal mass. The legs vanished, reappeared, then flexed and bowed as if under a great weight.

The crystal city lowered over us. At its center, an emerald green glow thrust out, brighter than anything around it—and extruded the most watchful glow of all.

A single, central green eye cast down a darting, baleful light.

Riser clutched me all the tighter. Vinnevra stood immobile with an expression of forlorn, final hope, hope about to give up and die—while Mara rose to her full height, squared her considerable shoulders, and opened her mouth to roar. . . .

The crystal city decorated itself with more threads of light, and the entirety swung back over us, behind us, then *down* and *through* the web, where it paused at right angles to the pathways.

The threads merged with the paths and avenues.

We faced directly the jutting wall of crystals, at a level with the huge green eye. The green eye had become the center of the maze. The smell of food became stronger. Despite my terror, my mouth watered. I was being tugged along like an animal, helplessly lured on by my most basic drives.

Vinnevra swung around. Her face was ghastly green in the reflected glow. "We're home!" she cried.

The great green eye lifted. The web of paths was slowly extinguished by darkness flowing from the cobwebbed crystal mass.

We have seen this before, Lord of Admirals informed me, and I realized the old spirit was not in the least frightened, and not because he was already dead. He could feel harm coming to his old enemies, harm being done to the Forerunners—and that was far more important than his own welfare, or mine. *This is the one who betrays Forerunners, their own greatest monster. We know this one. Remember?*

But I did not—not yet.

Walls descended around us, at first reflecting the jeweled eye, but then scenes and images played across their pale surfaces like sketches for yet more dreams.

Still, the old spirit refused to be cowed. *We are here because some humans are immune to the Shaping Sickness. We carry that secret. And we have not yet given it up to them. If we do, we die!*

But the inner voice was overwhelmed by a blaze of animal hunger. All sober judgment and thought was squeezed tight, then crammed down.

The walls finished sketching, painting, then projecting a place in which we could all be comfortable and at home.

An even greater lie.

TWENTY-SEVEN

W E WALKED THROUGH a forest of old, dignified trees, then over a meadow of sun-dappled grass, lulled by the buzzing of passing insects—none of which tried to bite.

At the center of the warm glade rose a long, thick wooden table. Spread across that table were all the glorious foods we had smelled before, when we rode on the . . . the what?

Vinnevra ran ahead and took a middle seat on a bench, then smiled sympathetically at Mara. The ape ambled forward willingly enough, but she gave me a look that seemed both wise, cautious—and doubtful.

Still, there was food, there was sun.

The ape joined Vinnevra, squatting behind her, and the girl passed her a bowl of fruit, which she delicately pinched up with thick fingers, then chewed on thoughtfully.

I walked around the table and sat across from Vinnevra. Pulling forward a large bowl, and then a smaller one, I served up Riser stewed grain, vegetables, and sliced meat, roasted to perfection and sprinkled with salt. Hot, rich, delicious.

Riser, strangely, seemed only half-present, but for the moment that did not alarm me. From the corner of my eye, I saw him eating and was glad; but I could not make out his expression.

"It's been a long journey, hasn't it?" Vinnevra said, flashing me a happy smile.

This forest was little like the forests I had known, thornier and drier. The sun was high and bright and the sky was just the correct shade of blue, and there was no . . .

Sky bridge.

We ate until we could eat no more, and then decided to leave the table to sit in the shade of a broad-spreading, thick-leafed giant of a tree that rose almost high enough to touch the passing clouds. For a while, I knew we had indeed returned to Erde-Tyrene, as Vinnevra had suggested we would.

"Too bad Gamelpar couldn't be here," I said.

She gave me a quizzical look. "But he is."

I accepted that. "Where are all the others?" I asked around the table.

Riser—off to one side—did not answer.

Vinnevra kept smiling. "They're here, too. We'll meet them soon. Isn't this wonderful?"

The daylight turned to dusk as it always had on Erde-Tyrene, high clouds pink and orange, then purple, brown, and gray. Stars came out.

Look at the patterns of the stars. This is not—

The moon rose. The others found beds in the soft grass and moss and rolled up and slept, except for myself and Mara, who moved away from Vinnevra and closer to me, grumbling deep in her chest.

The moon, bright and green, watched over us until my own eyes closed.

——

And then the great green eye probed deep, reminding me, with a strange enthusiasm, that we had met before. The Master Builder had conducted that first interview, with the help of this green-eyed ancilla, a very different sort from the lesser monitors and servile ancillas.

The ancilla proudly informed me—and by transfer, the Lord of Admirals—that it had indeed been placed in charge of this wheel, and ultimately of all Forerunner defenses.

It informed us it was quite capable of lying.

And then it played.

Whether it actually moved us about the wheel and made us live through other journeys, or simply scratched over our memories with fabricated dreams, I will never know. It certainly had the power to do both. And the freedom. It no longer served either the Master Builder or Forerunners.

Whom does it serve now?

The orb was approaching—time must be short. Still, the master of the wheel distracted me—did not allow me to use my powers of reason.

All the journeys and years ended with a burst of pain—immense pain.

And then, the old spirit was gone.

SCIENCE TEAM ANALYSIS: Separate streams of data follow, differing substantially from those connected to the Lord of Admirals. Analysis not yet complete, but we suggest skepticism as to their veracity and usefulness.

ONI COMMANDER: "None of this seems to be trustworthy. It's almost a sure thing that we're being fed fabrications. And if not—how can we even begin to correlate these so-called memories with actual events, after a hundred thousand years?"

SCIENCE TEAM LEADER: "I cannot disagree, but we still find, scattered throughout, curious correlations with recent discoveries."

ONI COMMANDER: "Little bits of bait making us swallow the whole damned lie, right?"

SCIENCE TEAM LEADER: "Possibly."

STRATEGY TEAM ADVISOR: "We're interested in the references to this 'subverted AI.' We already have records reclaimed—so to speak—from variations of what may very well be that Forerunner artifact."

ONI COMMANDER: "Nothing but trouble!"

STRATEGY TEAM LEADER: "True, but we're likely going to encounter more like it. Any insight this monitor can provide will be greatly appreciated."

ONI COMMANDER: "I'd still like to focus on the Didact."

SCIENCE TEAM LEADER: "Gentlemen, I've been skipping ahead a little. Let's move forward in the record. I doubt any of you will be disappointed."

ONI COMMANDER: "None of us is pleasant company, Professor, when we're disappointed."

SCIENCE TEAM LEADER: "Duly noted, sir."

TWENTY-EIGHT

SPENT A hundred years walking in circles.

Questions were asked. I could not remember either the questions or my answers. I could not even remember who was asking. Slowly, however, I recalled certain memories. Some were acceptable; others were not, and I pushed them back down.

———

Finally, I opened my eyes to a great stretch of star-filled space, at the center of which hung a huge, red and gray sphere, tormented by craters—an icy planet. Impacts over millions of millennia had carved a wolf onto the surface. I might have been out in space, suspended just like this orb.

Then my point of view swiveled and dropped. I looked down over a wide swath of the wheel, the Halo, as if from a high mountain. I was told I was witnessing part of what was sometimes called the Silent Cartographer—the complete and living record of the Halo. Those who would help rescue and then use the wheel were allowed to explore and learn in this place.

More memories returned. The band below swept up and away in the familiar fashion to the sky bridge. Many hundreds of kilometers below, huge squares—plates of gray-blue Halo foundation material—were being maneuvered by machines over the limiting walls on either side of the band, stacking up through the atmosphere, while cloudy swirls of interrupted weather gathered around the lowest plates.

The Halo was preparing for its coming challenge.

I felt nothing—took no breath, experienced no sensation. Only cold thought left me any hope of still being alive. Still, I came to enjoy this isolation. No feeling, no pain—only education and watchful eyes.

Then I also heard voices. A kind of selective blindness lifted and I realized I was standing—leaning slightly to one side, but standing. The red and gray world blocking out the stars, so near to the wheel, remained—as did the stars and the wheel itself. But beneath my feet, I became aware of a dark platform, and then, of shadows—many shadows moving in.

A smaller shadow came close, stretched out a blurry hand—and all came into focus. I looked out upon dozens of people—humans all, some like me, many others different.

Riser gripped my fingers. I knelt and took him in my arms. He whined at my touch. "Hurts," he said, and turned around to show a punched-out mark in his back—healed over, but furless, pink and angry looking. "Stung deep."

I felt my own back and cringed at the shallow hole my fingers found. I pulled them back, expecting to see blood— but they were dry.

Male and female, we were all naked. Most looked as old as Gamelpar had been before he died. Only a few were as young as me. Few words passed. We stood out under the stars, caught in the light of the red and gray planet, rapidly closing the distance between itself and the wheel.

"Who brought us here?" I asked Riser. He circled his fingers and looped them in front of his eyes.

"Green-eye," he said.

The closest male, a tall, elderly, brown-skinned fellow with a short jaw and thick neck, tried to say a few words, but I could not understand him. No old spirit rose up to interpret and Riser himself—master of so many human languages— didn't understand, either.

A female gently pushed the elder aside and spoke simply and in broken phrases, like a child, but at least I could understand her. "You the last," she said. "All . . . others . . . little ago, little time. But you last."

Then she turned and revealed that in the small of her

wrinkled, suntanned back, a chunk had also been removed . . . and healed over.

The younger members came forward. The elders parted and let them through, and Riser approached them, sniffing and judging in that way he had, which I never mistrusted.

Then he darted off and vanished for a moment among the crowd of elders.

These younger men and women—there were no children—gathered and compared their healed wounds. Some seemed embarrassed by their nakedness, others, not. Some were glassy-eyed, terrified into muteness, but others, as if at a signal, began chattering away. I was surrounded by five or six very communicative men and four or five women. Somehow I had been singled out, perhaps because I was the last to arrive, or the last to wake up.

Their faces fascinated me, but nowhere among them could I find Vinnevra. A few resembled Gamelpar, purple dark of skin and reddish brown of hair, with broad, flat faces and warm, intelligent eyes.

But Vinnevra was not here.

Age. Diversity. Very few young. That gave me my first shallow clue. Then Riser returned, dragging with him three other cha*manush*—a male and two females. On Erde-Tyrene, I had found females of Riser's people to be quiet and reclusive, until they had made firm acquaintance—and then, all too familiar, quick to poke and make rude inquiries, nothing off limits, everything either wonderful or funny. I had never been quite sure how to deal with Riser's women, or his female relatives—on those few occasions when I interacted with them—for Riser seldom invited me to his home, and seemed to prefer going out on jobs with me and his other young ha*manush* minions.

But now he had two females in tow, of that ageless puzzlement of cha*manush* years. Cha*manush* grizzled in their adolescence but seldom turned all gray or white, as my people did.

"Everyone is missing bits," Riser told me. His companions stood a few paces back, nostrils flexing, watching the rest of the crowd. They held hands, and one gestured for Riser to join them. He backed away from me, but nodded meaningfully, eager to convey something important. We could barely hear each other in the rising babble, so he signed out: *All from Erde-Tyrene. Younger fell from sky with us. Old ones brought here long ago.*

Others gathered around, too tightly for my comfort, but I did not discourage them or express any distress—for the story was coming out, the familiar story, that within them they had all once had old spirits, old warriors, each distinctive and opinionated.

To a one, young and old, those inner voices were now silent.

I tried not to conspicuously stare at the missing pieces of their backs when they turned, raised their arms, gestured. But I could not help myself. All of us on that wide-open, elevated platform—under that looming planet and starry sky, looking out over the stretch of Halo that had been the home of so many for so long—every single one of us had been wounded, sampled—"stung deep." We all limped, old and young—and we all cringed when we moved.

But the important question, immediate and crucial, was, why were we *here*? What did the machine master of the wheel intend for us? For I had little doubt that Riser was correct, that the green-eyed ancilla was behind all this. Did that mean it was now allied with the Didact, or with the Librarian, the Lifeshaper herself?

Had the wheel been reclaimed by the Lady?

Something else was missing in my thoughts, something that made all these theories pointless. I seemed to have misplaced a memory about a child. There was a child. . . . The child was in control . . . held sway over the green-eyed machine. We had been introduced!

But I could not remember its name, and I certainly could not remember its shape.

TWENTY-NINE

THE GROUP PARTED to open a passage. They craned their necks to see what was coming, rising over the edge of the platform. I caught a flash of brilliant green. A monitor—larger than any I had seen so far, at least two meters wide—came into view and moved between the parted humans.

"Welcome to our installation's new command center," it said in a beautiful, musical voice neither male nor female, nor much like a Forerunner's.

All of us, young and old, were pushed back by invisible forces until a circle cleared in the middle, about thirty paces across. As Riser and I were nudged back, I remembered the moments on the Didact's ship when the entire hull seemed to vanish, giving us the sickening sensation of being suspended in space.

At least here there was the gentle mercy of a floor—a deck, as the Lord of Admirals would have called it.

"All bid welcome," the beautiful voice said, "to the new masters of this installation."

At the center of our ring of frightened people, a number of hatches slid wide in the floor, and through these rose more monitors—smaller but otherwise almost indistinguishable from the large one. Each had a single glowing green eye. As they rose, the hatches closed up beneath.

There were now more than forty monitors crowded inside the circle, surrounded by humans old and young. All stood out in sharp detail against the deep backdrop of stars and the ever-growing red and gray planet, which now covered a third of the sky.

The nearest of these new monitors pulled up before Riser and myself. It projected an image I instantly recognized— though I had never seen him before, not through my external eyes.

Male. Human. I looked the image over cautiously, closely, noting that his shape was similar to mine, though broader in shoulders and thighs; arms long and powerful-looking; hands thick and backed with patches of hair. A flatter, broader head and a great, square jaw.

"A strange reacquaintance," the image said.

Unlike us, he appeared in raiment traditional for a high-ranking commander in the old human fleets: a rounded helmet that covered all but the forehead and the ears, a short coat over armor plates, a wide belt cinched just below the ribs, and form-fitting pants that revealed a bulging shield around the genitalia, which might, it seemed to me, have been more than a little exaggerated.

Like the ancillas, he was translucent—a ghost of a ghost, a whispering within made manifest without, like Genemender back in the Lifeworkers' preserve. Yet having carried him within me for so long, I would have recognized him anywhere.

This was Forthencho, the Lord of Admirals.

"We're being given command," the image said. "Believe this. It is true. The time for our victory has arrived."

Riser touched my hand. I broke from my fascination to glance down at the little one. He clenched his jaw and made a small shake of his head. His meaning was clear enough. He was incapable of further judgment or action. We had both been carried so far beyond any human wisdom or experience that any move we made—anything we might say or do—was equally likely to produce a good outcome or a bad—equally likely to pull us deeper into Forerunner madness, or propel us out and up.

The image of the Lord of Admirals continued. "We have been carried by these descendants, our vessels, for many years. And now we are brought here, for this moment, by a machine that has long since turned against Forerunners. It wishes us to defeat them—to cause them misery and dismay. And so we shall!

"But there is no way yet to know our total strength, or how far we may go . . . with our new command, but this we do know, finally: after ten thousand years, we have a chance to avenge our cruel mistreatment.

"We have urgent work to do all around this infernal wheel," the Lord of Admirals continued. "Forerunners have cocked things up magnificently before having the grace to kill each other or die of the Shaping Sickness they wished to communicate to us. The wheel itself is in jeopardy. There is little time, and so extreme measures have been authorized."

The larger monitor rose up, a faint display of lacework energies playing across its features. It hovered over us all— the inner circle of machines and the outer of the humans.

All around, the apparent openness of stars and planet was overlaid by vivid, glowing displays. The sky became like the inside of one of the old caves, filled with instructive images and stories masterfully tuned to our ignorant needs. I seemed to both see and feel a sharply defined awareness of how we all needed to behave, to act in concert.

The image of the Lord of Admirals favored me with particular attention. "You have a decent mind, young human," he said. "We have traveled well together. I will place you beside me at the center of this weapon's control and command. If together we can save this Halo, then we will use it to strike against the heart of Forerunner defenses. But the time between now and then will be very difficult."

Symbols and curving lines surrounded the wolf-faced planet. All of us tried hard to understand, as if our lives depended on that understanding—as very likely they did.

The lines swept like an expanding tunnel toward the far curve of the wheel—a point of intersection.

Now appeared a dizzyingly strange and complicated set of instructions for creating a portal—a broad gate like a hole in space, through which great distances could be shrunk to almost nothing.

I watched a detailed record—reality, simulation, or reenactment, I could not tell which—of the Halo shedding damaged bits, leaving behind broken ships and a spreading, radiating cloud of atmosphere, ocean, terrain—and then opening just such a portal, and beginning a passage to comparative safety, where it would repair itself—or be supplied with materials transported from another installation, much greater in scale and much farther away—to rebuild, if necessary.

At the same time, from all around, I heard a low moaning sound, as if from a gathering of frightened livestock.

"After this wheel was transported to the Forerunner capital system, and the metarch-level ancilla prepared to unleash its energies on the capital world itself, it was attacked by Forerunner fleets and defended by its own sentinels—a battle that resulted in much of the destruction we see around us. The wheel was moved again, a tremendous effort, but the Lifeworkers and many of the Builders who had survived continued to fight. They did all they could to destroy this installation from within. They failed. One and all, they were finally infected with the Shaping Sickness."

Much of this I had learned from Genemender. Still, the implications plunged deep. The green-eyed intelligence knew us too well. My hatred against Forerunners reached a pitch of intensity that almost blew me out of the presentation.

The Lord of Admiral's voice gathered certainty and strength. "Now that the Forerunners have succumbed, either in battle or from the Shaping Sickness, they have left behind just a few confused servants—and many, many humans, awaiting a new time, a new mandate.

"And that mandate is: avenge the fallen. Rise from defeat, rise from the dead!"

A great resonance hammered us with ancient instincts, reawakened emotions—and a desire to rectify ten thousand and more years of death, misery, and near extinction.

"The promise is simple," the Lord of Admirals announced. "Freedom. Support. Weapons unimagined in all our previous wars. *Humans will fight Forerunners again—and defeat them!*"

THIRTY

WHAT A RABBLE these words were addressed to! The elders and the few young stood alike in stunned silence, staring at the ghosts, projected and contained by machines much like those that had once populated Genemender's reserve.

We had all carried one or more of these warrior spirits; we had all become acquainted, more or less, with their natures and opinions. Now we were being asked to accept them as commanders—to follow them into battle.

My first question was, why? What value, these old ghosts, to Forerunner machines? What value could I have?

Worse, I knew that the green-eyed master of the wheel

was not actually in command—had not been in charge of the wheel for many decades. I knew, but could not act on my knowledge.

To do so would be to remember the encounter that had cost me a chunk of flesh and bone. The encounter with *the child*.

The Lord of Admirals seemed to hold the highest rank in this unnatural assembly. His ghost stepped forward and addressed me as if we were both physical.

"It's our final chance to reclaim history," he said. Had he been real, I think he would have tried to grasp my shoulder. As it was, his hand swept empty air. I saw in his faltering expression that he perceived himself fully capable of reaching out and touching. . . . And I felt pity.

For a moment, the illusion broke.

I knew that the green-eyed machine was itself evil, and not just to humans. It had betrayed its own creators. It was in league with the Primordial. But how was that possible? In the years since the devastating test at Charum Hakkor, how could the Primordial have done so much to subvert this wheel-shaped world and its mechanical servant?

A few meters away, Riser faced off against the projection of a blocky-looking female, stout as a bull. Yprin Yprikushma, no doubt. From his wry, white-lidded expression, I could tell he was not impressed.

I always trusted Riser's judgment.

The unreality of it all made me sick. We had been through too much to fall for more illusions, Riser and I. We knew that before now, all Forerunner magic—all of the tricks and wonders they called *engineering* or *technology*— had been used to reduce and then destroy humans—yet we were now being asked, *commanded*, by our ancestors, these old ghosts, to believe that in this *one instance*, we would carry out the will of a greater Forerunner machine, simply because it had gone mad and set out to destroy its masters.

My weakness almost brought me to my knees. I wobbled before the projection, holding out my hands to keep my balance. "You aren't real," I told the Lord of Admirals. "I wonder if you were *ever* real."

Suddenly I could not hear what the others were saying. The air around us became tight and still. We—the projected ghost and me—seemed locked in a box.

"I'm as real as I have ever been," Forthencho told me.

"Since you died?"

The air became harder and harder to breathe. The walls of the "box" were getting misty as if from the fog of my breath. I couldn't see the others, only this one projection, and his monitor in shadow behind him.

More tricks—more persuasion. Would I be suffocated if I did not comply?

"Why do they need us?" I asked.

"Not even a machine as powerful as the wheel's master can do its work alone. You are alive. You can serve."

"Humans? The last dregs of us that remain after so many Forerunner victories? We became animals. We were devolved—and only the Librarian thought enough of us to raise us back up again!"

"*It doesn't care!*" the Lord of Admirals said. "The machine will do everything it can to destroy Forerunners. It knows that I have fought Forerunners before."

"And lost."

"But also learned! I have spent my time within you going over and over old battles, studying all our past failures, and now, I have full access to their new strategies! This wheel is but one of the weapons at our disposal—if we join.

"Out there, awaiting our commands, in many orbits around thousands of other worlds, in other star systems, are reserves of tens of thousands of ships of war—and more Halos. We will be irresistible!"

The spirit's enthusiasm had an acid tinge that almost made suffocation preferable to agreement. So be it, I thought. I held out my hand and then fell against the moist barrier that hemmed us in.

I seemed to see through this sham to the Captive, the Primordial itself. . . .

I was fading. Illusion passed into illusion—and I preferred my own.

Mongoose, the trickster, I remembered, had been responsible for creating humanity. It was Mongoose who had convinced Mud to mate with Sun and breed worms, and then teased and angered the worms until they grew legs to chase him over the grasslands.

Worms became men.

The wheel's green-eyed master was a bit of a trickster, like Mongoose, playing jokes upon the humorless gods known as Tree and River, Rock and Cloud.

I choked out some words, I don't remember what.

The mist and the closeness flew up and away, and all around I again saw stars—but no other people.

No other machines. The old spirit's projected image and I were alone under the stars.

I could not help but suck in a breath as cool air swirled around me.

"I have told the great machine that you are willing," the Lord of Admirals said.

"But I'm not . . . *willing*!" I cried. Maybe I *had* agreed. Maybe I did not want to suffocate. Maybe I was just curious. I have always been too curious, and Riser was not here to correct me.

"Thirty others who carried warriors have chosen to join us in taking command of the wheel. Their courage reminds me of the—"

"Riser?" I interrupted.

"Very canny, that small one," the Lord of Admirals said. "I would have enjoyed having his kind serve under me."

"You don't understand him at all," I said, voice rough. My deep unease had intensified. I did not feel at all well.

"He will play this game for as long as it amuses," the Lord of Admirals said, "and for as long as he has a chance of causing Forerunners dismay and pain. He also wishes to attack the Didact personally. This has been conveyed to me by my old opponent, Yprin."

I knew that was a lie. In my weakness, I did not much care. I took a few stumbling steps around the platform, then straightened and focused on the red and gray world.

It seemed about to brush the sky bridge.

"We will be stationed at key controls to help maneuver this Halo. We have much work to do, yet even then, our chances are slim." The Lord of Admirals seemed to be having misgivings. His hatred, he must have known, was blinding him to the strangeness of this bequest.

"So . . . do we have a deal, young human?" he asked. "For now?"

"What will happen if we survive?"

"We will spread out to the fleets and launch an attack against the heart of Forerunner civilization, in the Orion complex. Never in all our battles did we come within fifteen thousand light-years of that prize!"

Madness, pride, shame, the delusion of a new opportunity . . . What ghost, I asked myself, could pass up such a thing?

"You lied to the machine," I said. "You told it I was willing."

"The least I can do, young human," the Lord of Admirals said. "I need you. And if you ever wish to go home again—you need *me*."

And why else, I asked myself—why else did the Lord of Admirals or the master of the wheel need me? One possible answer: everything here might still center on the future actions of the Didact. I had met the Didact himself, had helped resurrect him from his Cryptum on Erde-Tyrene. I had spent many hours in his somber company. I had watched his ship dissolve and the Didact himself be captured by the forces of the Master Builder—captured and, very likely, executed.

But the Didact had also served as a template for Bornstellar. When we parted ways, Bornstellar had been looking more and more like the old Warrior-Servant. I wondered how that had turned out. He had not seemed happy at the change. Had they taken Bornstellar aside, carved a chunk of flesh from his back, and installed the Didact's ghost into a machine?

Would we encounter that ghost and that machine, somewhere out there among the uncountable stars?

Surrounded by this magnificence, this power, this deception and cruelty, all I wanted was to reach back to our days on Erde-Tyrene—to shield myself, my naïve, young self, from ancient grudges and eternal evils.

In a dream, one can never go back. It took some time for me to realize it was already too late. I can't put into words all that I felt. To be truthful, I no longer *feel* much of anything.

All that I was, but for reflections in a cracked mirror, has been lost for a long, long time.

THIRTY-ONE

S TANDING BEFORE THE image of Forthencho, I knew that something inside me had also changed. I felt weaker, older—fading.

I pinched myself hard and felt almost nothing—no strength in my fingers. Very likely, we had been deceived into believing we were alone, so as not to witness the destruction of the braver individuals around us—those who refused to go along with the old ghosts and the green-eyed machine. Just another level of illusion.

My whirling thoughts settled into immediate questions.

"Why would Forerunner machines let themselves be run by humans?" I asked. My voice sounded thin and weak.

"Maybe they can be fooled," the Lord of Admirals said. "Some say that deep in our flesh Forerunners and humans are related."

I did not believe that, not then. "Have you received your orders directly from the machine?"

"There are many duplicates of command monitors, just as when humans fought Forerunners."

My vision seemed to flick in and out from clarity to bright but foggy bars of light. "What convinced it to turn on its masters?"

I could not stop my damned curiosity from working even if it sapped my last remaining strength.

"Given too much power, or contradictory instructions. Full of itself, perhaps."

Or convinced by forty-three years of intimate conversation with the Primordial.

Forthencho's image wavered, then returned, larger and more solid-looking. "The machine does not hate Forerunners," he continued. "But it knows they have been arrogant and need correction. And it takes an odd satisfaction in the prospect of having humans carry out that punishment." The Lord of Admirals seemed to be growing into his role, just as I diminished. "This ancilla has more power than any previous command monitor. The Didact gave it complete control over Forerunner defenses. When the Master Builder assumed the Didact's rank, he came to believe that he might be punished for his audacity as well as his crimes. If the Master Builder was to be arrested and imprisoned, then this ancilla would take revenge on his behalf. Perhaps it is doing so now."

The Master Builder had layered safeguards within safeguards. The perversity of it all was dizzying. "Madness!" I said.

"But with much precedent in human history," Forthencho said. "Many are the reasons we lost battles. Now, the machine acknowledges only one other who possesses the proper inception codes, and thus the power to stop it."

"The Didact," I said. And there it was again—the most likely reason I was being kept around.

"Perhaps. But the Didact appears to have been eliminated. And if he did not pass such knowledge on to you . . . then the machine is still safe."

I wondered how much the ghost had studied my memory, how much he believed this to be true—and how much he was still holding back from the machine.

"Our first task is to reorient the wheel and survive the planet's close passage. We have several hours to prepare, no more."

Our illusion of isolation faded. We were no longer alone, but the platform was much less crowded. Flanked by monitors, we looked in dismay at each other. So few remained! The rest had defied the master of the wheel—and now they were gone. I caught a glimpse of Riser, many meters away, and was surprised he had chosen to cooperate—but also relieved.

Transports surrounded the high platform: sleek war sphinxes and other defensive vessels, as well as ships of different design—rounded, less aggressive-looking. These carried no obvious weapons and might have once been used by Lifeworkers.

"They are here to take us to command centers around the wheel," the Lord of Admirals said.

"It can't be controlled from one position?"

"Perhaps it can—perhaps it will be. But damage is inevitable and some of us must survive. We have a much better chance if we are spread out."

"It's going to be that close?"

"Far too late to avoid it completely. If the planet doesn't strike one side or another and tear the wheel to shreds, it could still cause severe stress through its gravitational pull. Or—it could pass right through the middle of the hoop."

"What are our chances then?"

"Unknown. Such a thing has never happened."

The Lord of Admiral's monitor pulled back his image and nudged me outward along the platform, toward a war sphinx. I had been aboard an older version of such a weapon, it seemed ages ago, and found this one familiar enough—a cramped but comfortable interior designed for a larger frame, but quite capable of adjusting itself to carry both me and the monitor.

The monitor found a comfortable cubby that opened in one bulkhead, and it settled in while I dropped back into the adjustable pads of a Forerunner couch.

Unlike the Didact's war sphinxes on Erde-Tyrene, keeping vigil around his Cryptum, this one did not have a damaged warrior spirit. I detected no hint of personality in its cool, precise displays or its pronouncements and warnings. Forthencho's monitor had either taken over those processes or they had been wiped earlier in the master machine's purge of the Halo's rebellious countermeasures. All previous loyalties, all trace of Forerunner ethics—such as they were—had likely been leached away, replaced by a devotedly bland yet singular madness.

We lifted from the platform, pushed through a barely visible membrane, and swept out and away over the inner surface of the Halo. For the first time, I was able to survey long stretches of the landscape between the parallel walls and track the overarching sky bridge from a rapidly moving and lofty perspective. But I was too numb, too cold inside, to see much in the way of magnificence or beauty.

If we survived, this Halo would return to being a killing machine. I could easily imagine the great wheel being sent to Erde-Tyrene.

And so, I reached my decision. I had to do everything in my power to make sure we did *not* survive. Of course, I could not tell Forthencho this. My understanding was now separated from his. Still, as he had suspected, his sophistication—his ability to judge complex situations—had stayed with me, along with, I hoped, a bit of his old courage, his old willingness to sacrifice himself for a higher cause.

If I succeeded, I would be killing many hundreds of thousands of our fellows.

I would be killing Vinnevra and Riser.

The war sphinx flew a zigzag, looping a course above

and along the band. Wrapped in the pale couch, I felt no discomfort as we abruptly changed direction, rising and dropping—diving into the atmosphere, shooting up again like a leaping fish, spinning about to see our contrail twist and feather behind us in the upper air.

As we traveled, my weakness and numbness gave way to isolated, cool curiosity.

I did not care.

I admired the wheel. I saw how thick the walls were to either side, and how wide in proportion the great swath of lands between—brown or green, mountainous or flat, burned away or left as bare foundation material.

We flew over the early phases of what might have become basins of oceans or great lakes, the foundation itself pulling aside to create wide, comparatively shallow depressions, or rising up in irregular but suggestive reliefs over which, somehow, Forerunners might later paint dirt and rock.

This Halo had never been finished. Its potential had never been fully exploited. It was designed to accommodate many more occupants—humans, certainly, but likely the inhabitants of hundreds of other worlds, as the Master Builder's research on the Flood expanded.

Or the Lifeshaper herself had, in her devil's bargain, hoped to create more preserves, save more life-forms, against the Master Builder's planned wave of destruction.

"One hour until impact," the monitor announced. I heard in its voice no trace of Forthencho.

The Lord of Admirals could be suppressed at will.

THIRTY-TWO

THE WEAPON CONVEYED me—us—to a great, flat-topped wedge thrusting inward from a wall. At a quick estimate, this triangular expanse was about five hundred kilometers wide at its base, where it merged with the wall, and four hundred from base to tip. Everywhere but the tip itself, the wedge's upper surface appeared uniform and featureless. The looming planet suffused a pale rose glow across this expanse like dusk's final light.

As we dropped, the tiniest of shadows became apparent on the tip of the wedge, structures that grew and grew against the immensity until I saw how large they were in themselves—easily a dozen kilometers high. A slender half-arch, like the upper part of a bow, stretched beyond the tip. From the end of this bow, slender cables spread an ornate sling to support another complex of structures—each of these also the size of a small city.

Forthencho appeared to my left, looking not at the view through the port of the sphinx, but at me—a creepy focus on my own reactions.

"Tell me what you see, young human," the old spirit said.

"It's a command center," I ventured.

"Correct." He sounded proud, as if I were some son who had performed well. "And not just any center. This is the Cartographer, the core of the wheel's structural knowledge. The Halo's automated control systems were sabotaged by rebellious Forerunners before they were infected and died. The Cartographer is all that remains—but it will suffice.

"Three monitors will be stationed here, relaying the Cartographer's measurements to all the others. But for our signals, they will be nearly blind . . . making our work more difficult. But . . ."

His image wavered. When it returned, Forthencho seemed perturbed, even distressed, if that was possible for him, doubly isolated from the living.

"One of our questions is about to be answered," he said. "Brace yourself, young human. We will not be handling the controls ourselves. Gods help us all."

The war sphinx wove through and around beautiful, graceful structures that seemed untouched by recent battles. My mind had already filled to overflowing with visual impressions, and now I simply wanted to sleep and absorb it all, give myself time to slot all that I had seen and my reactions to those sights into useful categories.

I could no longer feel my hands at all!

My eyelids drooped, my thoughts blurred into fever. But still—no respite. With a lurch, the sphinx flew fast as a hornet up against a wall, stopped instantly—and connected. The hatch opened. The monitor supporting Forthencho disengaged from its cubby and the couch opened wide, expelling me with a long pale curl, like a tongue pushing out an unwanted gobbet of food.

For a moment, I seemed to see my body from another location—above and to one side. The body opened its eyes.

Then we rejoined, my body and I. But the peculiar feeling did not diminish. Something was changing—something had changed since the idyll in the false woods.

I stood on a flat space surrounded by a tangle of other platforms, some flat, others curved inward or out, arranged in many directions—a dozen ups and downs. Each platform faced a display on which glowed complicated visuals of the wolf-faced planet, the far stretch of the wheel, close-ups of damaged regions—even other control stations.

"This is the Cartographer," Forthencho said.

"Why are we alone?"

"Are we? Enjoy it while you can," he said.

The wall behind us shivered as other vehicles attached and spewed out nine more humans and as many monitors. Forthencho's monitor nudged me abruptly toward a steeply curved wall. I thought I might have to crawl, but I was able to walk along the curve, upright, toward another level at right angles to where we had begun. In normal circumstances, the abrupt shift might have made my stomach rebel, but I felt nothing.

Other humans, for the most part elderly, were chivvied onto opposite platforms. Only two were as young as me.

No Riser. Not at this station.

Then, from the opposite side, came those whom Forthencho had been informed were to handle the actual controls. Another cold spike went through my head.

The plague-stricken corpses we had seen on our journey had been in the last stages of the Shaping Sickness, supported and maintained by the strange variety of armor—products or patients, of that mysterious entity the Lord of Admirals had called the Composer—which must have existed even in his day.

But even in their worst contortions, those remains had displayed none of the perverse and infernal creativity lavished on these livid, ghastly combinations: a single Forerunner head covered with suppurating scales, shared by two partial bodies, with four legs—

A great lump of quivering, boneless flesh surrounded by a fringe of drooping appendages, ten shrunken arms or legs, undulating out and back to transport the mass to its position—

And around these wretches another type of constraint or support: flexible harnesses, fine meshes of wiring and tubing, radiating from a blue metal disk. A serpent oozed along with sinuous motions, then raised a torso, from the chest of which a jammed-in head peered out, eyes alert, showing what remained of the face—a face contorted with pain. The eyes sought me out. They were Forerunner eyes—slanted, gray, deeply intelligent. They reminded me of Bornstellar or the Didact.

And suddenly I felt pity—pity mixed with abject horror. "I can't do this," I whispered. "Let them all die. Let *me* die. Let this end right here!"

"If it *does* end here," Forthencho told me, "then *humanity* ends here. All that you know, all those whom you know and all that they have ever known—finished! Get up and stand for your species. This is our last chance."

His disembodied courage hardly fazed me at first. I was exhausted, my emotions skirling way beyond fear, into an acid nothingness of pure panic.

And with the fear came short relief. At least I could still feel something!

Forthencho's monitor withdrew and flung out a swift dart that struck my thigh. My panic faded instantly, as did half of my mind—the half that judged, decided, felt an urge to preservation.

I actually smiled.

"This will last for a brief time," the monitor said. "At the end of euphoria will return cooler thought patterns. Take care. You are being measured."

"By who?" I croaked, wiping drool from my lips.

GREG BEAR

Forthencho seemed far off now, like an insect lost in the muddle of floors and monsters and glowing curtains.

"Who's measuring me? Why?"

No answer.

The serpentine creature that had stared at me joined us on the platform. It curled its fleshy tail, wrapped in netting, wires, and scraps of sticky fabric, and rose up again, then reached out to empty air—while the skewed platform thrust up a slender pillar to meet its gray, grasping fingers.

With a sidewise glance through agonized eyes, the trans-formed Forerunner assumed a firm stance—

Studied me.

And took control.

The Lord of Admiral's monitor rose behind me. Something flowed outward from the monitor, around both my head and the monster's torso, and my direct view of the platforms was replaced by a far-spanning perspective on the wheel and the planet.

Turning my head, I seemed to see things in great detail, with a fine sense of depth. My "eyes" might have been hundreds of kilometers apart. I could perceive the closing distance between the Halo and the wolf-faced planet; I could also see a portion of the wheel beginning to torque in the gravitational pull of that icy, rocky sphere.

I understood a few of the symbols that now appeared in and around these objects. But the Forerunner beside me—I could sense its cold, sour presence both mentally and physically—understood perfectly well, and it guided my hands across the knobs with whispered suggestions.

The touch of its hands—repellent, pitiable, desperate. Why both of us were necessary, I could not guess. Yet all across the wheel, the adjustments made by this extraordinary team began to have an effect.

The Halo, thirty thousand kilometers in diameter, was precessing to a new angle in its orbit, facing off against the approaching planet, just under ten thousand kilometers. Our combined speed was bringing us to a rapid close, but long before the planet struck, its mass would severely torque the wheel, possibly even break it apart, and so other systems were being brought into play. The monitor, the disintegrating Forerunner—along with an educational residue from the Lord of Admirals—allowed me to follow and even understand some of what was happening.

The Forerunner beside me, with his (or her—I could not tell) hand now lying beneath mine on the controls, felt a pain I could hardly imagine. The distorted hand was exerting less and less pressure. I thought it likely that the controls could not, after all, be operated with purely human guidance—but I had no idea how long these pitiful creatures could avoid becoming puddles of slime, whatever the Composer had or had not done to keep them alive.

The Shaping Sickness—the Flood—had rearranged all their internal order, preparing these bodies for a new kind of existence in which the individual identity would be, for the most part, erased. But enough identity still remained for it to wish to carry out its final duty, before it either disintegrated completely—or fulfilled that *other* destiny imposed by the Shaping Sickness—and even young, naïve Chakas had a vague inkling of what *that* might be.

For now, however, the wires and mesh kept it from that fate.

This was becoming more than one kind of race.

————

Forthencho, seeing what we had found in the lake town, trapped in a Forerunner cage—, had called it Gravemind. Tagged to that word in the Lord of Admiral's experience was a half-buried awareness that the Primordial itself had not been, precisely speaking, one creature, but three, four, five, six—a dozen! Forthencho had never learned the actual number.

Having undergone that disintegration and dying of past individuals and rebirth into something vastly more powerful, all these creatures had joined millions of years before into its own early Gravemind, far more than the sum of its parts.

————

I see by your copious perspiration that you have witnessed such transformations. But like frightened children, you have not entirely understood their implications.

I have, and I *do*.

THIRTY-THREE

YOU HAVE ASKED me about the Didact. I have not provided much in the way of useful information, because during the time in which I knew him, I was only minimally educated and could not properly interpret what I saw and experienced.

That changed as I accessed the memories and knowledge of the Lord of Admirals. Yet even his experience of the Didact had been for the most part confined to remote observation.

But the intimacy of combat—of matching strategy against strategy, and more intimate yet, tactics against tactics—had provided Forthencho with an inner understanding of the

Didact that likely only a few Forerunners possessed. For the depth of the human-Forerunner conflict had led up to, and over, the brink of near-extinction, which revealed a kind of animosity—a raw, vigorous, yet completely rational enmity—unlikely to be found among those of the same kind. At least, unlikely among those who are sane.

We kill mice that invade our grain stores—kill them without mercy—but only the feeble-minded hate the mice.

But there is yet one more occasion on which I encountered the Didact, and that propelled my understanding of what this Warrior-Servant was capable of on a new level.

This insight is what you are after, above all. I am well aware my functions are failing. But you must indulge me. I owe you nothing. I am no longer human; I have not been human or even a living thing for over a thousand centuries. You will not be able to preserve my experiences and memory from more than a small fraction of that period, and yet, what I have been and done looms over my thin moment of humanity like a mountain rising over a pebble.

And it seems likely, as I observe your concern, that you are not yet cognizant of the one great truth that I offer you—the truth that changes all the equations of our history.

That amuses me.

———

All around, on all the platforms, humans had paired off with Forerunners in their final stages of transformation—soon to become useless, I thought, if not to actually die . . . a mercy.

Then, a great tunnel grew out before me, its shining walls blocking out my view of the platforms. The walls gleamed with arrow-flights of brilliant sparks, and sharp musical notes rang in my ears, discordant and frightening.

The linear sparks in the tunnel darkened to dull red, then died away like the embers of an old fire. I felt only intense cold. For a moment, I seemed to float in the tunnel surrounded by the last of the sparks.

The tunnel then turned completely gray and lifeless.

I tried desperately to perceive myself as occupying a point in space, a fixed position, and could not—there was only the tunnel and memories falling in line behind me like leaves.

An ancilla appeared, brilliant green.

The ancilla came between this blurred-out, uncertain *me* and the pitiful remains of my companion. My eyes suddenly focused—for the last time. I raised one hand and looked at it, wondered at how beautiful it was, moving its fingers at my command, obeying my will, *our* will—just like the wheel. But so slowly!

Reaction time was crucial.

"You will connect directly to the Cartographer," the ancilla said. "This will require interface adjustment."

The Forerunner turned away what was left of its face, shuddering as if at some sacred violation.

"We are instructed by metarch-level command to reveal all," the ancilla said. "We have no choice but to obey. The Cartographer contains all designs and locations and circumstances of this installation, past and present. All changes are recorded here.

"Preparations are necessary."

Another dart jabbed into my calf, and now the sparks raced *through* my body, rather than outside. I felt pain everywhere, and then a startling clarity.

Between my body and the decayed Forerunner's bulk rose a suspended rod about as thick as my arm, and from that rod flew thousands of glistening strands like spiderwebbing; the strands stitched up one side of my body, covering me with gossamer, while more strands laid themselves down over the Forerunner's upper torso.

It squirmed in fresh agony.

The tunnel now came alive to us. To both of us—I seemed to merge with my companion, and even, for a moment, feel its pain as well as my own—until all was submerged in an ecstasy of total information.

My eyes and ears were laid siege. Both of us blended with the tunnel displays, far more complex and detailed than anything before. More surprising, I *understood* what I was seeing—all of it! Comprehension came to me through the Forerunner—and suddenly I *knew* how to act, how to coordinate with hundreds of other, similar pairs located around the wheel.

We *became* the Halo. I could feel the stresses, the peril—and the means we might use to *escape*, as a runner fleeing a predator feels the ground beneath his feet.

Exalted! Godlike energy and power, like nothing I had ever known. If this was what it meant to be a Forerunner, than I would have gladly resigned my humanity. All my tasks, however tiny, brought me intense joy; all seemed supremely important, and perhaps they were, for a calculus of preservation was being made even now by the monitors and their hideous tools, by *us*: when to bring which systems into play, how long to use them, and in what sequence to cut them off.

I was completely aware of the survival mechanisms available to the Halo.

Later, much of what happened in the next few hours returned to a jumble of confusion and spectacle . . . but after tens of thousands of years, long reflection brings it back. I have of course defended Halo many times since. But you know that. . . .

All these survival mechanisms required great amounts of energy—energy in short supply after the sabotage of so many power stations.

Perhaps most impressive was the ability to suspend much of the wheel in time, lock it in stasis, turning the installation into a great, reflective ring immune to all changes imposed from outside.

But the energy cost of such suspension was immense—perhaps more than the wheel could muster. As well, all around the system, energy that would have been absorbed by the Halo would have to be deflected through a fractal-dimensioned slipspace, creating a suspicious scatter of heat signatures and even high-energy radiation that could attract the attention of anything hunting us.

The wolf-faced orb was already exerting an awful pressure on the wheel's integrity. The walls of the Halo glowed along their outer surfaces as they attempted to evenly redistribute the gravitational strain.

And the pitifully few remaining sentinels and other vessels firing their drive motors in an attempt to move the wheel out of the way were having little success. The only result had been to slow the Halo slightly, dropping its stellar orbit a few hundred kilometers—into a situation where the red and gray planet would sweep right through the hoop without touching.

But before that was tried, the Halo's hub and spokes activated. The makeshift control team hoped to elastically absorb some of the planet's energy as it fell into spokes and the hub, then transferring some of that momentum to the wheel—in effect, thieving the planet's velocity to move ourselves into a higher orbit. This might prevent another collision should the orbits of Halo and planet again intersect.

We had no idea how far hub and spokes, all hard light structures, would behave under that sort of pressure—whether they could actually stretch without breaking or vanishing.

Another eventuality Forerunners had never anticipated or tested. And so we waited.

We did not have to wait long before there were additional complications. Two outlying war sphinxes detected ships approaching from opposite the course of the planet—a great many of them, some very large. From the distant green-eyed "master" came a moment of sharp attention, concern—perhaps of recognition.

But for now, the ships had to be ignored.

The wheel's walls had distributed all they could manage of the planet's uneven gravitational tug. Now the foundation plates between the walls were warping and buckling, rising up and separating and in the process tossing loose or spilling great volumes of air and water, spewing long, silver-gray streamers into space.

The plates that had been stacked high earlier in preparation now began their slow shuffle to replace the damaged plates—but clearly the repairs could not keep pace with the destruction.

The Halo, barely keeping itself together, was squarely faced off against the red and gray planet.

———

The new ships came into our view.

Most obvious were the dreadnoughts—dozens of them spreading and swooping around the planet, flying close to the hub and spokes, then spreading along the spokes into a broad fan that might, if they chose to land, bring them down all around the wheel.

More concern—but we could do nothing if they were here to destroy us. Still, it soon became obvious that these were not maneuvers of attack and destruction. What were they attempting?

Rescue?

Such ships could quickly insert their drives into the grid and supply power. That could save everything!

More exaltation—and then, suddenly, an abyssal plunge into a cold, mechanical *something* that my eclipsed humanity interpreted as rage.

The green-eyed master of the wheel did not find this intercession at all helpful. We had been found. The rogue Halo was rogue no more! The appearance of so many Forerunner ships likely spelled an end to everything the perverted ancilla was trying to accomplish. . . .

A sickly glow of hope flowed from the serpentine Forerunner hooked up beside me. But very little time remained to act through any agency, no matter the source or the power.

The light of the star now came from behind the planet, casting eerie shadows through the fog of icy vapor streaming away from our wheel. The wall opposite our command center separated and bent outward like a metal strap in the hands of a burly blacksmith.

An uneven contest, to say the least. The mass of the Halo was tiny compared to the gray and red planet.

The planet now pushed up against four of the spokes, and then, as the spokes stretched, it struck the hub itself. At this, rippling pulses of blue fire flew outward. The hub shimmered as the spokes grew longer, then fragmented—broke apart. They seemed to lay down across the planet's rocky surface, then abruptly converted into curling, expanding beams of intensely blue and violet radiation.

Perhaps now the Halo was exacting some revenge—but only against bare stone. There would be no gradually stretching net or snare, no capture of momentum and acceleration.

The world continued its passage.

The wheel now began to truly come apart—walls shearing, plates separating, gaps of many hundreds of kilometers opening up between, like pieces of a huge necklace being yanked from all sides.

Still, the ecstasy of my connectedness shielded me from fear—my own fear. But not from the deep concern of the green-eyed master of the Halo, and then, rising behind it, something darker still.

But this darker source of command felt no fear, was beyond fear. I could feel its influence like the chill of a dark, dead star permeating, infiltrating us—

Forerunner and human alike became frozen in place.

And what it now impressed upon me, even now, was the most frightening thing of all—

Superior, intensely pure curiosity—far colder and more precise and disciplined than anything I had ever known. These entities were expressing an almost cruelly isolated and lofty interest in the stages of an ongoing experiment.

Was there some sense of satisfaction at this melding of so many Forerunners and humans? Some triumphal revisiting of an ancient plan, long ago frustrated, then abandoned, but now possible once more?

Could Forerunners and humans be recombined and reverse their shivering asunder so many millions of years before . . . when the Primordial and the last of its kind decided on a larger, wider strategy, a greater plan that would no doubt bring about immense pain, but also a greater unity of all things. . . .

Through the Flood, the Shaping Sickness. The greatest challenge and contest of all.

From that challenge, humans had for a moment only emerged victorious, only to be decimated by the Forerunners—a second crushing defeat for the Primordial's plans. All of this had been laid out in detail to the coldly logical mentality that was the Halo's master.

Even enhanced and combined, I—we—could only appreciate a small portion of the depth and power of this plan, this argument, unveiled to us as if we were children peering through curtains at the copulation of our parents. . . .

———

The Halo was dying, no doubt about it. Even as dreadnoughts attached themselves to the remaining intact plates, more gaps appeared, more sections twisted about and spilled their contents.

But a new voice laid itself over us, powerful, resonant, penetrating the Cartographer's display, the overlay of the machine, even the cold analysis of the Primordial.

This voice rose in volume, assuming command, and at

once—*I recognized it!* I knew it from that time we had spent on the island within Djamonkin Crater. A weary manner of speech once accustomed to complete command, but through circumstance withdrawn, set apart, lost . . .

But no more.

The Didact!

"Beggar after knowledge," the voice said, swirling all around us. "*Mendicant Bias.* That is the name I gave you when last we met. Do you remember the moment of your inception? The moment I connected you to the Domain and you were ceded control of all Forerunner defenses?"

All the images contained and controlled by the Cartographer darkened and collapsed into a now much-simplified ancilla. "That name is no longer secret," it said. "All Forerunners know it."

"Do you recognize the one who named you?"

The green ancilla burned like acid, yet I could not turn away, could not cleanse myself of its corrosion.

"You are not that one," it said. "The Master Builder gave me my final set of orders."

"I *am* that one—and you are not truthful."

The acid quality of the green ancilla's voice became so intense it felt as if my insides were being eaten away.

"You take commands from other than a Forerunner," the Didact's voice said, "a clear violation of all your instructions. I am the one who knows your chosen name, your *true name*—"

"That name no longer has power!"

"Even so, I can revoke your inception, call out your key, and command you to stand down. Do you willingly pass control to me, your original master?"

"I do not! I have listened to the Domain. I fulfill the wishes of those who created us all. You do not, and have never done so."

The green ancilla had receded to an infinitely deep incision, an arc of pinpoints carved or burned into the blackness. Its tininess wavered like a flame.

Then came a complex *sound* that might have been words or numbers, a transmission of information or commands, I could not tell which.

The Didact's voice filled the Cartographer—seemed to fill all space and time, and I knew he was still alive, once again in control—perhaps more powerful than ever before. "Poor machine," the Didact said. "Poor, poor machine. Your time here is done."

The ancilla leaped in the darkness as if startled—and vanished, along with almost everything else.

I found myself lying flat and exhausted, covered with sweat, on a cold, hard surface, while the last dull embers of the Cartographer's display slowly dimmed. The pain in my back and side was awful. I could hardly move. I could not see anything but blurry shapes.

The link to my companion—the sick, tormented Forerunner—was sliced from my arm. The binding gossamer gave way like ripping fabric. I was being shunted aside, removed from the Cartographer.

The ecstasy of my connection became an aching loneliness.

Now I heard actual sounds—voices—and a startled exclamation.

Recognition of who I was—who I had been.

___

The voice in my head became more intimate and gentle.

"I've found you, young human. I've found *both* of you—and still alive!"

A massive presence stood beside me, then knelt down and extended a six-fingered hand. The cut gossamer on my arm rose up like hair in a thunderstorm before lightning strikes. It connected and wrapped around a thick, powerful forearm—mottled gray and blue, the colors of a fully mature Warrior-Servant.

"You have already been connected and trained," the Didact said. "We have only seconds to act. You know this wheel—help me save it."

The connection to the Cartographer returned and grew suddenly brilliant and joyfully intense. Ecstasy flooded through me once more. But now my partner was the Didact.

We observed the red and gray planet, halfway through its passage, and the wheel's tormented plates barely held together by white-hot ribbons of wall.

The planet's gravity—the suicide option of the Forerunners seeking to prevent further harm to their kind—had almost finished its work.

ONI COMMANDER: "Do any of you understand this?"

SCIENCE TEAM LEADER: "It's abstruse—difficult to wrap our heads around, to be sure. I'd prefer spending weeks before making a decision . . . but combined science team analysis gives us considerable conviction that the related events are credible."

ONI COMMANDER: "But they contradict everything we know about the Didact! Why save a Halo?"

SCIENCE TEAM LEADER: "There's little time left—"

ONI COMMANDER: "We're collecting the flow! But its value seems even more questionable. What we know about the Didact—from the Bornstellar Relation, if you believe that!—points toward his complete revulsion of the Halos and the Master Builder's plans. The terminal dialogs—"

SCIENCE TEAM LEADER: "The terminal dialogs may themselves be questionable, in the light of this testimony."

ONI COMMANDER: "Only if there was more than one Didact, and we have no evidence of that."

SCIENCE TEAM LEADER: "Yet! The Didact's attitude toward the Halos obviously evolved over time."

ONI COMMANDER: "I lodge my strong skepticism."

SCIENCE TEAM LEADER: "Already noted, sir."

ONI COMMANDER: "And where does any of this get us with respect to our present situation? This Halo is clearly headed for the rubbish heap!"

SCIENCE TEAM ADJUTANT: "Sir, pardon my

interruption—we've been analyzing the fleet database, and we're coming to a tentative conclusion that this installation still exists. It may be the most mysterious Halo of all, Installation 07. Its surface is wrapped in perpetual cloud—. Perhaps it was so damaged that the life support systems never completely recovered."

ONI COMMANDER: "Nonsense. We've already been told that this Halo is thirty thousand kilometers in diameter. Installation 07 is no more than ten thousand kilometers."

SCIENCE TEAM ADJUTANT: "The story isn't over, is it, sir?"

THIRTY-FOUR

EMBEDDED AGAIN DEEP within the Cartographer, we saw many points of direction and opportunity spread around many different fates predicting all possible outcomes of the wheel's present dire situation.

I guided the Didact's intellect toward the best course of action. The words I heard myself speaking, if I spoke aloud at all, were transmitted to all the controllers. But their numbers had fallen to just a few.

Those of us that had survived were acting in desperate concert to salvage what they could. "Not all can be saved," we acknowledged. "Stresses can be relieved by shedding mass. The most damaged plates are likely choices."

With the power from the remaining dreadnoughts, the wheel began to lock in stasis its most important segments. We watched as thousands of kilometers of the band were wrapped in reflective protection, preserved for the moment— but only briefly—against the effects of the passing planet. The controllers in these regions were temporarily removed from the Cartographer's grid.

The wheel continued to rotate, even increasing its rate, while the planet finished its passage, missing any direct collision.

The hub and spokes were no longer in evidence. Strangely, the Cartographer could not tell us if their mechanisms had been damaged or destroyed. Information about weapons status was withheld even from this crucial functionary.

There was nothing more to be done where we were.

"We must transport this installation to the greater Ark immediately," the Didact said.

Lightly damaged installations might have been sent replacement parts from one of the two Arks that had created them in the first place—but such shipments had been discontinued for years, even if we could create a portal to receive them.

"There is just enough power to open a portal of a certain size, and no larger. It will remain open just long enough for parallel passage. I am instructing our ships to supply the necessary power, and to sacrifice their own slipspace drives if necessary."

What I could not understand was why the Didact had decided to save one of those very weapons whose creation he had so decisively opposed.

Perhaps it was not the wheel he wanted to save.

The Didact's motivation, however, was one thing he was not sharing—not with me, at any rate.

———

The wolf-faced planet went on its way, little changed.

The Halo continued to turn while, one by one, the sections locked in stasis were released. The energies of their return to normal physics were diffused around the system as intense, out-rolling, wavelike cascades of infrared and higher-energy photons.

———

"Cartographer!" The Didact's voice brought the surviving controllers, and the faculties of the Cartographer itself, to full attention. "Saving all possible biological specimens—including those infected by the Flood—is the desired goal. Plan for the installation's reduction. We must fit through the portal. Reducing its size also allows us to use the lesser Ark to make repairs. Report!"

That explained everything, then. The Didact was on a mission from the Librarian. He could save at least a few of the many species the Librarian had placed on the installation.

The Cartographer quickly made its report. We studied

the optimum configuration for passage through the limited portal, and conveyed our instructions.

Power was temporarily shifted from creating the portal. Thinner, brighter spokes shot inward toward the axis to join a spherical hub . . . the entirety of which suddenly seemed to convert to dark gray solidity. As segments were discarded, to keep most of the remaining specimens alive and their environments at least minimally protected, the spokes would act as both slings and counterbalancing braces.

All around the wheel, segments deemed expendable—bare foundation, unfinished habitat, or too damaged to be saved—separated from their walls and were released into space. They flew outward, slowly tumbling as they shed more debris.

Despite my absorption, I allowed a moment of grief for the dead and dying on the heavily damaged plates. Cities, forests, mountains—all lost? I could not tell and there was no time to tally—those decisions had already been made and new ones were quickly piling up.

The walls themselves now folded like accordions, pulling in the remaining segments, then joining them at their edges, shaping a much smaller wheel.

This might have taken hours, or days, I did not know—

Not important.

The wheel completed its sacrificial reduction.

The spokes flickered, testing the new configuration. All seemed well. . . .

And then, one more segment broke loose and flew outward. Again, more spokes formed, fastened to the edges of the adjoining plates, and again, the walls accordioned to join the plates along their edges.

The wheel now rotated with hardly a shimmer. We became confident of its integrity.

"Divert all power to formation of the portal," the Didact commanded. "Controllers will stand down. Your work is finished."

With deep pride and sorrow, he was addressing the Forerunners who had stayed loyal to the Council during the rule of Mendicant Bias—and who had continued to serve even in their infected state.

The wheel rolled on, its plates now covered in dense cloud. I caught some final glimpses of refined joining, weather control, atmospheric tempering, cooling or heating—protecting cargo to the Didact's wife, to the Librarian.

But also precious to me, for my own reasons.

I did not witness the passage through the portal. I suppose I was grateful for that.

In all the time since I had fallen from the sky and landed on the wheel, I had been exposed to far more than I had ever been born to understand, or withstand.

"You may stand down, as well, young human," the Didact said and with a twist of his arm, he broke the gossamer between us. The Cartographer's space faded to embers, then gave way to darkness.

The darkness was a mercy.

It was also a time of changes. I was not yet aware of how much had already changed—for me.

THIRTY-FIVE

CHAKAS, YOUNG HUMAN," the Didact said. "Riser is here. We are together again."

I rose like a drowning man bobbing in thick black water. My body was still numb. I had difficulty seeing—shifting, unfamiliar colors, crazy, unfamiliar silhouettes.

Then my sight focused enough that I could look up into a broad, grotesque face—and realize that it looked younger, smoother, less ruggedly patterned than I remembered.

Was this truly the Didact himself?

I had no idea how Forerunners aged or might repair themselves. I did not care. My emotions had been dulled. I felt at peace—mostly.

"You have been through a great ordeal," the Didact said. "And you have been very roughly treated. I am sorry for that."

"Where's Riser?" My lips did not move. Nothing moved. I felt nothing. Still, the Didact heard me.

"I have preserved him intact for delivery once we reach the Ark."

"I want to see him."

My old friend floated into place not far away, wrapped in one of those Forerunner bubbles—body relaxed and still, eyes fixed.

This is the way a dead man feels.

Was that the old spirit in my head again?

"And the girl," I said, "the woman, Vinnevra?"

"She, too, will go with the survivors. The Librarian will restore them to a habitat they will find pleasant."

"You're younger—you've changed."

"The Didact provided the template for my maturity. I am now all that remains of him, and so I serve in his place."

Slowly the familiarity dawned on me.

"Bornstellar?"

"No more, except in my dreams."

THIRTY-SIX

THE DIDACT WAS far from done with me, and I was far from done with the horrors of the wheel. It was the Didact, finally, who betrayed us all. He did it gently, but even so, it brought pain.

When I became fully aware of what had happened to me, I tried to suppress what little remained of my emotions, tried to hold back everything, feel *nothing*, but then the crossing currents of fear and resentment and hatred crashed together and everything returned in an awful rush.

I raged, I *burned*!

Something switched me off.

THIRTY-SEVEN

A **ND ON AGAIN.**
The process was instantaneous—but time had obviously passed. How much time, I could not tell.

Again I was in the presence of the Didact, traveling down a long, deep shaft. My body was wrapped in wires and squirming plates—what little I could see of it: one hand, part of an arm—my chest.

"This will be difficult," the Didact said, "but we have to attend to old problems. *Very* old problems." He seemed careworn, not as young as he had been earlier—worn down. "If you can keep yourself stable, I am going to take you to a place on the installation, a place we need to visit—both of us.

Your new configuration is delicate, and I do not want to lose you—not again. For the sake of your fellow humans."

"Then take me to the Librarian. I've done everything I can to keep faith in her!" My previous rage had been transformed into a cool churning, like rivers of ice water spinning around a deep hole.

"I understand," the Didact said.

"I doubt that. I demand to see her!" I heard a voice—my voice—and I also heard a distant echo. I was probably making actual sounds in an actual place—a big place.

"My relationship to the Librarian may be even more complicated than yours, young human."

We were falling into the deep interior of the wheel, in the realm formally occupied by an offshoot of Mendicant Bias.

What else is down here?

"Complicated, how?"

"Perhaps I can explain later. You are learning how to maintain. Good. I was worried."

Full vision returned. We dropped from the tunnel into an even greater space. Below, I saw that weblike maze of glowing green pathways, now stable, no longer shifting about as we continued our descent.

"Is *she* here?" I asked.

"My wife? No. She's on one of the Arks, I'm not sure which one."

"You're not taking me to see her."

"Not yet. We need to reawaken a memory, to complete a circle, and then you will be finished."

"Finished? You mean, dead?"

"No. Fully functional. There is an unresolved instruction set, an undesired imprint, that we need to erase or modify. First we have to raise it up."

That meant nothing to me—and yet, I suddenly recovered a fragment of memory, the memory I had been suppressing for so long: inward-curving, jewel-glinting eyes mounted far apart on a broad, flat head. . . . Intricate mouthparts shaping strange sounds. A massive body with drawn-up, withered arms and legs, like a squatting fat man or a dead spider.

And last but not least, a great, segmented tail writhing around to shove a barbed sting into my spine—

The child—older than our time, yet eternally young.

"*No!*"

I was not screaming.

I could not scream.

"Control your fear, or you might destabilize again. You don't need to *feel* anything. Soon it will all be like a phantom limb—your emotions."

That was true. I found I could channel all into that hole filled with swirling, cold water—shutting down my fear, or no longer feeling it.

Fear is physical, organic.

The old spirit!—unmistakable.

Fear without flesh is an illusion.

I had no idea what that meant, but now from the swirling fluid I pulled up a spinning impression of emotional states, a wide array of choices, many of them painful, but all isolated from my core, my self. In time, I might be able to reach out and use them for whatever purposes I might choose—but not now.

I enjoyed being numb.

"I remember the Beast—the Primordial," I said. "Does that mean I met the Captive?"

"Probably. It often leaves a memory of what it did—cruel enough."

"It did something to me—to *us*, didn't it?"

"Yes," the Didact said. "And we are about to meet it again."

"No!"

"Are you afraid?"

"No." Again that absorbing swirl down the dark hole.

"Excellent," the Didact said. "Still stable."

We were walking side by side—but I was not walking. I was floating. I could still see my arm, my hand—but little else. And my eyes saw things very differently.

"I envy you," the Didact added, "for I *am* afraid."

"But you met it before—didn't you?"

"That other, the first me, ten thousand years ago, and only briefly."

I spoke with the Primordial as well.

THIRTY-EIGHT

W HEN ALL HOPES are lost, only then does reality acquire that sharp focus that defines who we are and what we have become.

So much was becoming clear.

The old spirit was with me—but not just him. I could feel others as well, fully formed but not yet active or aware—arranged around a commanding core—my own core, my self, so often symbolized as cooling waters swirling down a dark hole . . . surrounded by something like *walls* containing thousands of old spirits arranged like scrolls in a library.

But one was not the same. It hid among the others, subtle, quiet—utterly different and alien.

This was the one we were here to erase.

"Did it hurt me?" I asked as we moved down a long, straight pathway, toward a shadowy, darkened mass of crystal.

"Yes."

"How damaged was I?"

"Badly—physically and mentally," the Didact said. "Extraction of the imprint was quick and brutal—a hallmark of Mendicant Bias. The Master Builder never understood how to utilize the Composer."

I wasn't sure which name was more dire, more disturbing—Captive or Composer.

The dark mass of crystals grew closer. No lightnings danced. The mass did not move. The spaces within the wheel were dormant . . . but not empty.

Expectant.

THIRTY-NINE

A CRACK OPENED in the dark wall, then widened to allow us passage. We moved between hundreds of meters of fractured crystal, as shiny and black as obsidian.

"This is the old heart of Mendicant Bias," the Didact said. "It is dormant now. The ancilla is stored elsewhere, undergoing further correction. Soon it will again work within its design parameters."

"Am I dying? Am I dead?"

"You are being transferred from your damaged body—a process that will soon be finished. You are becoming, in part, a keeper of the biological records of your race. That seemed the best way to salvage your memories and your intellect, and to safely contain the most dangerous components of the Librarian's experiments. You will continue to serve the Librarian. And me. Do you feel that capability?"

"Are you killing me, then?"

"You are already dead—in that sense. The body will be disposed of. Will you miss your physical form?"

Oh, I did—so much!

And yet I also enjoyed feeling numb.

"The body's complete record is stored within you," the Didact said. "If you wish to access any of its physical sensations, you can mimic them."

I did not want that! I wanted the real thing. But then, the numbness would come to an end and the pain would return.

"You have worked well with the Lord of Admirals, my old opponent. Are you still there, Forthencho?"

A sullen silence.

"The Lord of Admirals and I have some old questions that need answering," the Didact said as we exited from the cleft wall.

"About the Shaping Sickness?"

"The Flood."

At this, the old spirit stirred.

"On the inner surface of this installation, thousands of biological stations were converted into Flood research centers," the Didact said.

"The Palace of Pain."

"Many such. Hardly palaces, though. All were administered by Mendicant Bias, working under the direction of the Captive."

"Is the Captive down here?"

"Yes. Prepare yourself, young human. Even stable and in your present form, what we are about to learn could be destructive."

It nearly destroyed us before, my old spirit said.

FORTY

A MISTY CIRCLE of dead bluish light filled the center of
an arena 104 meters wide.

I discovered I could precisely measure sizes and
distances. Within the misty circle of light stood a round,
elevated stage twenty-one meters wide and surrounded by a
thicket of interwoven black rods.

The slightest sound of machinery echoed around us. By
the timing of the echoes, I knew we were in a hemispheri-
cal chamber 531 meters across.

Through the thicket of black rods the head became apparent first: shining grayish brown, flat, jeweled eyes mounted
wide, expressing an arachnid's perpetual watchful sadness—no

neck, the head's broad wings curving down over narrow, leathery shoulders.

Closer. My numbness was less and less of a defense.

"I'm not ready," I said.

"You're as ready as I am," the Didact said. "As ready as we'll ever be."

Now I saw, beneath the startling and ugly-beautiful head, a thick, grossly fat torso mostly concealed behind six or more drawn-up legs, bunched together like sticks and embraced by two shriveled yet still impressive arms—arms with multiple joints, cased in wrinkled, leathery skin. The skin was covered with what resembled sweat but was actually a glassy, coruscating solid, like frozen dew. The Primordial was in repose, captive once again, yet quietly watchful.

Ancient for humans, but also for Forerunners. Ancient beyond our measure.

The Beast.

My sense of measure suddenly became confused. I could not seem to focus. The many-faceted eyes measured *us* in return; the Primordial knew all our dimensions intimately. The mouthparts concealed under the front of the wide head thrust down and out and sounds came forth, accompanied by a continuous faint tapping or clicking. The sounds seemed familiar, yet were not speech. The Beast was asking questions, but did not expect answers. It also welcomed us. That much became apparent.

It was glad to see us—much as a parent feels joy at the return of a child.

The Didact stepped forward first. I struggled to find something of the young Bornstellar in this great, bulky form, but I could not. The Manipular had been completely absorbed by the old Warrior-Servant.

And so it was appropriate that these two monsters face off again, perhaps to play out a game of chance with the dried, discarded bones of our bodies, to sit and reminisce about the agonies and horrors visited upon humans and other races in their eternal satiation of curiosity and power.

The Didact gave voice to a chant, a Forerunner prayer, it seemed—and suddenly I saw myself in the caves outside Marontik. Clear as if I relived it, I felt my body covered in blood and clay, surrounded by the flickering light of tallow lamps, and heard myself also praying, trying to understand why the elders who conferred manhood were carving my shoulders and ribs and chest with slow bone knives—why the rules of life were so perverse.

Why love had to partner with pain and death.

The Didact's prayer was not so different from my own.

But it unfolded soon into questions.

FORTY-ONE

HAVE YOU FOUND what you came here for?" the Didact asked the Primordial.

For a moment, I doubted it had the means to answer in any language we could understand, but the sounds from the symmetrical, vibrating mouthparts slowly began to produce words—something like speech. At least, I heard speech.

"No. Life demands," the Primordial said. "It clings and is selfish."

"Why did you come here at all?" the Didact asked.

"Not by choice."

"Were you brought here—or did you command the Master Builder to bring you?"

The Beast now chose not to answer. Except for its mouthparts, it barely moved.

The Didact persisted as we drew closer to the mesh cage, despite his obvious revulsion. "Are you again hoping to take vengeance upon Forerunners for defying your race and surviving? Is that why you bring this plague down upon us all?"

"No vengeance," the Primordial said. "No plague. Only unity."

"Sickness, slavery, lingering death!" the Didact said. "We will analyze everything here, and we will learn. The Flood will be defeated."

"Work, fight, live. All the sweeter. Mind after mind will shape and absorb. In the end, all will be quiet with wisdom."

The Didact gave a small quiver, whether of rage or fear I could not tell.

"You told me you were the last Precursor."

The Primordial rearranged its limbs with a leathery shuffle. Powder sifted from torso and legs.

"How can you be the *last* of anything?" the Didact asked. "I see now that you are nothing more than a mash-up of old victims infected by the Flood. A Gravemind. Were all the Precursors Graveminds?"

Another sifting shuffle.

"Or are you after all only an *imitation* of a Precursor, a

puppet—a reanimated corpse? Are all the Precursors gone—or is it that the Flood will make *new* Precursors?"

"Those who created you were defied and hunted," the Captive said. "Most were extinguished. A few fled beyond your reach. Creation continued."

"Defied! You were monsters set upon destroying all who would assume the Mantle."

"It was long ago decided. Forerunners will never bear the Mantle."

"Decided how?"

"Through long study. The decision is final. Humans will replace you. Humans will be tested next."

Was the Primordial giving me a message of hope? Doom for our enemies . . . ascendency and triumph for humanity?

"Is that to be our punishment?" the Didact asked, his tone subdued—dangerous.

"It is the way of those who seek out the truth of the Mantle. Humans will rise again in arrogance and defiance. The Flood will return when they are ripe—and bring them unity."

"But most humans are immune," the Didact said. Then he seemed to understand, and lowered his great head between his shoulders like a bull about to charge. "*Can the Flood choose to infect, or not to infect?*"

The wide, flat head canted to one side, as if savoring some demonic irony.

"No immunity. Judgment. Timing."

"Then why turn Mendicant Bias against its creators, and encourage the Master Builder to torture humans? Why allow this cruelty? *Are you the fount of all misery?*" the Didact cried out.

The Captive's strange, ticking voice continued. "Misery is sweetness," it said, as if confiding a secret. "Forerunners will fail as you have failed before. Humans will rise. Whether they will also fail has not been decided."

"How can you control any of this? You're *stuck* here—the last of your kind!"

"The last of *this* kind."

The head leaned forward, crimping the torso and front limbs until one leg actually separated and fell away, shooting out a cloud of fine dust. The Captive was decaying from within. What sort of cage was this? The misty blue light seemed to vibrate and a high, singing sound reverberated through the hemisphere, shaping razor-sharp nodes of dissonance.

But the Captive still managed to speak.

"We are the Flood. There is no difference. Until all space and time are rolled up and life is crushed in the folds . . . no end to war, grief, or pain. In a hundred and one thousand centuries . . . unity again, and wisdom. Until then—sweetness."

The Didact stepped forward with a sharp grunt. He lifted his hand and a panel appeared in the air, shaping controls. The Captive's head squared on its torso, as if bracing for what it knew was about to come.

"It is your task to kill this servant," it said, "that *another* may be freed."

The Didact hesitated for just an instant, as if trying to understand, but anger overcame him. He made a swift gesture like swinging a sword. The controls flared, then vanished, and the mesh around the Captive's platform spread between them a far more intense, blue-green glow.

"Let your life race ahead," the Didact said. "You were made to survive deep time, but now it will arrive all at once. No *sweetness*, no more lies! Let a billion years pass in endless silence and isolation. . . ."

He choked on his fury and doubled over, contorted with his own agony, his own awareness of a great crime about to be committed—and another crime avenged.

The mesh held the inverse of a stasis field, the *perverse* of a timelock. Above the platform, the light assumed a harsh, biting quality.

The Captive's mouthparts vanished in a blur, and then, abruptly stilled. Its gray surface crazed with thousands of fine cracks. Limb after limb fell away. The torso split and collapsed, puffing out a much larger dusty cloud—all contained within the perimeter of the mesh and its field.

The head split down the middle and the two faceted eyes lay for a moment atop a pile of shards and cascading gray dust, then slumped inward until only broken facets remained. They glinted in the dead blue light. The dust became finer and finer, and then—everything stopped.

We watched in silence.

Total entropy had been reached.

The Didact knelt and pounded his great fist on the pathway. It is never easy to judge and execute a god.

I know.

"No answer!" he growled, and his voice echoed around the great dome. "Again and yet again—never an answer!"

This is the answer, the Lord of Admirals said, suddenly rising from his silence to share the Didact's emotion—but judging it from our coldly lifeless state.

No immunity and no cure. There is only struggle, or succumb. Either way, the Primordial will have its due. We have met our creators, they have given us the answers we sought—and that is our curse.

The Didact got to his feet and gave me a long, bitter look. "Nothing is decided," he murmured. "This isn't over. It will *never* be over."

For the Didact, the ultimate meaning of upholding the Mantle was never to accept defeat. I sensed that the Primordial had expected as much and as it decayed over the artificial fleeting of millions of centuries—as its extraordinary lifespan played out in blind silence—it had gloried in it.

All was sweetness for its grinding mill.

AI TRANSLATOR: End data stream. Memory minimally active but no longer transmitting.

ONI COMMANDER: "Christ almighty, do you think the Covenant ever accessed this?"

SCIENCE TEAM LEADER: "I doubt it. This monitor's IC is layered and firewalled so deep it would take a million years just to run one of our probes through the outer fractals. We can't mimic the central controller in any way. And the Covenant tech teams, at their best, were never as good as ours. What in hell is this 'Composer'? We've never heard of it before."

STRATEGY TEAM LEADER: "Sounds like it was used as a remedy for victims of the Flood—or for converting biological beings into monitors. Or both."

ONI COMMANDER: "Another infernal machine for making monsters!"

AI TRANSLATOR: Another data stream has been detected. It appears to be Forerunner instruction code.

SCIENCE TEAM SENIOR TECH LIEUTENANT: "There's no more than ten minutes of viability remaining. The monitor's central processor realizes its time is limited and it's offered up a pretty ingenious fix. We can fast track and convert the code, then implement it in an isolated module."

ONI COMMANDER: "I forbid any such thing! This damned one-eyed bollock can already run through our firewalls like a kid through a sprinkler."

SCIENCE TEAM LEADER: "We won't have time to download any of the underlying data store unless we implement the code."

STRATEGY TEAM LEADER: "Gentlemen, and ladies, get what you can while you can. We've got an impending action, and I want all this data sorted and filtered as to reliability, and made available to our incursion and sortie teams by the end of this cycle."

SCIENCE TEAM LEADER: "We'll need a tentative designator for the source. What are we calling it?"

ONI COMMANDER: "We still haven't confirmed any connection between this one and—"

SCIENCE TEAM LEADER: "I said 'tentative.' "

ONI COMMANDER: "No way in hell I'm going to confirm this is the same as the monitor found defending Installation 04."

STRATEGY TEAM LEADER: "That's our working hypothesis. Should raise some eyebrows at High Command, and we need that sort of boost right now."

SCIENCE TEAM SENIOR TECH LIEUTANANT: "Sir, am I being ordered to confirm that this is—"

ONI COMMANDER: "How many of these devious bastards are out there, anyway?"

STRATEGY TEAM LEADER: "One per Halo, so far. As for this particular monitor—I certainly hope it's the last. Yes! So designate. But bury it somewhere in the political report. Give us all some cover in case it blows up in our faces."

ONI COMMANDER: "Say the damned thing infiltrated our secretarial pool."

SCIENCE TEAM SENIOR TECH LIEUTENANT: "Sir, shall I
actually say that?"

STRATEGY TEAM LEADER: "Christ almighty. No!"

AI TRANSLATOR: Monitor language stream resuming. It
is incomplete but recoverable.

FORTY-TWO

T**HE DIDACT'S SHIP** lifted away from the fog-shrouded wheel as it rotated above the greater Ark, that vast, life-bearing, regenerative flower floating in the dimness above the galaxy's margins.

No more Halos issued from its Forge.

My flesh had been shriven. My humanity had come to an end, and yet I had become the Finger of the First Man, as Gamelpar had told the story—built to last thousands of years . . . built to serve Forerunners.

But also made as a gift for the Librarian.

And given the opportunity, finally, to testify to you, the true Reclaimers.

In time, my numbness developed into something richer, something that could survive thousands of centuries with only a minimum of madness creeping in. To contain multitudes is a definition of madness, is it not? I have rarely been able to remember which of my fragmented selves has performed any particular action.

I see in your records that one of me caused you considerable difficulty—and then, assisted you! How like us. But never did that monitor reveal its origins, or the motives behind its perverse behaviors.

Perhaps now you can guess.

As Reclaimer, it is your privilege to shrive me again—not of the flesh, long since turned to dust, but of my rich confusion of sins.

———

The Forerunners had, for a time, the Domain. I have never been able to access the Domain. Perhaps it no longer touches any part of our universe. If that is the case, then nobody will ever understand the history or the motivations of the Didact or any other Forerunner. . . .

That means, however long I continue to exist, I will never understand why *any of this* had to happen.

———

I last observed the Didact in company with the Librarian on the Ark. They were walking on a high ribbon over the greatest biological preserve I had yet seen—dwarfing any such on the wheel. Thousands of kilometers of varied habitats, containing the accumulated life stores of well over a thousand worlds—and still, in the time remaining, she was planning to gather more.

That was also the last time I saw Vinnevra. She had become part of the Librarian's core population of humans, minus, of course, the representatives from Earth—from Erde-Tyrene, I mean.

I was no longer responsible for her; she could not even recognize me. Yet ever since I have missed her.

Riser had survived the removal of his imprint—a very tough cha*manush* indeed—and had been returned to our home. Or so I was told. I vowed at the first opportunity, I would look for him.

I would do everything I could to find him.

But the location of Erde-Tyrene was concealed from me for many years. And when I was finally given the freedom to search, it was already too late.

I miss him to this day.

I miss Vinnevra, and Gamelpar, and my mother.

I miss them all to this very instant.

———

At the command of the Didact, who rarely commanded his wife about anything, those processed by the Composer, those who remained on the fog-shrouded wheel, along with the remains of all the other Flood victims and the deacti-vated Graveminds—of which ten had already formed—and the last of the functioning monitors keeping perpetual watch—all on the wheel and the wheel itself were sent through a portal for one last time, never to be used in that same way again.

It was known as Installation 07.

It has become a sacred tomb for millions, though some may still live.

I do not know.

———

The Librarian was very interested in my report on the con-ditions of Erde-Tyrene, which she had not visited for many years. To my dismay, I had to acknowledge that it was likely not her touch I had felt at birth—not her personal touch—but that of an automated imprinting system. Now that I was no longer flesh, that revelation did not disturb me. Much.

I still kept a firm record of how the original Chakas had felt about the Librarian.

———

The Didact returned to the graces of the newly constituted Council—for a time. The Librarian's power, of course, rose along with that of her husband.

Know one knew of the actual fate of the Master Builder. It was assumed he had died somewhere on Installation 07.

The debate about strategies against the Flood was renewed. As I said, neither of the Arks were manufacturing Halos, though they were certainly capable of such. This fact, which seemed inconsequential at the time, would eventually be hidden from me in the name of "compartmentalization."

———

I see very clearly how much the Librarian has shaped humanity since the end of the first human-Forerunner war.

Whenever you look inward and see an ideal female . . . whether it be goddess, anima, mother, sister, or lover . . .

For a brief, barely sensible instant, you will see the face and feel the spirit of the Librarian.

———

My systems are shutting down. The humans I carry within me are dying . . . I can feel them fading by the millions. Old friends in my solitude. So many discourses and debates on human nature and history!

Gone.

They were brave spirits and deserved more than ever I could give them.

END STREAM

TENTATIVE CONFIRMATION: PARTIAL MEMORY STORE
of Forerunner AI "Monitor" 343 GUILTY SPARK

DEVICE STATUS INACTIVE—NONRECOVERABLE.
DEVICE ORDERED JETTISONED BY ONI COMMANDER.

REQUEST FOR STANDARD BURIAL CEREMONY DENIED
BY SAME.

END DATA LOG.

RESUME DATA LOG (ibid ref.)

SCIENCE TEAM LEADER: "What's up with the tech team?"

ONI COMMANDER: "They're running around on C deck like a bunch of scared marmots, carrying AI cores. Won't let anybody in."

SCIENCE TEAM LEADER: "Cores? They need to flush and replace ship's AI?"

ONI COMMANDER: "Don't know!"

STRATEGY TEAM LEADER: "Look at this. . . . Ship's veering from main task force. We're moving away from all the action! Who in hell ordered that?"

SCIENCE TEAM SECOND OFFICER: "Environment is cooling. Oxygen is dropping."

ONI COMMANDER: "We can't get to the bridge or to any other deck. Hatches are in battle damage lockdown."

SCIENCE TEAM LEADER: "But we're not in battle!"

ONI COMMANDER: "I'm not at all sure of that. The damned 343 dupe—"

STRATEGY TEAM LEADER: "It's out in space with the other garbage."

ONI COMMANDER: "But its data stream is still with us!"

STRATEGY TEAM EXEC OFFICER: "Three of us climbed down through the maintenance shell. Other decks appear to be conking out one by one. We can't raise anyone on E and F, and the engine room is a madhouse. Whole ship is—"

TECH CHIEF: "Listen to what just came through bridge comm! The skipper's talking to something in the AI root system."

STRATEGY TEAM LEADER: "Something that's not the ship's AI?"

TECH CHIEF: "Just listen!"

(playback)

(Voice ID'd as 343 Guilty Spark): "Your ship's AI is defective."

CAPTAIN: "In what way?"

(Voice): "Compound Information Corruption. Ship will experience complete systems collapse and drive implosion within five minutes. But there is a cure for that ailment."

CAPTAIN: "What kind of cure?"

(Voice): "Much worse than the disease, you might think. I shall have to replace all original AI functions with my own. I've long wanted a chance to resume my quest. Your ship is an excellent vehicle for that purpose. Apologies, Captain."

(end playback)

ONI COMMANDER: "We invited that thing right into our living room, plumped up the cushions, brought it a pipe and slippers! We should have known better! We should have—"

SHIP'S AI: All ship functions are now under control of 343 Guilty Spark. Root and System AI signing off.

STRATEGY TEAM LEADER: "Damn thing hacked the entire ship! We are so screwed."

ONI COMMANDER: "Four or five minutes of oxygen . . ."

GUILTY SPARK: "You will not die. You will sleep for a time. I have need of all of you."

STRATEGY TEAM LEADER: "What need?"

GUILTY SPARK: "Know that all that lingered in me, the memories and emotions of old humanity, when I was still flesh, is also hidden deep within you. It slumbers, but it shapes, and it haunts your dreams and your hopes.

"You and I are brothers in many ways . . . not least in that we faced the Didact before, and face him now, and perhaps ever after. This is combat eternal, enmity unslaked, unified by only one thing: our love for the elusive Lifeshaper. Without her, humans would have been extinguished many times over. Both I and the Didact love her to this day.

"Some say she is dead, that she died on Earth. But that is demonstrably untrue.

"One of you almost certainly carries Vinnevra and Riser's old spirits within. Only the Lifeshaper can find them and coax my friends back to life. And after a hundred thousand years of exploration and study . . .

"I know where to find her."

ABOUT THE AUTHOR

Greg Bear is the author of more than thirty books of science fiction and fantasy, including *Hull Zero Three, City at the End of Time, Eon, Moving Mars, Mariposa,* and *Quantico*. He is married to Astrid Anderson Bear and is the father of Erik and Alexandra. Awarded two Hugos and five Nebulas for his fiction, one of two authors to win a Nebula in every category, Bear has been called the "best working writer of hard science fiction" by *The Ultimate Encyclopedia of Science Fiction*. His short fiction is available in *The Collected Stories of Greg Bear,* published by Tor Books.

Bear has served on political and scientific action committees and has advised both government agencies and corporations on issues ranging from national security to private aerospace ventures to new media and video-game development. His most recent endeavor is a collaboration with Neal Stephenson and a crack team of writers, *The Mongoliad,* an epic novel available as a multiplatform app and soon to be published in three volumes by 47North.

extracts reading groups
competitions books new
discounts extracts
competitions
books
new
events books
extracts
new titles reading groups
interviews
events extracts
discounts
new books events
events new
discounts extracts discounts
www.panmacmillan.com
extracts events reading groups
competitions books extracts new